THE RIFT

BOOK ONE OF THE GRID TRILOGY

CLIVE HARDWICK

Also available from Amazon by Clive
Hardwick

CHANTER'S HIDE

All characters in this book are fictitious and any
resemblance to actual persons, living or dead, is
purely coincidental

This book is dedicated to my son, Matt, who has been a constant source of encouragement and support from day one. I love you mate.

BOOK ONE – THE RIFT

PART ONE – DANNY

ONE

The festive livery of Christmas Eve was marred by a damp, dismal fog. Danny was looking forward to hot mince pies and cream. He peddled his Raleigh with gusto, his breath pluming before him. Although only a month away from his fifteenth birthday, he loved Christmas. Seeing the magical expectation on Sam's and Tara's faces as they anticipated Santa's visit always reminded him of his own wonder before the myth was obliterated.

It was years ago now, at least seven, maybe even eight, when Danny was awoken by a podgy bloke in a red suit humping his first real bike into his bedroom. His dad had been putting on weight for a time. Danny watched through half closed lids as 'Santa' propped the bike against his set of drawers, his false beard dropping to his chest as he stood up and rubbed his back. To be fair, Danny had known for a time that the incredible present deliverer was on a par with the bogeyman – fictitious.

Tonight though, Danny had been at Rob Carney's house playing GTA and he had lost track of time. He was pedaling like stink when he ran into the man in the long, black coat. Even though the bloke went down like a skittle, he was on his feet in seconds.

"I'm so, so, so sorry," Danny said. "I didn't see you."

The man smiled. "Don't worry Danny, no harm done. Make sure your bike is all right."

Danny automatically checked his bike before thinking what a waste of time it was. He had run into a human being, not a brick wall.

"It's f......," he began. The man had vanished as quickly as he had appeared. Danny felt a shiver run down his spine as he realized the stranger had known his name. He jumped back on his bike and pumped the pedals like there was no tomorrow. That was the first time he met the man he would later know as Seth.

Plenty was to happen in the meantime however, mostly of a particularly unpleasant nature. Danny peddled back home like a boy possessed and, as the evening passed with his family, playing games, which they had done for a few years now, his concern about the stranger diminished. His dad sat with one bottle of beer in front of him all night but never stopped feeding his face with crisps, nuts, and sweets, doing his best to add to his considerable girth. Mum, on the other hand, had no more than three nuts but became extremely relaxed, a little verbally challenged and increasingly louder as she drank gin and tonic as if it were lemonade, the mixture favoring the gin more with each pouring. These observations meant little at the time. It would only be in retrospect that the importance of Danny's parents' eating and drinking habits would become apparent.

Danny's full name was Danny Kaye. It was his mum's choice – she loved the old musicals, especially his namesake. His brother was Sam, and he was eight at the time, his sister Tara – six. Danny always thought he was the mistake, quite a bit earlier than the folks would have liked but loved, nevertheless. Mum and Dad were Kate and Tom and, as a family, they were happy.

So, that was the Kaye family, playing Yhatzee on Christmas Eve, dice rattling, laughter and banter filling the house, as it should be. By the time Danny was ushered to bed he had, more or less, forgotten about the man in black and as days became weeks, then months and years the man never crossed his mind again.

Christmas Day was wonderful, as usual, for kids with no responsibilities or financial burdens. Danny woke up just before eight and wandered downstairs, trying to curb the excitement and anticipation normally associated with children of a much younger age. He was fifteen, nearly an adult, for God's sake – he was not about to let the side down. He walked into the living room with an expression, hopefully akin to severe boredom. Sam and Tara had, obviously, risen a little earlier and were surrounded by wrapping paper, bows, tags and, more importantly, toys.

"'Morning kids, "he said in his best big brother voice. "Merry Christmas."

Tara came running up to him with a doll in her arms.

"Look Danny, her name is Sophie, and she pees her pants. "

"Very nice Taz. "

Sam was too engrossed in his Lego to give Danny a glance.

Danny scanned the base of the Christmas tree to see if 'Santa' might have left something for a teenage music fan. At first, he was dismayed to see only the torn remnants of his siblings' gifts.

Tara followed his gaze and explained solemnly, "Father Christmas din't bring you nothing cos you been a bad boy. "

At that point Dad came in from the kitchen with a slice of heavily buttered toast in his hand.

"Happy Christmas Danny boy, "he said, a sad smile on his face. "I see Taz has given you the bad news. "

"Yeah, bad, bad Danny, " he replied, playing along with the pointless but apparently, necessary game.

"Mother, " his dad called. "Didn't Santa bring Danny anything at all?"

On cue Mum made her appearance, which left a lot to be desired. Her eyes were puffy and bloodshot, her face pale and sickly looking.

"I think these might be for him, "she said with a bilious grin. "I found them on the doorstep. "

They went through this charade for a bit longer, before he was presented with what he'd asked for, an iPod, headphones, and gift cards for downloading 500 songs. After they ate a superb and exceptionally large Christmas dinner, which Dad consumed at a record pace, even having seconds, the family settled down for the afternoon. Mum and Dad fell asleep in front of the TV, Mum still looking off colour and tired after cooking the festive meal. The kids went upstairs and played with their presents and Danny borrowed Dad's laptop to download songs all afternoon. A good time was had by all.

The holidays were soon over and the remainder of Danny's penultimate year in school began. He was reasonably bright but drifted along never really applying himself, wanting his education to be done with so he could get a job and earn some money. He was the same as a lot of kids, opinionated and misguided. The more his parents tried to drill into him that qualifications were essential and if he could pass enough exams he could go off to university, the more he free wheeled, ensuring that would never happen.

Tuesday, the 3rd of January, he caught the school bus from their village, Lower Benton to Alverton Secondary, just outside Stratford-Upon-Avon. His mood was gloomy, but he was resigned to returning to the classroom and knew, after the first day, he would be back in the routine. He wasn't aware, however, how much his life was about to change.

Bullying exists in all schools and is, clearly, a nightmare for the recipients. Danny had been lucky throughout his school life to avoid such treatment although he'd witnessed enough of it. Like most, he felt sorry for the kids being bullied but, most of all, glad it wasn't him. That was about to change.

He had seen Lawrence Carter a few times before the Christmas break. His family had moved to the area from London and he had joined Alverton in October, after half term. He was in the same year as Danny but in 5c, Danny was in 5b. He was a big lad, with a sour expression, as if someone had just cracked a stink bomb under his nose. Just before breaking up, Danny had seen him knocking about with Richie Sproggett, a dim lump who, prior to Carter's appearance, had been a real loner – probably not from choice.

After eating his lunch on that first day, Danny went back to the classroom and took out his new iPod and settled down for 40 minutes of peace with his music. He'd been sitting with his feet on his desk for about five minutes when the door opened and in came Carter, Sproggett and another meathead who he'd only heard people call Smithy.

"What do we have here? "Said Carter with an expression indicating the stink beneath his nose had intensified.

"His name's Kaye, "said Sproggett. "Danny Kaye. "

"My mum was watching him over Christmas, dancing about in the rain with an umbrella, "Carter said, a sneer flaring his nostrils even wider.

"That was Gene Kelly, "Danny corrected him.

"It was who I say it was twat-head, "Carter said. "Now give me that iPod before I smash yer face in. "

"No, "Danny said defiantly, knowing this would not end well.

"Richie, Smithy, grab the little shit. "

Before he could move, Carter's henchmen pinned Danny to his chair while Carter ripped the iPod from his hand and the headphones from his ears.

"Tell the screws and I'll tear you apart, Kaye. Understand? "

Danny nodded but deep inside fury was surging fruitlessly. That was the first time he encountered Lawrence Carter and learned that anger alone was wasted. It needed to be trained and channeled.

Throughout the next few months, he was subjected to more abuse, mostly verbal but very threatening, nevertheless. He was pinned down by Carter's disciples on several occasions whilst the man himself frisked him. After the first couple of days when he realized he was now a regular for the bully's attention, Danny made sure he never had any money or items dear to him about his person. Strangely enough he never felt afraid, just frustrated – powerless and disgusted with his own inadequacy. He dreamt of being Jack Bauer or James Bond and kicking the shit out of the three of them, but that was all they were – dreams.

He came home from school on the Thursday before the Easter break. He walked in the back door muttering expletives, knowing his mum would be having a nap before cooking dinner and his dad still at work. He had his hands rolled into fists, his anger and frustration at an all-time high.

"Who's a cowardly bastard? "asked his dad, emerging from the dining room.

"Er, nobody. Why aren't you at work? "

His dad let out an almighty sneeze and wiped his nose and eyes with what appeared to be an, already sodden handkerchief. "The boss sent me home, "he said in between sniffles. "In case I infected the rest of the staff. Now, answer my question. "

Danny hadn't intended saying anything, he was going to deal with this on his own, but suddenly he couldn't help himself and the whole thing came tumbling out. By the end there were even tears in his eyes.

"Don't worry son, we'll sort this," his dad said through gritted teeth.

"Damned right we will." his mother stood in the doorway, her eyes bleary and still very tired looking. "First thing tomorrow we'll ring your headmaster."

"No," Danny pleaded. "I can't be a grass, Mum."

Dad shot her a look. "Go and have a shower and sort yourself out," he said sharply. "We'll deal with this."

"I can't tell the teachers Dad," Danny said. "It'll get round the school and everyone will hate me."

His dad put his arm around Danny's shoulders. "We won't be telling anyone son. People like this Carter need to be taught a valuable lesson and it's one not covered in the curriculum."

Danny knew where this was going and said, "But all three of them are bigger than me Dad. And there *are* three of them."

"That's why you need an advantage, Danny. I've never mentioned it before but in my teens, I used to get into quite a few scraps myself and I found I was rather good at fighting, in fact I gained a bit of a reputation as a hard nut. "He patted his paunch. "I know it's hard to believe now but there wasn't an ounce of fat on me in those days. Anyway, most kids made sure they didn't upset me and if they did, they were sorry. That was until I came up against Billy Arnold."

"But I've heard you talk about him. I thought you were good friends."

His dad smiled. It was one of those rolling back the years smiles, all misty and vague.

"We are, but it didn't start out that way Danny. Come on we'll go into the lounge and I'll tell you all about it."

As they left the kitchen, he grabbed a handful of tissues and blew his nose with an almighty honk. Once in the lounge he flopped onto the sofa and patted the space next to him. Danny sat and waited while his dad finished wiping his nose and looking for somewhere to deposit the soiled tissues. He shrugged and stuffed them into his trouser pocket.

"The first time I met Billy, we had a humdinger of a scrap." He went all misty again and sighed. "And I started it."

"Why, what did he do ?"

"I caught him snogging the girl I was going about with at the time, Kathy...Jone...Johnston, that was her name. I was pretty keen on her, she had a mass of wavy, black hair, pretty face with a little snub nose and legs that went on...."

He coughed and went a little red in the face. "Her looks aren't

 important, " he said." The thing was – she was supposed to be my girl and there's this kid I'd never seen before kissing the face off her. I just saw red."

"How old were you ?"

"Just turned seventeen. I'd just finished my first year at the local Tesco, on fruit and veg with this old bloke called Harold. I can't remember his last name, in fact, thinking about it, I'm not sure I ever knew. Everyone just called him Harold. I think he'd been there since the store opened. Anyway, that doesn't matter. Like I said, I caught Billy with Kathy and went mad. I launched myself at him, expecting to give him a good hiding and send him away with his tail between his legs. It didn't quite turn out that way. I caught him with a couple of punches early on but I'm sure that was because I surprised him. After that he danced around, blocking, or avoiding every punch I threw, whilst giving me a bloody nose with matching cuts on my cheeks and eyebrows. He sat me on my backside, I got up and I was back down again. This went on until, for the first time in years, I realized I was beaten, so I stayed down feeling a mixture of anger and admiration. As I sat there, he held out his hand to pull me up. I ignored it, of course, and scrambled to my feet. I remember glaring at Kathy and then back at him. Anyway, to cut a long story short, he had no idea she was going out with me, she'd told him she was a free agent. " He paused to wipe his nose again and Danny wasn't sure if there wasn't a tear or two in his eyes but that could have been the cold. "When he found out what had gone on, he dropped her like a stone and apologized to me. I mean, I tried to beat the crap out of him, and he apologizes for beating it out of me. It turned out that his uncle owned the local boxing gym, and he was the best they had. Apparently, he'd had a dozen fights, only amateur, but they'd all ended with the other chap failing to make the count, so a knockout each time. From then on we were practically inseparable for a couple of years and I even went to the gym with him for a few months."

Danny was surprised he hadn't told him this before but then again, no-one likes to admit to being thrashed, especially to his own son. He didn't see why he was telling him now though and said so.

"Well, when he was nineteen Billy had a bad motorbike accident and his left leg was pretty smashed up. He had pins and stuff stuck in it and his years of dancing around the ring were finished. As you can imagine, he was devastated at the time but, nevertheless, carried on with the gym and became a trainer instead, working with the young lads. He still does, the only difference being that he now runs the place. His uncle retired a few years back. "

Danny had never been stupid, maybe a bit slow sometimes, but now the penny was starting to drop. "You want me to go to his gym and become a boxer," he said, a little uncertainly.

"You're off for the next two weeks for Easter. I intend to give Billy a ring tonight and ask him to take you under his wing. I don't want you to become a boxer, unless that's what you want, of course. I want you to learn enough to be confident in your ability to teach Carter an important and painful lesson. It'll take a bit longer than your Easter break but I'm sure the knowledge that it will happen will carry you through. What do you say son ?"

Danny shrugged then grinned. "Bring it on."

TWO

Saturday morning, he was riding his bike to Arnold's gym feeling extremely nervous and apprehensive. When Dad had suggested this course of action it seemed a good idea but now the doubts were creeping in. He couldn't remember ever having a fight in his life and here he was, going to, supposedly, learn to box. His dad had wanted to come with him, but he thought this was something he had to do on his own. Although Dad had talked about Billy Arnold, Danny had never met him so that added to the apprehension. As he crossed Albert Street and rode down Winfield Road, the gym came into view and the butterflies in his stomach turned into hornets and he nearly turned back. It was only imagining the look of disappointment on his Dad's face that drove him on.

He leant his bike against a wall where most of the paint had flaked off and what was left had a kind of leprous look. He took a deep breath and pushed open the door. He didn't know what he was expecting but was surprised when he had to dodge the swing of a punch bag as it slammed the door shut. The kid responsible nodded and muttered an apology then carried on beating the crap out of the swinging, heavily patched object. The smell of the place was not pleasant, the main odours being sweat, muscle rub and a slightly overpowering mixture of suspect drainage and general decay.

As the door slammed shut the only person old enough to be Billy Arnold turned, smiled, and walked towards him. The limp wasn't prominent but there.

"If you aren't Danny Kaye, I'm Madonna," he said with a grin. "You're the spit of your dad, son. How is the chubby, old lump?"

"He's fine Mr. Arnold, says it's time you and he went for pizza or something."

"It's about time he laid off the pizza, along with the burgers, the spuds, the pasta and all the other fattening shit he shoves down his throat. I've told him, he's a heart attack waiting to happen, but does he listen? No. I just hope you're a bit more receptive to my advice." He bent down until they were face to face. "What do you say Danny, are we going do this and kick these bullies' arses?"

Danny liked Billy already. Unlike Dad, he was tall and lean, his face friendly and tanned, his auburn hair full but flecked with grey. He reminded Danny a little of Harrison Ford.

"We are," he replied with a huge grin.

"Give me five, my boy." Billy laughed when Danny slapped his hand. "If you don't mind hard work Danny, pretty soon you'll have no problems. Between us we'll make a man of you."

"Where do I start Mr. Arnold ?"

"First off, it's Billy. Second, we're going to have to put a bit of muscle on those scrawny little arms and legs. So, like I said, before we get you on the bags and in the ring, the hard work begins. Are you still with me, young man?"

Danny was a bit disappointed not to be getting on with things a bit quicker, but Dad had told him to listen, do as he was told and not question anything Billy said.

"I'm with you Mr....er... Billy."

Billy held up his hand. "Hit me again partner."

They both laughed as Danny slapped his hand once more. That was the last time he laughed that day. He spent hours doing sit-ups, star-jumps, humping medicine balls about and, generally, adding to the unpleasant aroma of Billy's gym. This was the start of a new Danny, not necessarily a better Danny as future years would show. That's for later though.

Sunday morning, he dragged his aching body out of bed, pulled on a pair of shorts, a t shirt and his trainers and hit the streets. Billy had told him to run every morning, increasing the distance by, at least, a quarter of a mile each day. He'd also said he wanted proper running not 'this pansy jogging crap', as he put it. So there Danny was, running *not* jogging, grimacing a lot as he exerted his sore and shocked muscles for the second time in two days. Whilst he had been with Billy yesterday, he had talked to him a great deal as he sweated and panted and yeah, did a lot more grimacing, about discipline and dedication. Billy had said that to be a decent athlete took 80% hard work and 20% natural ability and even if Danny wasn't a natural boxer, if he gave a 100% in the work department, he would be more than competent enough to achieve his goal. Billy had also told him how, in the early days, his body would beg him not to be so cruel and that if he listened to it, he would wash his hands of him. As Danny ran, he was finding it extremely difficult not to listen to his body as it screamed at him to stop punishing it. But he didn't. He wasn't going to let Billy down, or his dad, or himself for that matter.

It turned out that he had quite a bit of ability and over the next two months he grew stronger, faster, and started to spar with the other kids at the gym and hold his own. After ten weeks, Billy said he thought he might be ready. Danny had learned so much by this time and had come to respect Billy and look up to him in the same way he looked up to his dad. He had become such an important part of Danny's life but in this case, he had to disagree with him. When he told Billy, he thought he was wrong and that he'd know when he felt the time was right, Billy grinned and slapped him on the back, "Just testing kid," he said. "When you are and you've sorted out what you need to, I'd love it if you carried on here, Danny. I'm not getting any younger and I think you and me could make a good team."

Danny told him he'd think about it but knew once he was confident of dealing with Carter and his henchmen, he'd be done. He'd keep up the running and generally keep in shape because he quite liked the way it made him feel, sharp, strong, and clear minded but what he was doing with Billy was a means to an end. He didn't have any desire to become a boxer or a trainer for those who did, but he couldn't tell him that, not yet anyway.

He carried on for another two months. He was still receiving attention from Carter and had to hold himself back a couple of times. When the time came, he wanted to make sure he was capable of putting the three of them down. He wasn't ashamed to say that he was looking forward to it. He was going to make sure they didn't treat any other poor little sod to similar abuse.

On Monday the 15th July , the last week before the summer holidays, he went to school with no fear, no apprehension, only impatience. The morning dragged as he longed for lunchtime, the time when Carter and his goons would come to taunt him, Carter always blatantly ramming his own iPod in his face. When the bell rang at the end of double maths, the ugly bastard turned and grinned at him. This time Danny grinned back and gave him the finger. Carter's face flushed with anger and, after he made sure Mr. Jennings had left the classroom, he and his two puppets swaggered over to Danny. Danny stood up and waited, unable to stop the smile that insisted on plastering itself across his face.

"I believe you've finished with that iPod twat-head," he said evenly. "I think I'll have it back now. I hope you haven't stuck too many of your Neanderthal songs on there."

Carter looked as if he were about to explode, which is what Danny wanted, not that he was worried.

Uncontrolled anger in an opponent is what every boxer wants, it makes them reckless, predictable, and easy pickings. Billy's coaching had changed him totally, he was focused and confident of his own ability. At that precise moment he was relishing what was to come and had no doubt of the outcome.

As he came close, Carter's hands were balled into fists, which he obviously intended to batter Danny with, but there was also confusion in his eyes. Why had the worm turned? Danny could see the cogs of his dumb brain turning. Just to wind him another notch he said. "Come on retard, let's see what you've got."

Carter stormed forward. Danny stepped easily to the left and landed a pile driver in Carter's solar plexus. The stupid sod was suddenly bent double, gasping and groaning but managed to croak, "Richie, Smithy, get him and hold him."

"Yeah, come on meatheads, do as your master commands," Danny said coldly, his fists by his side a la Muhammed Ali.

This was the first time he'd seen fear in their eyes. Something was happening here that shouldn't be. But they were thick enough to do as they were told. Smithy almost tripped over Carter as he practically fell on Danny. Danny stepped back and fired three powerful jabs, feeling Jonesy's nose break beneath the second. He still had one eye on Ritchie as he came in from the right. He met his feeble attempt with a massive hook that, he found out later, broke his jaw. By this time Carter had regained a little of his composure and was idiotic enough, after what he had just witnessed, to have another go. He swung a useless, wide punch. Danny watched it, as if in slow motion, trying to connect. He blocked it easily and hit Carter twice, squarely, in the mouth, knocking out his two front teeth. Carter slumped down and Danny stuck his foot on his chest.

14

"I'll relieve you of that now," he said, trying to ignore the pain from his bruised and cut knuckles. "He yanked his iPod back but threw the headphones back at Carter. "I don't need your earwax though."

The bully was still spitting blood when Danny said, "If I ever catch you bullying anyone ever again, I will knock all of your teeth out. Do you understand me?"

Carter nodded and spat again, and Danny couldn't help thinking – I hope he's got a national health dentist, this could cost his folks a fortune otherwise. He laughed out loud and as he turned to walk from the classroom, a cheer went up. As he had been dealing out overdue justice, he hadn't realized he had an audience. There were kids in the doorway and at the windows as well. From then on Carter never went near anyone else and Danny vowed never to go near the dentist that attended to his front teeth.

For the remainder of his school life he gained a reputation from the younger kids as some sort of superhero who maintained law and order, warning the prospective bullies that a path in that direction would end in a world of pain. Occasionally one of his so-called peers would try his luck and throw a punch or two. He was very restrained and kept their punishment to a minimum. He was still running and, generally, keeping in shape and going to Billy's every Wednesday night. He did help with some of the young would-be's but was still firm about becoming a more permanent fixture. He loved Billy but even though he didn't know the direction his life would take, he, somehow, knew that he was destined for something more important. He also knew that it wouldn't be anything academic as the only GCSEs he would be allowed to take were English Language and English Literature. He wasn't as concerned as his parents, although his mum didn't seem to be concerned about too much at all these days. Her drinking habit had become, well, more habitual. Her and

Dad seemed to row constantly, and Danny and his siblings just took themselves off to their bedrooms and did their own thing. Sam had developed a passion for model aircraft, whilst most of his schoolmates were stuck on PlayStations or X boxes. Sam didn't really have any friends to speak of, but then that went for all three of them. Danny had lost touch with Rob McCarney and now his best friend was a bloke the same age as his Dad and apart from Billy, all he had were classmates, who weren't mates at all. Tara had always been a loner and ever since she'd learned to write had begun creating her own little literary worlds. Danny did sneak a peek at some of her later stuff and, for a girl of her age, it seemed surprisingly good to him. He always had visions of how their lives would be – his brother and sister. Sam, with his intensity and concentration, oh and a love for chemistry at school, would, obviously, become a well-respected scientist and Tara would be the next Jane Austen. As for himself, although he felt he was sort of waiting for something, he had no idea what that might be. He had bought a cheap guitar a couple of months ago and had learnt a few chords but all it had really done was make him aware of how good the guys he listened to were. Dad loved his sixties and seventies music, even though he wasn't born until 1976 and Danny had grown up listening to The Beatles, The Stones, Cream with Eric Clapton, and The Yardbirds with Jeff Beck. His dad could play air guitar brilliantly but lately, Danny doubted if he could reach a real one with the size of his belly. He kept telling him he needed to lose weight, it wasn't good for him. All his dad said was that he'd been spending too much time with Billy. Even at the age of sixteen, he could see there was no point in trying to tell Mum that she had a problem. As far as she was concerned, life was the problem, gin the solution. So, although there was a lot of love in his family, there was also a hell of a lot of dysfunction. But they muddled

16

through and six months later he left school with a B and C in E. Lang. and E. Lit. Time to face the big, bad world. It wasn't long before he became aware that jobs of any description weren't easy to obtain. True, he didn't have a clue what he wanted to do but he wanted to earn money doing whatever it was.

It turned out the only job he was qualified for, was as a washer up and glass collector at "The Black Dog", the local pub. He couldn't even serve behind the bar because of his age. They did have music on Saturday nights with local groups and folky sorts, and they got paid. He started to work harder on the guitar and found he didn't have a bad voice either. He was no John Lennon, but he was fair. After a couple of months, he talked Roy Matthews, his boss, into letting him sing a couple of songs the following Saturday. Everybody in the pub knew him and the worst that could happen was that they'd think he'd done it for a laugh. As it happens, he was rather good.

THREE

From then on, he became a regular "turn", doing three or four numbers before the main attraction came on. Roy slipped him a tenner each week and some weeks he received more applause from the punters than the group who were getting £150.00.

He had no illusions about his musical abilities, he did it for the extra cash and because he enjoyed it. Unlike a lot of kids his age, his head was firmly screwed on and never went anywhere near the clouds. He was just a washer upper in a village pub who could sing a bit. He wasn't going to set the world on fire, but he was reasonably happy for the time being. His dad kept getting on his case about finding "a proper job" and although he knew he was right, there was no hurry. He had no responsibilities, paying a mere £30.00 to his dad each month for his board and lodgings. His life was a doddle and he knew it, just drifting along, enough money to buy whatever he wanted, which wasn't that much, Looking back, he wasn't like most sixteen-year-olds, arsey, whining, little gits who hated their parents, having no comprehension of the sacrifices they had made to bring them up. Mentally, he was older than his tender years and was appreciative of everything his folks had done for him. In a lot of ways, he was a model son – but things change. The arrival of Joey King turned his life on its head.

After his little set in the pub, towards the end of May, he was putting his guitar back in its bag after giving a not too shabby performance of The Beatles' "You've Got To Hide Your Love Away" when this kid came up to him. He had long, blond hair and a pretty, angelic looking face. He looked about fifteen but turned out to be nineteen and became a major influence on Danny's life for quite some time. That sounds as though it was a good thing – it wasn't. After all this head screwed on, model son stuff, it was hard to believe he could be so easily lead and such a total dick.

That night Joey King came up and complimented Danny on his set.

"You're pretty tasty feller," he said. "But if you and me combined vibes we could be lifting the wedge these other losers are shafting from the man. "He pointed to Danny's guitar." Take that sucker out and let the King show you what he means bro'."

His blue eyes were intense, and Danny just found it impossible to even think of not doing what he'd asked. He unzipped the bag, took out the guitar and handed it to him. Joey took it gently, shook his mane of blond hair and played. The hairs on the back of Danny's neck stood on end. Joey's fingers mesmerized him as they swept, butterfly like, over the strings, playing an amazing accompaniment to The Beatles song he had just played. He handed the instrument back to Danny and said, "I don't know about flies man, you could catch a pig there." Danny's mouth was wide open, and he closed it quickly. "That was incredible," he said.

"Yeah, I taught 'Slowhand' all he knows, " Joey said with a grin, showing a set of perfect, white teeth, Even though Danny wasn't gay and had never understood how one male could ever have those kind of feelings for another male, he couldn't help thinking how good looking this guy was. After listening to his dad's CD collection and watching him with that air guitar, his reference to 'Slowhand' was not lost on him. He'd always loved Eric Clapton's playing but never seen him play an acoustic guitar like Joey King.

"You're so good," he said. "Why the hell would you want to play with me?"

Joey flashed his pearly whites again. "'Coz I've got a voice like a duck farting chap."

That was Danny's introduction to Joey King and a completely different lifestyle.

From then on, he and Joey became friends and bandmates. Joey came to Danny's house regularly, where they would work out songs – even his dad thought they were good. Joey was very respectful to him and charming to his mum. In fact, the way she looked at him used to make Danny cringe. She was like a love-struck teenager, making big cow eyes at him and becoming suggestive as the alcohol started running more freely through her veins. It seemed as though his dad had washed his hands of her. Danny was just about to turn seventeen, so not a kid anymore and could see their relationship falling apart. He was sure his dad still loved her, but his mother had another love now, more powerful than any other – the bottle. The arguments between them had stopped by this time. His mother would just not admit that she had a problem. It was a mess, but Danny, Sam and Tara still loved them both as indeed, their parents loved them. His dad was taking more and more comfort in food and still piling on the pounds. Danny found it hard to decide which was worse, the booze or the over-eating. Still, they all got on with their lives and Danny was thoroughly enjoying his. He and Joey were doing whole nights at "The Dog" by this time and getting quite a reputation. The extra money was brilliant, and he'd even doubled what he gave to his Dad each month. He was still, currently, being a good, decent human being, working hard and enjoying playing as a duo with Joey. They began playing other pubs around Stratford and Warwick and he had all the cash he wanted. They were happy days. They decided to call themselves 'Danjo' (not very original, admittedly) but didn't think it mattered what they called themselves. They were better than half decent and people came to listen to them.

Danny became selfish where home-life was concerned. He told himself there was nothing he could do that would change anything, which allowed him to lead his own life, care-free. The fact that he never tried, never attempted to persuade either of them to look at what they were doing to themselves, didn't occur to him at that time. Later he would feel so guilty and responsible, but then, life was good, and he didn't think it could be any better. Plenty of money and doing what you like doing is pretty much everyone's idea of ideal. But the icing was about to be piped onto the cake. They were playing at a pub called "The Cutlass" and had just finished their first half with their version of Oasis' "Wonderwall". Danny put his guitar, now a secondhand Gibson J-45, back on its stand, turned to go to the bar to get an Orange Juice and practically fell over this gorgeous girl in front of him. "God, I'm sorry," he said.

She shook her head, the silkiness of her luscious, long, red hair a vision in the subdued lighting. "I'm not."

He fell in love there and then. She was beautiful, her eyes large and mesmerizingly green. The only word he could think of then and still think now was – perfect. She was, as they say, drop dead gorgeous.

She held out her hand. "I'm Beth," she almost purred, or maybe that was his imagination. "You're cute Danny, do you want to buy me a drink?"

"Y...y...you're lovely," he stammered, showing immediately, his inexperience with the fairer sex.

She giggled and that sound was better than any music he had ever heard. At that moment he had never been happier. Unfortunately, that feeling was going to give him his highest high and his lowest low.

After the gig Beth asked if he'd walk her home and he was over the moon. He nipped to the loo to ring his Dad, telling him he'd be a bit late. He didn't have to tell him why, the way he felt must have been apparent in the sound of his voice.

"A young lady wouldn't be the reason would it?" his dad asked jovially.

"She's beautiful Dad," Danny said enthusiastically. "She only lives about half a mile away, so I won't be too late. I just didn't want you and Mum worrying."

"You're a good lad Danny, enjoy yourself," his tone suddenly took on a serious edge. "I'm sure I don't need to tell you to behave like a gentleman and treat her with respect, do I?"

"No Dad," Danny said with a sigh. "See you later alligator."

"Yeah, in a while crocodile."

As he and Beth made their way to her house on the opposite side of the village, he was walking on air. He'd lost the nervous stammer, although a host of butterflies were fluttering around in his stomach. Halfway there she put her arm around his waist and the stammer returned, but to his arm not his voice. It went up towards her shoulder then dropped, then went back again and down again until Beth said, "Put your arm around me Danny, for Christ's sake." She lifted her head and kissed him on the cheek. "I do love young, inexperienced, little boys though. They're so sweet." Her arm tightened around his waist and he was glad it was dark because he could feel his face burning and knew it must be as red as the Christmas tablecloth they had at home. He put his hand on her shoulder and was on cloud nine. Her shampoo and perfume were a heady mix of raspberry and an intoxicating musky fragrance. Although he'd never taken drugs of any kind, he could imagine that being high would be like how he felt then, breathing in that wonderful aroma and being so close to heavenly bliss. He made feeble attempts at conversation until she said. "There'll be plenty of time for talking later handsome. Let's just enjoy the vibe. You feel the vibe, don't you Danny?" Her eyes were wide, and he thought he was drowning.

Unfortunately, the stammer was back as he tried to surface and answer. "Y...y...y...eah I do,"

She gave a burst of that tinkly bell laugh again. "I've never met anyone as cute as you, it's almost unbelievable. It's a shame you won't stay that way because it's so endearing." She kissed him again, this time closer to his lips. His head was so full of blood by this time it felt like it was about to explode. If there was a record for blushing, he would have won it hands down.

They walked the rest of the way in silence, but it wasn't awkward, it was dream-like, and he realized that if you have nothing that needs saying, say nothing – enjoy the vibe.

They arrived too soon at Beth's house, a semi on Redlands estate, a nice, respectable area, like Danny's. In fact, they could have been bookends, holding the village in their masonry hands.

"This is me Danny," she said softly. "Do you want to see me again?"

"I'd like more of the vibe, yeah," he replied with a soppy grin.

"See, the cuteness is already being tarnished. Come here." She put her arms around him and lifted her face towards his. "Kiss me idiot," she said, her eyes greener than ever. When his lips met hers, the whole of his body tingled but he kissed her without a stammer. It was the most amazing moment in his life.

"Call me, Danny-o," she practically whispered, as she went up the path to her house. "I'll be waiting."

He didn't walk home, he flew. He was higher than a kite. It was unfortunate that feeling had to be so short lived.

Over the next couple of months, they saw a great deal of each other, and he loved it. She came to all Danjo's gigs and when he sang any love song, he sang it to her. She'd be swaying, her hair a red, silky sea, her eyes sparkling, her movement so sensual. He loved her. Years later, when he looked back at his time with Beth, he would still get a feeling in the pit of his stomach, a confused ball of love, lust, hatred and loss with the love and hatred fighting for supremacy. But at that time love was all he felt for her. Over those weeks, when he wasn't working or playing, they were together. He became proficient in the art of kissing, or so she told him, and, as far as his introduction to heavy petting was concerned, it just blew his mind. To touch Beth in that way was immense and to have her touch him was just incredible. Although they had not gone beyond this, it was only a matter of time before an opportunity arose where they took the next step. Both of their mothers were home most of the time and when they weren't it was only to pop to the local shop or something like that. They both loved their daytime TV with Beth's Mum drinking endless cups of coffee whilst indulging, Danny's plumping for something a lot stronger. So, it was a case of having nowhere to go. He had already decided that Beth was the one for him and when they 'did it' it would be special.

That time came unexpectedly when Beth's Auntie Jackie became ill with a virus that left her bedbound. Being a spinster she had no-one to look after her so Beth's mum went to nurse her, leaving Beth to do all the cooking and cleaning for her and her dad, which she was pissed about but it also gave them time to themselves, between her finishing college and Danny starting work and before her dad came home. Luckily, he had a good job within British Gas and worked late most nights.

Beth had it all worked out. It was down to logistics and making sure they didn't get caught. If they did, neither sets of parents would be happy, to say the least, and her dad would be devastated. and Danny liked him, he was a

24

decent sort, never talked down to him, always treated him like an equal. The day and time were set, and Danny had never been so nervous in all his life. He had dreamed about this so many times and just wanted it to be perfect. He realized he was young and naïve but, that was the whole point.

He arrived at Beth's at the appointed time and rang the bell. She must have been right behind the door because she opened it immediately. She wore a short, black, silk dressing gown, the tie hanging loosely, her cleavage showing through the gap, her long legs crossed in a mock demure stance. She looked as perfect as any woman could. "Come on in Danny-o," she said with a wink. "Today could be your lucky day."

He couldn't help himself, he put his arm around her, slammed the door shut with his heel and carried her up to her bedroom. The nerves had somehow disappeared. That afternoon was amazing, and it wasn't until after, she told him it was her first time as well. That did it, he cried, he couldn't help it. He was her first and she was his. It was meant to be, or so he thought then.

For the next twelve months life was a dream, He had a beautiful, intelligent, sexy girlfriend, a good mate and a life that was good. Danjo's reputation had spread and they were making decent money gigging. He still worked at "The Dog" but had reduced his hours considerably. The music thing was getting into his blood and he'd even written a couple of songs. They were soppy things about Beth, but he didn't think they were too bad. He never played them to Joey because he knew he'd take the piss. They were a little trio and he'd even cajoled Beth into singing a song with them. It was this gorgeous song off one of his dad's albums by a group called 'Fairport Convention', called 'Fotheringay'. He had always sung it on his own and, although not in the same league as Sandy

Denny, he did a reasonably good job. Beth's breathy, hesitant vocals took it up another notch and it always gained a lot of applause from their fans. There they were Danny, Beth, and Joey in a little bubble of their own, a bubble that, soon after Danny's eighteenth birthday, would not only get popped but savagely ripped apart. It would be the start of so much shit and misery, and the beginning his own decline from decent human being into something else.

Until then, he had the most amazing time, his life was filled with love and music, what more could anyone ask. He and Beth made love in a variety of places and positions and he started to contemplate asking her to marry him. It was only their youth that stopped him. He believed they would be together forever anyway, so there was plenty of time to make it official. In the meantime, they enjoyed their lives together. The start of the rot was when Joey started on the drugs, He'd been smoking weed for a long time and had offered it to Danny on several occasions. Luckily, Danny had never had the inclination to smoke at all, so had no desire to start filling his lungs with anything other than fresh air. Joey even offered it to Beth but, after a brief flirtation with tobacco earlier in life which had caused extreme nausea, she also declined.

FOUR

It was early November when he learnt that something more serious than weed was getting into Joey's system. His eyes began to lose that brilliance that drove the girls mad and he started to fumble some of his solos. When Danny asked him if everything was all right, he just mumbled something about feeling under the weather. Danny was, after all, only eighteen years old and had not seen a great deal of the shitty side of life. He didn't know how a drug user looked. Joey said he was under the weather and Danny believed him. Well, at first. When, after weeks, he hadn't improved, Danny suggested that it may be a good idea to see the doc'.

Joey laughed in his face and said, "You're such a naïve sort Danny and that's what I love about you. I don't need no doctor."

And so, it went on, Danny still wondering what was wrong with him until Roy Matthews said to him after a gig at 'The Dog'. "Either he stops snorting or you two don't play here again."

The penny still hadn't dropped. "Snorting?"

"He's on coke or some other shit." He looked at Danny with an expression that seemed to combine disbelief with genuine concern. "Don't you know he's using?"

When he thought back to this conversation, Danny was both ashamed and proud of his lack of experience in this field. He said, "Using what?"

"I mean cocaine not Coca Cola, how old are you Danny?"

"He's on drugs?"

"Hallelujah. As I've said get him clean or don't come back. You're a good kid. If I were you, I'd drop him. He's bad news."

From then on, their relationship deteriorated. Danny tried to help him, get him off whatever he was sticking up his nose, but it wasn't happening. At the time he was stupid enough to think that telling him what he was doing to himself and how he was destroying their partnership would be enough to bring him to his senses. Danny had never been near anything stronger than paracetamol in his life and thought Joey would just stop doing whatever it was he was doing. He had experience with the effects of alcohol, thanks to his mum, but drugs were a whole new ballgame. He stuck with him though because he was his mate, they'd had so many good times and he did, literally, love him like a brother. Seeing him destroying the good side of himself and letting the shitty side take over was killing him. At that time, he didn't know that his problem was going to impact so severely on his own life and become the beginning of his own descent into self-destruction. Joey's actions brought to the surface, for the first time, the evil everyone carries inside. Most people find little difficulty in keeping it where it belongs, its sharp claws only slipping through occasionally and quite easily forced back. There are lines that most wouldn't dream of crossing. There are times when the desire is strong, but something inside kicks in, like a trip switch. The paedophiles, perverts, serial killers and down-right evil bastards have, somehow, had this switch bypassed. Certain events, however, at key points in life can bypass that switch as well, and Joey's drug fueled actions were a beginning to Danny's own switch not only being bypassed but ripped from its moorings. From being one of the happiest individuals on the planet, he was about to have his heart and brain stuck in a blender and royally fucked up. He would look back on the times at school, when he dispensed well deserved justice, spending quality time with his dad and, of course, his life with Billy and get a warm glow. He was a decent kid; he wasn't nasty for the sake of it; shit he was a hero to the younger kids who he saved from the same fate he'd been made to suffer.

It wasn't that long before he was forced to realize that, without professional help, Joey was on the road to ruin. He'd even taken to shoplifting to fund his problem and it was the first time Danny witnessed this that reinforced what Roy had said to him about Joey being trouble. He'd heard the expression - cruel to be kind - on a few occasions and thought this was the time to test its validity. He told Joey that if he didn't get help with his problem, they were finished, he'd wash his hands of him.

The words Joey used then would come back to hurt him in the not too distant future, although, at the time, he put it down to his miserable condition.

"You're such a dick, Danny. You haven't got a fucking clue, have you?"

These words wouldn't just come back to hurt him, they would contribute to him hurting Joey.

It was back to just him and his guitar and, without Joey, the number of gigs he got were halved. Not only was Joey a brilliant guitarist but he was a bit of a comic as well. Without his input Danny was just another kid with an okay voice who could play a few chords. Roy gave him regular work but that was because he felt sorry for him – plus he liked Danny. He increased the bar work again, now old enough to serve the punters but he was just going through the motions. He and Joey had been special and losing that knocked him for six. He still had Beth but that was different, but even she seemed to be changing. She missed quite a few of his gigs due to a course she was doing at night school, learning to be a nail technician. He felt as if they were drifting apart and the more he tried to stop that from happening, the worse it seemed to become. He loved her and was sure she felt the same, it was just things were getting in the way. He was that upset and confused he spoke to his dad about it. He was very understanding and, although his and Mum's relationship wasn't all that it had once been, he'd had a lot more experience with the opposite sex than Danny had. He suggested that since the break-up of him and Joey, he'd maybe lost the spark that had first attracted her to him. He told Danny not to let Joey King ruin his life like he was ruining his own. If you want her Danny, he'd said, you've got to show her, make her feel special, make her feel like she's the only girl in the world. I know it sounds corny, son, he'd added, but corny works well with women. They love to be treated like princesses. He also advised him not to become predictable, a boring mouse of a man. Women liked reliable but they loved spontaneity. Danny took on board all his dad's words of wisdom and went away to plan his first 'spontaneous' act. He knew that on Wednesday she was going to be home alone, doing some homework for her course, though he couldn't understand what that would entail. He was supposed to be working that night but had managed to get Rich Evans to do it with the promise of an extra tenner to add to his normal pay from Roy. He bought a nice bottle of wine, a huge box of her favourite chocolates and a dozen red roses. He would surprise her and show her how much he loved her into the bargain. He was looking forward to an extremely romantic evening.

He arrived at her door just after seven feeling pleased with himself. He knocked and waited – and waited. He wondered if she'd popped out to the shops or something, so he took out his phone and rang her. He heard her ringtone, Rihanna's 'Rude Boy' coming from her bedroom above the front door. After a few seconds she answered.

"'Lo Danny boy." Her speech was slurred, and he was confused.

"I'm at the front door, are you still doing your homework?"

"Nah, 'ad to pop out. Am at the shop."

30

The fact that she was lying to him was obvious, even to him. The reason, however, eluded him, but not for long. He tried the door and found it was unlocked. He went in and climbed the stairs, a knot in the pit of his stomach. When he opened her bedroom door, that knot blossomed into a ball of raging fire. They were in her bed, him, and her, fucking, drugged up to the eyeballs. Terrible pain fueled that fire when Joey said, "Hey man, how's it hangin'?". His former best friend and former girlfriend were stuffed full of shit and in bed together, naked. He had never known such hurt and such anger in his life before. He dragged Joey out of bed and just kept hitting him. Tears were streaming down his face and snot and spittle shot everywhere as he said over and over "fucking bastards, fucking bastards." He would have killed him if Beth hadn't thrown herself at him and begged him to stop. He backed out of the room trampling over the roses and chocolates. He picked up the bottle and threw it against the wall. "You fucking bitch," he said through the sobs that racked his body. That was the start of the shit.

Within the space of a month or so he had gone from having everything he wanted to an emotional tornado. At the tender age of eighteen he knew the emptiness that heartbreak brings, the fury that betrayal causes and just how much other people can fill your life with happiness and how easily than can fuck it up. His dad had a song in his collection called 'Ball of Confusion', by the Four Tops. That was how he felt. It would have been bad enough to find out Beth was seeing someone else, for that person to be his best friend and adding the drug thing to that – it was mind blowing, gut wrenching, heartbreaking shit. He did what every self-respecting teenager would do under the circumstances, wallowed in self-pity, which would have been fine had it stopped at that. Unfortunately, the pain he was suffering turned into something more than

31

misery. His head felt as though it was about to explode, and he entered a period of darkness so deep and savage it nearly destroyed him. He stopped playing altogether; he didn't have the heart anymore. In fact, during that time, he wished he didn't have a heart at all. He'd read somewhere that songwriters produce their best songs at times like that. The last thing Danny felt like doing was writing a song. He kept on working for Roy but could see the man's patience running out. He was hardly the life and soul of the party and a miserable barman is not good for business. Danny thought Roy was working up to letting him go but, obviously, finding it hard after what he'd been through. As it happened Danny made it easy for him.

It was about 10.00p.m. Friday night when this dipstick, Dave Dunster, came into the pub. He'd had a few already, that was apparent, and he swaggered up to the bar. Danny had never liked the bloke, he was always trying to wind people up, trying to find their switches. He seemed to delight in taking the piss out of people, finding that little trigger to set them off. He was a big, ugly bastard who reminded Danny of Bluto out of the old Popeye cartoons. He got away with his jibes because people were scared of him. He was just another bully who relied on his size and appearance to intimidate people.

"All right Dan," he said, a big grin showing off his uneven, discoloured teeth. "Pint of bitter mate." He looked around the room at his audience before continuing with. "Haven't seen that hot bird of yours for a while, or your guitar playing buddy, come to that. They're not getting it on behind your back are they, my old son?" Danny tried to keep his calm. He said, "I think you've had enough Dave; you'd better leave before you upset someone."

"Come on Dan, I'm sober as a judge. Have I touched a nerve maybe? I hear they're having a druggies and whores party down at 'The Swan'. You want to pass it on."

He looked around again, happy with his work. When he turned back Danny broke his nose, leapt over the bar, and shoved the obnoxious bastard onto the pool table and gave the fat slob what he deserved – a good hiding. Bloodying his knuckles on the piece of shit felt good, really good. Roy was good enough to let Danny give Dunster his just deserts before he sacked him. That was the start of the roll and from then on Danny was rolling deep.

FIVE

He sunk into a blue funk, spending most of the time alone
in his room listening to stuff he'd downloaded from one
of the torrent sites. It was mostly old albums he'd heard
his Dad playing, the one he listened to most was 'The
Wall' by Pink Floyd. It suited his mood. That was when he
started drinking. He raided his mum's stash, half a dozen
bottles of gin in her knicker drawer. If she noticed one
was missing, she didn't let on. There he was, headphones
on, Roger Waters' masterpiece savaging his eardrums,
grimacing every time he took a slug of the old Mother's
ruin. Luckily, he was left alone, Mum and Dad hoping,
that given time, he'd get over his little upset and be good
old Danny again. That, unfortunately, was never going to
happen. His brain wouldn't let go of the image of Beth
and Joey, wasted and naked. So many emotions boiled
inside him and if not for the booze numbing them, he'd
have acted out Floyd's 'One of My Turns' and smashed
the bloody room up. The money he'd saved from the
good times was being spent on vodka, a spirit that didn't
make him shudder every time he took a swig, like the gin
did. He just welcomed the oblivion that alcohol gave him,
after half a dozen large ones he was just another brick in
the fucking wall. He'd sleep for a few hours, a dreamless
sleep, an alcohol fueled coma. When he woke up with a
banging head and a mouth like the bottom of a bird cage,
he'd take another couple of heavy measures to alleviate his
suffering. He remembered the way he'd started to look at
his mum when she was pissed, an expression of disgust
tinged with pity, yet here he was not only following in her
footsteps but overtaking her. He was a mess, soon to
graduate to total fuck-up. He found out that when your
girl and your best friend screw you over at the tender age
of eighteen and you've had little experience of the shittier

side of life, it blows your mind. He wasn't proud of any of
the things that happened after he finally decided to leave
his room and Pink Floyd to their own devices and inflict
his bad self on the world.

The first time he ventured forth, he'd had a couple of
liveners to set him on an even keel. He hit the cashpoint
and drew out fifty quid. It was early September and still
warm, not a cloud in the sky. After so long stuck in his
bedroom, the sun hurt his eyes. A couple of hundred
yards down the road from the bank was a dingy old pub
called 'The Crown'. He was still squinting when he pushed
open the door to the bar. The air was thick and limited
light was allowed through the grime coated windows. He
walked up to the bar, his eyes adjusting to the dimness.
The place was nearly empty. There were a couple of old
geezers playing dominoes and a bloke in a boiler suit
stood at the bar with a pint in front of him. By the
different coloured stains covering his work clothes, it
wasn't hard to work out his profession. The telly was on,
showing some race meeting. The painter, who was
obviously a betting man, was watching intently, his lips
twitching, eyes practically bulging from their sockets. As
Danny took out a tenner he yelled 'Go on my beauty',
nearly deafening him. He followed this up with 'Yes, yes,
yes,' quickly followed by a long 'Nooooooooooo, you
fucking bitch.'

Danny looked at him and the bloke glared back, as if
blaming Danny for his horse coming in second. "Do you
have a problem?" Danny asked him, holding his gaze. The
painter looked him up and down, seeing his clenched fists
and replied. "No mate, I ain't."

Danny ordered a triple vodka and sat on a bar stool. The
painter left soon after and Danny spent over thirty quid
before he staggered out into the twilight. On the way
home he called into the off license and bought another
bottle. That night he was going for total oblivion.

From then on, he turned into a self-pitying, self-centered, waste of space, pisshead. As luck, of the bad variety, would have it he still had quite a stash in the bank due to his playing days with that bastard, Joey. They'd earned a fair bit and as he didn't need to spend his on bloody drugs, it had accumulated. His wages from the pub had more than covered his day to day needs. He had money to fund his rapid slide into selfish fuckdom and didn't need to resort to theft as some shits do. His dad, bless him, tried to talk some sense into him. As most of the time Danny was either drunk or passed out, he didn't have a very receptive audience. In retrospect, when Danny thought of the way he'd treated him, it made him sick to the stomach. Even his mum tried to talk to him, maybe thinking she was more on his level. None of it worked, he was on the road to self-destruction and nothing was going to stop him. Mum and Dad could slap up as many diversion signs as they wanted, he'd just stagger past them in a drunken stupor. He was losing weight, just eating shit like sausage rolls and pasties and the odd cheese roll from the pubs he was now frequenting. He became the Landlords' friend, someone who could take a lot of booze without causing trouble and filling their tills in the process. Although he hadn't caused any trouble, he'd had a few minor altercations where a threat or quick dig had sufficed and, consequently, had earned him a reputation for someone not to be messed with.

This stage of his life went on for twelve months or more, routines – good or bad, are hard to break and alcohol is, obviously, very addictive – and he was addicted for sure. Life without vodka was unthinkable, that's when he could think. He drank to stop the thinking, always yearning for the drink that would send him to that dreamless state that only a drug of one kind or another can do. Addicts who find no reason or desire to give up their addictions tend to drift away from this world like smoke in the wind way before their time.

Unfortunately for Danny, something did give him a reason to stop drinking. The date was January 14th, and it was 5.00 p.m. He'd been in the pub from eleven, got back home about four and had that last drink to send him away. He had no idea how Mum managed to wake him – once in that state he was normally out of it for hours and when he did resurface was still on another plain. This day was different – hugely different. She shook him and in seconds he was back in this nasty world. She was screaming at him and tears were rolling down her face. He was trying his hardest to focus and hear what she was screeching about. He propped himself up on the bed and noticed a couple of uniformed women at his bedroom door. He was about to ask them what the fuck they were doing there, when pennies that hadn't been present for a long time started to drop. Something serious had gone down. It's strange, he thought, no matter how smashed you are, how out of it, some things just cut straight through it and bring you back to this fucked up life with a bang. He'd thought his life was shit and couldn't be any worse when, suddenly, what was left of his heart was ripped out of his chest.

Everything suddenly slowed down, his alcohol addled mind trying to find other reasons for the devastation that was his mother and the presence of two WPCs. His mum shook with the sobs that wracked her; the screeching having become an awful mewling. He swung his legs off the bed and stood unsteadily, hugging her in a clumsy, drunkard's smother grip. He beckoned to the police officers with a nod of his head and they came into his room.

"Dad?" He managed to croak, feeling nauseous, sour booze-sweat coating his forehead. "Is it my dad?"

The looks on their faces told him what he didn't want to know at all, ever. After months of not really knowing one day from the next, he was now aware of the day of the week and his bloodshot eyes could make out the time to be just after six. When he thought there was no way, in this hell that is called life, that it could be any worse, his mother fell to her knees and the sound that came from her lips was the most terrible he'd ever heard. It seemed to come from the depths of her soul, beginning as a slow, mournful, hollow plea, rising in intensity until she was screaming. "Not my babies, please God, not my precious babies."

Danny looked toward the policewomen, his eyes begging for denial. Both shook their heads and one of them said. "I'm so deeply sorry. If it's any consolation, they wouldn't have known anything about it, they didn't suffer."

"No," he yelled. "It's no fucking consolation. You come here and tell me my dad and my kid brother and sweet, little sister are dead and then talk about consolation. Are you insane?"

He realized he was shaking and needed a drink. He needed a drink so badly, needed to drink and drink and drink until he reached the oblivion that would take away the pain, that would fill this hole that was his heart and drown it for good. He broke down and slid to the floor next to his mum. They hugged each other; their bodies racked with a grief neither of them could understand. He didn't even know what had happened and at that moment it didn't matter. He didn't know how long they sat like that, all he knew was, when he pulled her to her feet and sat her on the bed, it was dark outside, and the WPCs were long gone. He poured them both a large vodka and they sat in silence. It was then that he needed to know.

"How, Mum?" he asked softly. "How?"

Her tone was flat and empty. "Car crash," she said. "Your dad had a massive heart attack. They hit a lorry head on, killed instantly apparently." Then it was back, the realization, the horror, the indescribable hurt and they were sobbing again.

"I kept telling him to lose weight," she wailed.

Then the guilt hit him. Billy Arnold had told him on several occasions that his dad was a heart attack waiting to happen and Danny had known he was right. What had he done about it? Nothing. He'd watched his dad stuffing crisps and chocolate into his mouth and shook his head. So, all he did to help his dad was to shake his stupid head. He took the glass from his mum and said simply. "We both stop this now."

He didn't look back. He ransacked the house and poured the contents of almost a dozen bottles of vodka and gin down the sink. He'd decided not to drink anymore and that was how it was going to be. He was resolute. His mum, on the other hand, had been in the clutches of the demon for a great deal longer than he had. It was her life and to ask her to stop at such a traumatic time in both their lives was never going to be easy. He kept telling her that he'd stood by and let Dad bring about his own death and, in the process, Sam's and Tara's as well. He wasn't going to make the same mistake again. She was all he had now, and he was going to make sure that didn't change. He could see that she understood but alcoholism is a terrible disease. It bends and destroys the mind and savages the liver, not content until its hold is complete. It becomes a God, a true religion and like most religions it requires sacrifice. Alcoholics become soulless husks whose only cognizant thought is for the next drink. Danny made an appointment with their GP and made it clear to Mum that he didn't intend to let her face this on her own. The disappointment on her face was not lost on him and he realized this was going to be harder than he'd first thought. To give up any drug, you must want to, and he

39

could see the fear in her eyes, the terror at the thought of losing the crutch she had leant on for so long. He was suddenly aware how most people rely on something or other to get them through this life, whether it be religion, drugs, booze, food, or any other poison needed to get them through the night. In the last couple of years, he had had to cope with more than someone so young should have to. To lose his dad and his siblings and have his best friend and his girl betray him could have destroyed him but it didn't. Somehow there was something inside him that absorbed this devastation and converted it into fuel, making him more resilient, even if it was slowly desensitizing him. As his life rolled on, he became very pragmatic, his emotions buried deep, his main concern his mother's rehabilitation. He'd managed to get her into an NHS programme for alcoholics in Stratford and, although it was a slow process, he saw the light seeping back into her eyes. The triple funeral had practically destroyed her, and it had been a long slog from then on. They were turning a corner though; he was sure of it. Normality was creeping into their lives; he'd even managed to get a job at Stratford Tesco, on the fruit and veg section, of all places. On his Dad's death the mortgage on the house had been paid off so with his new job they managed to keep their heads above water. He thought it would probably do Mum some good to get back into employment, but one step at a time. Days became weeks and then months and soon she had been 'dry' for six months. He'd stopped searching the house for hidden bottles because he could see for himself that she was clean. Their lives, though not what could be described as exhilarating, were now on an even keel. They had both come to terms with their lot and were getting on with it. Occasionally they even laughed, a sound not heard for a long time in the Kaye household. Saturday night became their movie night. They watched the oldies eating crisps and popcorn, snuggled up on the sofa, mother and son. He'd never forget those times.

Time passed uneventfully until a year had gone by. The anniversary of the accident was hard, as they knew it would be and it was the first time since giving up the booze that Danny really craved vodka. He could see his mum was struggling with her demons too. Strangely they spent the day in their own little bubbles. At a time when they should have been comforting each other, they hardly spoke, dragging themselves through twenty-four hours of torture. Why anniversaries are worse than all the other days is a mystery but, somehow, the loss seems to be amplified, the scab covering the pain ripped from the angry flesh beneath. His mum took herself off to bed earlier than usual after hours of television programmes, none of which they watched. It was only on to smother the awful silence that hung like a rancid dust sheet over the world that day. When he looked back, he found it hard to understand how they allowed their grief to be so personal, so exclusive. During the previous twelve months they had become closer than they had ever been but, on that day, it was as if they were strangers. When Danny passed her bedroom door a couple of hours later, he could hear his mum sobbing but instead of going in and hugging her he shuffled along the landing to his own room where he sat on the bed and wept himself. There they were in the same house, sharing the same, unbearable loss yet crying like babies in separate rooms. Looking back, it seemed like total madness but then it was what it was, somehow, they each needed to own their grief. To share it would have seemed disrespectful.
The next morning was a bright, sunny affair and when Danny came down to the kitchen his mum was already there, a cup of coffee in her hand. Her eyes were still red and puffed from a night of tears and little sleep. He must

41

have looked similar because she said, "I guess you had a bad night as well." She nodded towards the kettle. "It's only just boiled; this is my third."

"Too much caffeine isn't good for you," he said, just for something to say.

"Should I go back on the gin then?" she said, giving him a black look.

He was taken aback, and it obviously showed on his face. "I'm sorry Danny." She pushed her fingers through her hair. "It was a hard day's night."

They both smiled. Dad was always slipping Beatles song titles into everyday conversation. The most used was 'From Me to You' which surfaced every Christmas and birthday.

"Never mind, here comes the sun," Danny said as he poured hot water onto a spoonful of coffee granules.

They sat in silence until he got up to go and shower and get ready for work.

"Why don't you throw a sickie," his mum said. "You do look like shit."

"Thanks Mum, I love you too."

"I think they'd understand, under the circumstances."

He shook his head. "I need to go." And then the thought that she might need him to stay with her hit him. "That is unless you want me to stay here with you today."

She held up a hand. "No, being as I had such a bad night, I'm going to take a sleeping pill and go back to bed, I'm shattered. If it helps, go and throw some spuds about."

And so, he went to work and left her. He would always regret that.

SIX

Danny had never been very tactile but after the accident and the shit with Beth and Joey he'd become very withdrawn. With Dad and the kids gone, Mum, without her alcoholic crutch, was similar. They loved each other but didn't go in for displays of affection. Since the anniversary, their Saturday night movie sessions had disappeared and they normally spent the night in their separate rooms, as they did the rest of the week, doing their own thing. His mum began struggling with insomnia and got a prescription from the doctor's which, if she attended a six-monthly review, was on repeat. She started to sleep through the night but seemed a bit fuzzy for most of the day. Again, he didn't see a problem. He always thought that after a year or so she'd get over it and be able to lay off the pills. He'd never considered himself to be stupid but, looking back, he considered himself an insensitive, thick bastard. Maybe he was too concerned with his own emotions, plus his role as primary bread winner. For the first time in his life he was beginning to think about his future. The job at Tesco was all right but the thought of 'throwing spuds about' for the rest of his life was not appealing. He'd started playing guitar again, but it was more out of boredom than anything else and it certainly wasn't something he could consider as a career option. For a time, they both drifted through life. He was working as many hours as he could (shop work is not the best paid of jobs) to pay the bills and put food on the table whilst his mum floated along on a sea of sleeping tablets. Once he suggested that it may be of benefit to her and the household budget if she got herself a part-time job. Her response was not favourable, to say the least. She broke down and wailed about being a burden, saying that his life would be much better if she wasn't there. She said

43

she couldn't face leaving the house, let alone having to make small talk with people she had nothing in common with and who she probably would dislike anyway. She stormed off to her room and slammed the door. Needless to say, Danny didn't broach the subject again. They were treading water, neither of their lives going anywhere. It was an existence, each of them carrying so much pain around that was never talked about, concealed in impenetrable boxes, buried as deep as possible. There are probably millions of people in this world doing the same. Some cope with it better than others. As the months went by, after the anniversary, Danny's coping strategy was showing signs of wear. When life is filled with emptiness and routine, cohesive thought is the enemy. To be able to wander through tedium and not scream your lungs out is a gift. Unfortunately, it was a gift he didn't possess.

Dragging himself to work every day was becoming harder and putting the smiley face on for the benefit of his co-workers and customers was now a severe strain. He imagined it resembling a rictus grin, rather than a genuine smile. His head was ready to explode, the inner scream slowing crawling up and squeezing his vocal cords. After work he would go back to a house, no longer a home, with his mother either in her room or gazing at some garbage on the TV, her eyes glazed. On a few occasions he tried to talk to her about her medication, suggesting that she try and wean herself of the sleeping tablets. She would just say she was fine and go back up to her room, where she'd spend the rest of the night. It was getting to the stage where they rarely saw each other. They no longer shared any mealtimes. By the amount of weight she'd lost, he doubted that much in the way of food was passing her lips. He would cook meals for her, but she would just move the food around the plate until he took it off her. He felt as if he was fighting a losing battle. When he said

to her, "Come on, Mum, you've got to eat something."
She would ask him why.

That time felt like the oppressive, grey stillness that often precedes a savage storm. He felt that something was going to happen, something had to happen. Their lives could not possibly continue like this for much longer. They were both slowly disappearing, the colour that once blazed through their world was becoming a faded sepia. They were becoming old, tattered photographs in a forgotten album, shadows with no sun to bring them to life.

Then the storm came. It was Thursday evening and Danny had finished a double shift. He was knackered, miserable and wanting nothing more than some food, a shower and bed before he had to get up and do it all over again. As soon as he had unlocked the front door, he knew something was wrong. He'd read stuff like this in pulp fiction crap before and thought – what a pile of shit. How, when nothing appears to be different, can anyone know that there is? He could hear the TV, as was the norm, and other than that it was like any other night. But he had this feeling in the pit of his stomach; he didn't want to go down the hall. He called out to his mum and waited for a response. After a few seconds he called again, louder this time. The TV was just a low rumble so he knew she couldn't fail to hear, but still she didn't reply. As he forced his way down the hall, his feet not wanting to move, he'd begun to sweat. He had never been religious, but he started to utter a plea to God to make everything normal. He promised him he'd carry on with his life as it was if He could just make sure his mum was all right. He'd never complain again.

The staircase came into view, as if in slow motion, the landing and top few first. As he moved forward it was as if his eyes were walking down the stairs. When they reached the bottom, any belief in God was gone but it didn't stop him screaming at the non-existent fuck.

His mum's twisted body lay, pale and lifeless. A few feet away was a smashed gin bottle, a tiny puddle almost apologizing for not being bigger. There was no pain on her face, no shock, no horror. She looked peaceful and as the tears rolled down his cheeks, he envied her.

SEVEN

The following weeks, he was going through the motions, a robotic husk, glazed and tired. The funeral was a very small affair as Mum had only one living relative, a cousin in Australia, who was in no position or, had no inclination to spend the time and money to attend the funeral of a person she hadn't set eyes on for about thirty years. As for friends, if she'd had any, they were long gone. Even in her younger days, when Danny was a boy, he couldn't recall her mentioning any girlfriends. There were half a dozen acquaintances and Billy Arnold, who only came to support Danny. Although he was one of his dad's best friends, he didn't really know his mum. Danny just kept thinking that not so long ago his life was wall to wall sunshine and now he had nothing. In the space of three years he had lost both his parents and his younger brother and sister. It's the sort of thing people read about and feel really sorry for the poor sod left behind, but only for a few seconds, until they turn the page and read some juicy tidbit about some celebrity or other. It was the sort of thing that happened to others. Only this time, it had come home.

After the funeral, when all the legal stuff had been sorted, he put the house up for sale. He was beginning to hate going through the door. He carried on at Tesco but only until the house sold. Once that money was in his account, he was out of there. He decided that he would rent a small flat and reassess his life, or so he told himself. What he really wanted to do was curl up into a ball and cease to be. The house was only on the market for a couple of weeks before it was snapped up. Its location, in a small, leafy village, a stone's throw from the M40 made it very desirable. It went for the full asking price of £239,000.00. He gave Tesco a month's notice and began searching for a flat. He didn't want anything flash, just serviceable and reasonably priced. By the time all the paperwork on the house had been completed and the cash was sitting in his account, he'd found a one bed-roomed, ground floor place on the outskirts of Warwick. It was only ten years old and clean and tidy. He moved what furniture he needed in and sold the rest through eBay. He made enough to pay his first three months' rent.

There was no leaving party for him. The people who he had worked with had bought him a card and a bottle of Scotch. They had no idea of his past encounters with the demon drink. He accepted both gratefully and felt both relief and a sense of loss when he left work for the last time. In a way it had been the only thing keeping him going, the only reason to wake from hard earned sleep. He really had no idea what his future held, He had no plans, just an overwhelming desire to rid his mind of any cohesive thought.

He unlocked the door of his new home and didn't go out for a week. He slept, sat, and stared at the TV, even though it wasn't on. He stopped shaving and showers became less frequent. He found it hard to move. He had heard the word depression in the past but hadn't realized what it meant until now. He was devoid of anything other than a growing blackness. He was sinking into himself, into the putrid, stagnant pool that was his being. The only thoughts he had now were of self-destruction. He began to wonder if there was an afterlife where he'd be reunited with his family but, mostly, he didn't care. He just craved total oblivion.

Strangely, the bottle of spirits bought as his leaving gift saved his life.

He had decided to stop trudging through the shit that was his life. He had even sharpened an already very sharp kitchen knife so it would glide through skin and vein as it would through butter. As he put the sharpener down, he nearly knocked the bottle of scotch off the surface. The golden liquid reflected the sun's rays and put everything on pause. Suddenly he was desperate to feel the spirit's heat burn the back of his throat. A last drink, one for the road, so to speak. He grabbed a tumbler, unscrewed the cap, and listened to the glug, glug as the whiskey filled the glass. He swallowed half, wincing as it went down. After so long without a drink it wasn't long before he was feeling a little lightheaded. He carried the bottle and glass into the lounge and slumped onto the sofa. He left the knife in the kitchen; it would still be there when his current business was finished. His obsession with the demon that resides in alcohol was back and the only thought he had then was to reacquaint himself with that obsession. Oblivion can be found in many ways, if not permanently, and his desire for that finality was not forgotten. It was just on the back burner until he'd enjoyed his last shot at the temporary stuff. He sat and drank, his body becoming accustomed to the heat of his old friend, his only true friend. A friend that soothed; never scolded, never pointed out the stupidity of some of his decisions.

Two hours later the bottle was empty but his desire for the demon was even stronger. He lurched to his feet, steadied himself, made sure he had his wallet and left the flat. He had intended to go to the off license two streets away but as he was passing the 'Red Lion', he heard Pink Floyd's 'Another Brick in the Wall' playing. David Gilmour's solo cut through the rancidity surrounding his brain and his fingers started to caress that air guitar that his dad had loved to play. He went through the open door and was surprised to feel the chill of air conditioning. He went to the bar, not bothering to look around. He was here to drink, to find that last seductive kiss of temporary death. He slapped a twenty on the bar and asked the barman for a bottle of vodka and a glass. The barman

49

explained with an apologetic smile that if he wanted a full bottle it would cost £24.50. He lay down another tenner and told him to keep the change. He had a few quid in coins in his pocket so he wandered over to the jukebox and stuck on more Floyd, Hendrix, Doors and Cream. There was a great selection of oldies. He decided then that when he did the deed, he would put The Doors' 'The End' on repeat. A smile nearly surfaced at the thought of symbolic shit like that. He took his booze over to a table in the corner of the bar, sat, drank, and listened to kickass music.

He was halfway down the bottle when a dark-skinned girl came in. She was a stunner, her hair a mass of curls, her classic features enhanced by the darkest brown eyes he had ever seen. Her figure was exquisite, she wore a red crop top with, obviously, no bra and white shorts. Her long legs ended in a pair of Doc Martens. As she approached the bar, three gobby twats followed, all making lewd gestures and remarks. Danny was about to see if he was still as handy pissed as he used to be, when the girl grabbed the leading twat by the bollocks and said in a broad northern accent. "What part of fuck off d'you have a problem with knob head? D'you want me to twist these little bastards off?"

One of the other two came at her but before Danny could stand, she ducked, twisted (twisting twat one's goolies a bit more) and fired a Doc Marten into the idiot's face with three short, sharp jabs. Danny heard bones and teeth crack as the punk slumped to the floor, his mouth a mass of blood and broken teeth. She eyed twat three with venom and said, "Fancy your chances shithead?"

He, apparently, had a modicum of sense. He shook his head and practically ran from the place. She let go of twat one's nether regions and punched him in the face. "Now, do one before I get angry."

They scuttled out and Danny couldn't help applauding. She turned and glared at him.

"Who the fuck are you?"

Before he could say anything a man in a long black coat appeared by her side.

"Steady Phil," he said. "He's your new best friend."

He looked strangely familiar, but Danny couldn't place him until he said,

"Hello again Danny."

The years fell away, and he was that kid again, cycling home on Christmas Eve. The man before him had not impinged on his thoughts at all for most of the time between. Yet here he was again, and their first encounter was a vivid memory suddenly.

"I see you remember me," the man said with a smile. "Once seen, never forgotten, eh?"

Danny sat and gazed, temporarily speechless. The stranger's smile broadened, the creases at the side of his mouth deepening. He seemed to exude confidence, from his collar length silver hair down to the tips of his black, calf length boots. His face showed signs of age and the vitality of youth in equal measure, making it impossible to discern his age. Intense blue eyes lit up his angular features. He waved a hand in the girl's direction.

"This is Philomena," he explained. "But call her that at your peril. Her preference is the rather masculine abbreviation 'Phil'. I can't understand it myself but that's probably because I've seen too many winters." He sighed and held his hand out in Danny's direction. "Phil meet Danny, Danny…. Phil."

"He don't look much," she muttered, eyeing Danny up and down.

"Maybe not at the moment," said the man in black. "But once we have convinced him that there are better things to do with his life than end it prematurely, I'm sure you'll see the potential."

Danny had watched this exchange with a strange curiosity, the drink still impairing his thought process to a substantial degree. There were many questions swimming for their lives inside his flooded brain but the only one that managed to surface was this one.

"Who are you?"

"I'm sorry Danny, how remiss and intolerably rude of me. My name is Seth and I'm pleased to meet you properly, at last." He held out his hand and Danny shook it automatically. Seth pointed to the bottle and glass on the table. "I suggest you bid farewell to your false friend and allow us to endeavor to introduce purpose back into your life."

Danny burst out laughing; this joker was like something out of a Charles Dickens' story. Once he'd managed to control his hysteria, he splashed more vodka into the glass and took a large swig. "I suggest you vacate the premises and allow my false friend and I a little privacy," he said, proud of his eloquence, under the circumstances.

It was Seth's turn to laugh, the sound deep and melodic. "Excellent Danny, I can see you have retained your sense of humour – admirable."

Danny grinned back and waved his hand in a shooing motion. "Cut along then, I'm rather busy."

"I apologise my boy but I really must insist. Put down the glass and come with us."

The laughter was gone, and those blue eyes no longer held warmth. Danny was suddenly angry. "Fuck off, the pair of you. I don't even know why you're here bothering me."

He raised the glass again and vaguely remembered glimpsing something from the corner of his eye before feeling a sharp pain in his neck. Then the oblivion he had been seeking arrived.

PART TWO – DAVE

ONE

Dave's life was about to end, and it was no surprise to him. When riding against an unwavering wind, it's only a matter of time before the wind's power is greater than the ability to resist it. His head was on a block and there was a mountain of a man towering over him, muscles bulging, veins visibly pumping blood and Dave couldn't help thinking – at least this is going to be quick. He'd never, in his relatively short life, pictured himself like this, which was – on his knees, neck on a poorly crafted wooden block, hands tied behind his back with a fucking great sword hovering over his head. The truth was – he wasn't ready to die. If that blade separated his rather good-looking head from his reasonably fit body, nothing would change. All the shit he'd been through would be for nothing. He wasn't worried though. He had friends; at least he thought he had. That very, very, sharp blade was about to end their friendship forever and, although normally, he was a reasonably calm person, he was beginning to think, 'okay I know you guys like a bit of fun but this is getting a little too close for comfort'. The muscle-head with the sword was giving it large with a few pre-heading sweeps – working the crowd, so to speak – for which Dave was rather grateful. There were a lot of oohs and aahs as the sword nearly took off his ear. The blade was aloft, reflecting the sun's rays. It was a nice day for a public execution – Dave couldn't have wished for better weather for having his head lopped off. It certainly beat the past few days with all the pissing rain. Dave found nothing good about rain, apart from helping spuds and carrots and the rest of them five a day, tasteless things to grow. He was not a lover of most vegetables, leaning more towards pies and puddings and things of a stodgy nature. This was not to say he was fat; he wasn't – far from it. Dave was one of the lucky ones, those who could eat anything they liked without putting on an ounce. At this precise time, however, there were more important things to consider than his dietary preferences – his head, which, if the people he had called friends didn't soon take down this son of a bitch, he would be losing. When he had been dragged up onto this rather elaborate platform (someone had even painted it red, he presumed so the blood would blend in), he had had no qualms on the outcome. Now, he was not so sure.

The meathead with the blade was enjoying his time in the limelight. He was even wearing some head-cap mask thing that looked as though it had been cobbled together by his mum at the last minute. Unfortunately, Dave never found out if that was the case or not. There was a collective sigh from the blood thirsty spectators, which could only mean one thing. He braced himself. Suddenly, something parted his hair at a rate of knots, he felt a sharp pain in his wrist and the rope holding his hands together fell away.
"Grab the sword mucker." This came from far away but was, obviously, the dulcet tones of 'Ringo' aka Frank McGee. Dave had just enough time to turn onto his back before another of Ringo's arrows pierced his would-be executioner's eyeball. Dave don't know if it went through his brain or if that was like a walnut suspended, somehow, in the middle of that big, ugly head of his, from the back of which now protruded an arrowhead. The lump dropped the sword, having more pressing business. Dave only just managed to catch it by the hilt as it attempted to finish off the job it had been about to do. His reasonably fit body leapt up and onto its feet, his hands waving the sword around, in front of the six guards surrounding him. The surprise was over, and they were looking mean, really mean, like fucking pissed.

55

"A little help wouldn't go amiss here guys," Dave yelled. "I don't mind a joke, but this is turning into a bleeding pantomime."

"Keep your hair on 'Pansy'." 'Pete the parsnip' slid from the crowd with the grace of somebody who slides well and quickly when he decides to. He was swiftly followed by Jack Hardy and Harry 'the coach' Shaw. Dave remembered thinking, as one blade became four, with 'Ringo' as back up, we must sort out a nickname for Jack. His, as Pete had already mentioned was 'Pansy' because his surname was, and still is, Potter. Harry's should be self-explanatory to most, except the wealthy or the sufferers of travel sickness. There they were – Dave, Pete, Jack and Harry facing six town guards. They'd had to deal with worse odds. There was a bit of circling and jabbing, weighing each other up before the guards went for it, the usual lumbering charge, accompanied by the twatish war cry shit. It took Dave and his mates about five minutes to do the business. Dave didn't like to blow their communal trumpet, but they were good. That was one thing; they were trained well before being hurled into this total madness. Pete's name was Davies, and his nickname came about because he had a face that resembled a parsnip, sort of broad at the top, going down to an extraordinarily thin chin and unusually lined. Frank was just a Liverpudlian and huge Beatles fan - hence 'Ringo' (easy) and, as things went, they didn't need any more of his archery skills. The crowd had seen a lot more than they bargained for but seemed quite happy with the extended footage. That was the thing with the peasants of the 12th century, they appeared to love watching others having their lives brought to an untimely end. Although Dave and co. dispatched the guards with ease, it had to be said in their defense, they never killed anyone who wasn't trying to kill them. The Famous Five, as they tagged themselves, apart from a little thieving, were honorable. Even the thieving was from the wealthy, powder-puffed buggers who screwed the little man. It will be explained shortly, who these friends are, where they come from and what they are doing in the 12th century. H.G. Wells wasn't just a writer, he was a visionary.

They made their getaway pronto, before reinforcements could make things more tiresome. Dave had to admit that coming so close to meeting the Reaper had not invoked the satisfaction the Blue Oyster Cult seemed to think it would. He did fear the bastard. Any road up, as they say in Macclesfield or somewhere round there, they were on their toes again.

"What the fuck were you doing, Ringo? I'm sure if it'd been your head on the block, you'd have fired that pissing arrow a bit quicker than that."

"If it had been my head on the block," said Ringo, with a smirk. "I don't think they'd have allowed me to have my bow and arrow by my side, you know like a cuddly toy, a little mate to take with me across the river Styx."

"Fuck off you Scouse twat," Dave said, unable to keep the grin from twitching the corners of his mouth. "You're always such a smart-arse."

"I am from the city that produced the group that changed the world. I'm allowed to be a smart-arse and, incidentally, you need to work on your witty repartee. It's a tad too basic, our John would have made mincemeat of you."

"You and the bleeding Beatles," Pete said. "I never liked the bastards anyway."

"That, my old parsnip, is because you're a total moron. You think rap is music when it is, so obviously, a load of dicks effing and blinding and indicating that most of the population would like to shag their mothers. I mean, come on, for fucks sake, grow up."

This is what got them through – the banter. It may seem as though they were a bunch of fearless jokers but, that was not the case at all. Each day could be their last, that's why the pay off, if they made it, would make each of them rich men.

"I love Dolly," said Jack, nodding his head slowly, his face contorted into a sad, lustful kind of expression.

"You love her tits," Dave said. "You hate country music."

"Not when she sings it I don't."

"Do you have any of her CD's?"

"No, but I've got a DVD."

"Why doesn't that surprise me, I'll bet there are some questionable stains on the cover."

"It was like that when I got it off eBay. I don't know what you're suggesting."

"You're a wanker." Harry was a man of few words. He was never one for flowery exaggeration.

They turned as one and gazed at the fine specimen that was "the coach" with his hunched shoulders, hooked nose, and mop of prematurely, grey hair.

"Don't you start," warned Ringo. "You love the fucking eighties, the decade that music forgot."

"Some of us enjoyed the music of our youth," he said.

"We never felt the need to pillage our grandparent's vinyl collection."

There followed a unified shout of "Piss off", to which the coach held out his hands and shrugged.

"The truth hurts my friends, the truth hurts."

They were a bunch of mates, really good mates, the kind that would die for each other. Dave had heard that said on the other side so many times, mostly under the influence, which was mostly bollocks, to say the least. This wasn't, this was the real deal.

So there they were, Dave Potter, Harry Shaw, Pete Davies, Frank McGee and the yet to be nicknamed Jack Hardy in the year of the bastard 1148.The bastard bit had been coined by Ringo because all of them, until a few months ago, had been enjoying the comforts of 2022. When 2022 is traded for 1148 it's a bastard. What's a bigger bastard is ending up in 1148's equivalent of London and having to travel, mostly on foot, to pissing Scotland with nothing but one's wits to rely on. There were no planes, trains, or automobiles of any description in the 1100s, just horses and a cart or two. These belonged to either the hard-working farm types or mean and miserable soldier sorts who tended to travel en masse. Not wanting to rob the working man and trying to keep as low a profile as possible with the authorities, these beasts of burden weren't really an option for the Famous Five. They rambled over hill and down dale and were doing all right until Dave had an ale or two too many in an inn going by the name of "The Duck on The Pond" in the village of Bauminster. This posh twat was grabbing hold of the landlord's daughter in an inappropriate manner. It was apparent she wasn't enjoying the attention, even though she was suffering it well. The grim smile on her dad's face said it all. It wasn't Dave's business and, as already stated, they were trying to keep a low profile. But the upshot was, she was cute, Dave was a little worse for wear, plus he'd never been one to stand by and watch decent folk getting abused by arseholes. Before Pete could grab him, he was in the twat's face. "You touch her again," he threatened said twat. "And I'll take your face off, you fucking, powder-puffed cock." Out of the corner of his eye he saw Ringo shaking his head, but he remembered thinking, what he'd read about his hero, John Lennon, he would have probably reacted in a similar way. Anyway, the tit swiped Dave across the face with this lace hanky thing and was about to say something when Dave's fist stopped him, breaking his nose and a couple of nicely made wooden teeth. Well it turned out he was the local bigwig and suddenly the place was like an army garrison, bloody soldiers all over the place. Dave took out four of them, but they seemed to multiply, He dropped one and two more took his place. Before he let them take him, he saw his buddies blend into the background with Jack giving him the old thumb and forefinger circle. So, he stopped fighting and let them cart him off to a straw carpeted cell which reeked of shit, piss, and vomit. That reinforced his conviction – there is nothing good about living in the twelve century. He was waiting to be tried or questioned, at least, so he could give his side of things, mitigating circumstances and the like, but what happened was that he spent a night having his olfactory senses assaulted. He even added to the stink himself, after a night on the beer. In the morning he was dragged out into the sunlight and to the executioner's block. He remembered seeing the dick in the powdered wig in a ringside seat with his red nose, black eyes and spare set of teeth, grinning like a loon. Dave winked at him and would have given him the finger if his hands weren't tied behind his back. He took pleasure, however, in the shit's obvious chagrin with Dave's lack of remorse or fear for what was to come. That's how he ended up with his head and body about to become strangers. Not something he would have advised adding to a bucket list.

Once they were clear of any further danger, Dave looked at the others and said, "This time travelling shit is not all it's cracked up to be."
"I don't recall seeing any brochures extolling its virtues," said Ringo. "It may be a little more bearable, however, if you learned to keep your nose out of the local knob's business."
"So, you're saying you'd have let him carry on pawing that young girl?"
"Yes, and if you weren't too pissed to notice his extensive entourage, you probably would have as well. We're not here to act as judge, jury and executioner, Shit happens –

it always will. Some dick fondling a waitress's tits is a poor reason to almost get your head chopped off."

Dave looked at him, knowing he was right but craving recognition for his gentlemanly behavior. "Twats like that need to be put in their place though," he said stubbornly.

"Mate, it's like anything – you have to weigh up the odds before you go steaming in. You're not fucking Superman."

"Why are you always so bleeding sensible?"

Ringo shrugged. "Just the way I am." He paused. "Mind you, if I'd have had another couple of jugs of that scrumpy, I'd have decked him myself."

Dave laughed. "You're an arsehole. You know that don't you?"

"Yeah, but an arsehole that just saved your miserable life, sunshine. Talking of which, I don't believe you have expressed your gratitude."

Dave bowed to him. "Thank you, you might be an arsehole but you're handy with a bow and arrow, I'll give you that."

TWO

It is time to explain how Dave and his friends came to be time travelers. They all answered an ad in one of the nationals for 20 – 40-year-olds to take part in a scientific study of the parts of the brain associated with stress and fear. How and why some people react aggressively, and others take flight, why some are wired differently to others. The ad said that the study would last for at least six months and during that time, board and lodging would be provided with three square meals a day and an allowance of £250.00 per week. Dave thought the thing itself sounded like a waste of time but being paid that amount of cash and having all your grub cooked for you was more than tempting. Especially as he and most of the others were sponging of the state and surviving on a pittance. It was a no brainer, as the brainless say. So, they all arrived at this complex in Richmond, a massive place with all mod cons. All the rooms were en suite; it seemed like a frigging five-star hotel. They were met by, whom they assumed to be, the head honcho, a geezer called Jerome Wagstaff, a giant of a man with a beard that would make a lot of rain forests jealous. There were exactly forty applicants. They were given a tour and Dave thought the place was bloody impressive. There was a fully equipped gym, a spa, three games rooms, one housing six full sized snooker tables. In fact, impressive didn't cut it, awesome was what it was. The restaurant was like Dave imagined the Hilton to be. But with all this opulence they weren't made to feel like commoners having a taste of the good life. Jerome was a cracking chap who made them feel right at home. He had no airs or graces, just a great down to earth bear of a bloke who kept cracking jokes. Yeah, Dave loved Jerry from day one.

After the tour they were shown to their rooms – although they were more like apartments. There was a lounge with leather sofas, a fuck off, wide screen TV, Hi Fi system connected to Spotify, state of the art laptop, shelves of books and CDs, all of which had been chosen carefully from the preferences section of the application form they'd all filled in. The phrase home from home came to mind but this place kicked Dave's shitty bed-sit into a cocked hat, pulled it out, stamped on it and put it back. It was amazing.

They were given an hour to settle in, freshen up, have a crap, or do whatever before dinner was served. He took a shower in something out of a movie, there were three heads, which could be set at different angles and pressures. It was an incredible experience. Up until now a shower was a thing to be fitted in just to keep clean. From now on he was going to look forward to entering the little cubicle and spending a good twenty minutes indulging in another worldly showering adventure.

Dinner was a four-course affair and, obviously, cooked by MasterChef winners. Dave had never tasted food like it before. He didn't realize that food could be so flavorsome. He was in heaven and was immediately hoping that when the ad had stated - at least six months, it was a very conservative estimate. The restaurant, however, looked nothing like it had during their tour. There were now forty individual tables and as they entered the room, they were shown to their own tables and asked not to communicate with any of the other guests. So began their journey into not so wonderful weirdness.

Once they had eaten their fill, from a starter consisting of scallops and prawns with fancy shit (including edible flowers) in this incredible sauce, through a fish course of salmon and trout (Dave couldn't help thinking of the

Cockney rhyming) into a main of lamb done three ways, shank, amazing lollipop jobs and liver in a red wine and rosemary jus, followed by a raspberry sorbet with chocolate cylinders and elaborate sugar work, they were all stuffed. The only thing that would have improved it would have been an ice-cold pint of lager but all they had was water, not even a bottle of poncey wine. Once all the tables had been cleared, a couple of blokes dragged in a small platform and placed it in the middle of the top end of the room, so they were all facing it. A couple of minutes later old Jerome strode in and jumped up onto the tiny stage.

"I hope you all enjoyed your first meal with us," he said with a grin. "I must apologise for, what may seem to most of you, an unusual and very unsociable set up, but for the first day, while we assess you all, we would prefer it if you didn't form any alliances that may interfere with the programme. When we have processed you, we will split you into eight groups of five, which is when your interaction with the other members of your group will begin. To explain a little more I would like you to meet my partner in crime, Christian Spalding. He and I will be carrying out your assessments together."

Jerry stepped down from the platform and folded his arms, looking towards the door leading into the restaurant. They all followed his gaze, waiting for his buddy to arrive. Dave was freaked out when he heard "Good evening folks" boom out across the room. His eyes shot back to the small stage where a tall, thin individual with shoulder length blond hair now stood.

"Sorry for the mis-direction," said, what turned out to be, Christian Spalding.

"If there are any would be magicians among you, you'll appreciate the significance of such tactics."

After getting over the man's surprising appearance, Dave was still trying to get his head around how such a deep, booming voice (akin to that bushy bearded bloke's, Brian somebody or other) could come from this thin, waif-like geezer.

"I won't keep you long," Christian continued. "Just to say that over the next two days we will find out how you all tick, down to the last tock, which is absolutely necessary before starting the trial. Now I'm sure a lot of you are thinking – how can they get to know us that well in such a short time? All I'll say is 'we haff vays'." He let out a great barking laugh that just wasn't right. A sound like that didn't come from such a body, it just didn't.

"I will warn you that the next two days will be exceptionally long and very intense, but we believe that, afterwards, you will know yourselves better and feel more at ease in your own skins. I'll leave it at that, for the time being. Go to your rooms, relax, and get a good night's sleep. An alarm will wake you at six a.m. and breakfast is at seven prompt. Anyone who thinks they can snooze for an extra half hour will miss out on the most important meal of the day. We make no allowance for slackers. You've signed a contract, agreeing to our terms and if you abide by them, you will be very well looked after. If not, there will be consequences and any recidivists will suffer our wrath." Another burst of booming laughter filled the room, but the look Dave saw in Mr. Spalding's eyes contained no mirth. "Goodnight, we'll see you in the morning. You will be shown back to your rooms individually. There will be no comparing notes at this stage. Sleep well."

Once Dave was back in his room, he heard a click and when he tried the door, he found it was locked. That was the moment he realized that something very odd was going down here.

He settled down and watched an old episode of "Game of Thrones" on the 50" Sony TV, wishing he had a few beers to go with it. It's funny how quickly a person gets used to something a whole lot better than their normal life and then wants more. There were times when he almost felt ashamed to be a part of the human race, but he'd always prided himself on his shallowness. He'd always found these deep fuckers to be miserable bastards. So, he watched Jon Snow being very heroic, honest, and totally moral, which is hard to pull off when you're sticking a great big, bastard sword in somebody's guts, but it makes great TV. By the time the show had finished he was feeling wacked, it had been a long and very strange day. He made himself a coffee and listened to Rihanna being a dirty bitch before 'turning in'. The bed was amazing, just like in Goldilocks and the three bears, not too soft, not too hard – just right. Am I going mental? He wondered. He wasn't normally this much of a divvy. Pretty soon after he slipped beneath the silk sheets, he was dead to the world. He remained that way until six o'clock when that old geezer, somebody Cotton, yelled 'Wakey, wakey' through the tannoy. At this point, having been unemployed for more time than he wished to admit, he was not used to mornings. They were things that slid by without him having to witness their passing. He normally surfaced about one with a gob like a badger's arse. He suddenly wondered who came up with that simile and why. What makes the rear end of a badger different to any other mammal. He got up, made another coffee and, although he gave up smoking two years ago, was dying for a fag. This place was really fucking with his head. He finished his coffee and went for two of the three S's, shit, and shower. He couldn't be arsed with a shave. The shower, however, nearly made him late for the old breakfast. He really loved that shower.

At seven sharp, there was another click, and a knock on the door.

"Come on in, pal," he called, and in came the same bloke who'd locked him in the previous evening. The tag on his midnight blue shirt told Dave his name was 'Jason'.

"Am I going to be locked in here every night, Jason?" He asked.

"I just follow orders sir," Jason replied.

"'Course you do." Dave was beginning to think that this clinical trial was more like a military operation.

Jason accompanied him to the dining room, where the set up was like the night before. The place was three parts full and most folks were sat, eyes ahead, obeying the rules. This was beginning to piss Dave off; he'd never been a fan of authority. As he followed his 'jailer' to the back of the room he made eye contact with another chap who, by the look on his face, felt as aggrieved as him.

"All right mate?" Dave said, and as the other bloke was about to reply there was this high-pitched whining sound that slowly increased in intensity until they were all sticking their fingers in their ears. He'd never known a sound to be painful before, but this bastard savaged the brain and Dave was almost on his knees when it stopped, and Spalding's voice boomed out. "You were warned about interaction at this stage. What you have just experienced is a very mild reminder. Any further flaunting of the rules will result in a much harsher punishment."

Dave was becoming seriously pissed off with the high and mighty shite. Fair enough, the digs were second to none and the pay would tempt everyone, except the most severely work shy of the species. What was so bad about throwing back the duvet, swinging the old pins out of the pit and eating a very hearty breakfast before a hard day's mental probing. He supposed it was the old authority thing again, plus the way they were going about it. Being locked in a room, albeit a plush, Hilton style pad, told who you could and couldn't talk to, sort of went against the grain. Looking round the dining room he could see the different expressions on the inmates' faces. There were a few that mirrored his, a lot that just showed resignation and some that were, obviously, petrified. The unknown can be an unsettling little bastard. Some welcome it with a 'bring it on' attitude whilst others hover between frightened interest and terrified trepidation. It's strange how the choice of breakfast also highlights the difference. England is, after all, the home of the full English; the best start to any day, whether it's eight hours laying bricks or a good session down the pub. He counted eight of the group munching on the old bacon and eggs while the rest were nibbling on croissants or daintily spooning in what looked like sawdust, but he assumed was muesli. Why would anyone want to eat something that looked like it had been scooped out of the bottom of a bird cage? He couldn't even entertain the idea, never mind put it in his trap. No, Dave was tucking into the F.E. with toast on the side and yet more coffee. As with dinner, the previous evening, they weren't rushed and he couldn't help thinking it would have been pleasant to have a chat with some of the other prisoners over this leisurely meal, compare cells, find out if their showers were the same bollocks as his. Ordinarily, he wasn't the most sociable of sorts but in a situation like this, he could see some comfort in sharing the experience. Fuck, I'm sounding like some bloody psychologist or something, he thought.

Breakfast came to end and the tension in the room was almost tangible. He got the impression that most of his colleagues were feeling that this well-paid little jolly was turning into something a bit more sinister. Personally, Dave was getting ready to make his feelings known, especially the brain ramming screech they'd all suffered, after his innocent morning greeting to a fellow resident. He had never been known as a hard case, never looked for trouble but, on the other hand, had never been one to turn away from a scrap. If trouble found him, he wasn't one to run. That is unless the odds were more than two to one. He wasn't a pussy, but he wasn't a thick twat either. Good old Jerome came in and apologised for the earlier assault upon their senses and urged them to think of the rest of the trial as a journey of self-exploration. Although Dave liked the chap, he couldn't help thinking what a load of bollocks he spouted. In the next few weeks, his affection would increase but his assessment of Jerry's oratory skills would increase even more. When they got down to the nitty gritty though, his fondness of him blossomed. Jerome was a good bloke, with his heart in the right place. The same couldn't be said, unfortunately, for the skinny Brian Blessed (Dave had just remembered his name), known as Christian Spalding.

THREE

They we were all replenished, one way or another, and old
Jerome came in smiling like the old Cheshire cat.
"Now you've all been fed and watered," he began. "We
will get down to business. As mentioned last night you will
be split into groups of five. I'll call out your names and
would appreciate it if each group would follow our
stewards as their group is completed."
And so, he started reeling off names, some of which,
nearly made Dave laugh out loud. Who calls their kid
Bingo, especially when their surname is, well it doesn't
matter, Bingo for Christ's sake? His last name was
Buggings, by the way. Bingo Buggings – did they despise
the poor little bastard that much? Maybe they'd got their
hearts set on a girl. There are some weird bleeders about.
The group stood as one, waiting for their individual names
to be called. For their group, Dave's was second after old
Harry and then, obviously, the rest followed. That was the
birth of the Famous Five. Although none of them had
read the stories by Enid Blyton concerning this little band,
Jack, who was a bit of a general knowledge freak pointed
out that one of them was a dog and two were girls. Not
wanting to spend time and brain power trying to think of
another moniker, they ignored these minor facts.
They filed out of the dining room behind some fellow
called Derek, who resembled a more muscular version of
Sly Stallone in his 'Rocky' days. Dave whispered to Frank
(soon to become Ringo) how his biceps were bigger than
Dave's thighs. Ringo said he was sure the muscular
bastard was cracking walnuts between his buttocks as he
walked. Dave said it was either that or he'd shit himself.
Dave and Frank hit it off from the start, Ringo was a
funny fucker and Dave loved funny fuckers. He had a
touch of the John Bishops about him although his accent

wasn't as broad. After all the clips he'd seen on telly of his hero, John Lennon, he did sound a lot like him. Whether this was the way it was or whether he'd worked on it, none of them ever found out. It didn't matter, he was a funny fucker and had the archery skills of Oliver Queen (Arrow). Although, at that time, he was just a funny fucker, the archery skills came later.

Derek led them into this room with leather chairs, coffee tables and a drinks machine. The walls were painted white and there was one window that looked out onto the car park. It seemed very clinical. They were told to help themselves to tea or coffee and he left. The cappuccino was the best Dave had ever tasted, especially from a machine. They were left for half an hour and they chatted, and, from the start, they got on, really clicked. However, they'd chosen the members of the groups, they'd done a bloody good job. Before they knew it Christian made an entrance. No diversionary tactics this time, he just walked in through the door. Obviously, he opened it first and didn't pass through it like a ghost.

"Right," he said.

"Dave, you don't mind if I call you Dave?" He held out his hands in a sort of 'tell me to fuck off if you like' sort of way. Dave didn't, he told him to knock himself out. Something, by the way, very shortly, he would want to do himself.

"Well Dave, we'll have a bit of a chat to you first, if you don't mind," Christian said with a smile that was not only false but reminded Dave of how he would imagine Esther Rantzen to look if she was high on coke. It was quite disconcerting. "Would you like to follow me?"

"Why me?" Dave asked.

"We have to start with one of you and as you are the only one to flaunt our rules so far, we thought it might as well be you. You don't have a problem with that, do you, Dave?" The way he said Dave's name made his skin crawl.

He really didn't like this fucker. But it was either telling him where to stick his trial and going back to beans on toast for dinner or going along with it and earning a fair wedge, whilst having blinding scran. Dave wasn't daft, well not that daft.

"No, Christian," he replied, with as much smarm as he could muster. "Please lead on."

He got the impression that the dislike was mutual and started to wonder how this was going to pan out. He had never been one to suffer fools or be nice to twats that pissed him off and he was getting the distinct impression that Christian was of a similar mind. Dave had been sacked from a few jobs because he refused to do as he was told by jumped up tits who annoyed the fuck out of him. In fact, one little bastard, Mr. Duffing, Duffy, something with Duff in it, pissed him off that much he had him by the throat. He was lucky to get away with that without the old bill being involved. He had to eat about twelve humble pies and do more bowing and scraping than is acceptable to the meanest son of a bitch. There were six other blokes, who'd managed to stick the stupid job and this wanker for years, grinning from ear to ear, only just managing to stop themselves cheering. That, as far as Dave was concerned, said it all. People like that, who take joy in making other folks lives a misery, shouldn't be allowed to live, unless they vow to change their ways. That should be a law.

Dave followed Christian out into the corridor and down to the right. He was being severely childish, making faces behind Spalding's back and giving him the V's. They seemed to walk for ages, up and down these bloody corridors until they came to a pair of glass doors. There was a keypad on the left-hand side which Christian keyed in 9175 to gain access. He did it quickly and tried to shield what he was doing with his scrawny body. It, obviously, didn't work. Dave couldn't help chalking one up to him.

72

Beyond the glass doors everything became very laboratory looking with steel benches covered in kit that resembled stuff Dave vaguely remembered from the physics lab at school. On the right-hand side of this huge room were four doors. The thin man took Dave to the third and they went in. Sat behind a desk was old Jerome. To the side was a chair resembling something from a dentist's room, next to a weird looking machine. Christian closed the door and indicated the dentist's chair with his right hand. Dave looked at him and shook his head. "I had a check-up a month ago," he said, "I'm fine."

"Sit in the chair or leave Mr. Potter, your decision."

As Dave sat down, he wondered what happened to the friendly, Christian name business.

"Let's just make you comfortable," Spalding said, with what can only be described as a sadistic grin. He took out what looked like a small TV remote control, pointed it at Dave and pushed a button. The grin widened as, suddenly, steel bands slid noiselessly from the armrests and footplates of the chair and imprisoned Dave.

Dave glared at him and looked over to Jerome, who looked very apologetic and even mouthed a 'sorry'.

"What happens if I want to leave now?" Dave asked Christian.

"You made the decision not to when you sat in the chair David."

So, it started off with Dave, then Mr. Potter and now David. Dave swore to himself before he left this fucking asylum, he would drop this bastard, he was really starting to get on Dave's tits. But for now, he had to tell himself to play it cool, not let the sadist see how much he was getting to him. When the fucker went down, he wouldn't be expecting it, Dave's fist in his face a complete surprise. He nodded. "Do your worst."

That is an expression Dave had heard used many times but when he employed it this time, he wasn't expecting to regret saying it. Restrained in a dentist's chair with heavy steel bands, might make one think – why? He didn't, although this willowy wanker was pissing him off, this was an official trial, endorsed by the powers that be, wasn't it? "This is a modified lie detector," explained the thin man, pointing to the machine at the side of the chair. "In a moment we will hook you up to it and have that little chat, I mentioned earlier." He nodded to old Jerome, who got up from behind the desk and took his position between the machine and Dave. He stuck electrodes on the back of both of his hands and two at his temples. As he positioned the last two, he leant forward and whispered, 'Tell the truth Dave, tell the truth.'

So began the 'little chat', more like the fucking Spanish Inquisition, as it turned out. As Jerome resumed his position behind the desk, Christian began the interrogation.

"We'll start off with a couple of basic control questions." This was, unusually, normal – name, date of birth and so on. It didn't stay that way for long though.

The first question 'proper' was 'Have you ever stolen anything?'

Dave had done a bit of thieving in his younger days but thought this might not go down well so he lied. It was at this point that he understood why he was so heavily restrained. He had no clue know how many volts shot through his brain but it fucking hurt and made him bite his tongue. "Fucking bastard," he said through gritted teeth. This seemed to cause Christian an enormous amount of pleasure.

"Speak truthfully and that will be the only time you feel the wrath of the 'Interrogator'." The bastard almost chuckled.

From then on Dave suffered over an hour of very personal questions, as personal as 'Have you ever looked at your mother in a sexual way.' He was thankful that his mum was 18 stone and resembled a female Sid James. He loved his mum but – sexually, come on. He told the truth, even when he felt ashamed, and by the time the session had finished, though it sounds corny, he felt he did know himself better. But he still hated that scrawny, sadistic bastard and his intentions toward him hadn't changed.

From then on, this so called "trial" became weirder and weirder, not to mention bloody hard and extremely uncomfortable. The plush rooms with all the creature comforts and the en suite with the dog's bollocks of a shower were gone. Instead Dave and his new friends slept in one room on mattresses as thin as fucking rice paper. To liken it to an army barracks would be an insult to good old squaddies. They had one blanket each and a pillow, well more like an empty pillowcase, whether an impression of a pillow lurked inside was debatable. It was just as well it wasn't the middle of winter because there was no visible sign of any form of heating. The gourmet grub they'd been served before was also a thing of the past. The term for their meals from then on was, Dave believed, 'basic rations'. They all complained of course and were told to grin and bear it. They were, after all, still being paid the same amount of cash and although the scran was basic, it was free and marginally better than beans on toast every night. They became a tight knit group, which was, obviously, the intention. Through hardship, firm bonds are formed. Somebody must have said that, Dave thought it was some geezer like Churchill. It was hard. They were all bums who were used to surfacing about 1.00p.m. and then getting busy lazing the rest of the day away, pausing at dinner time to put the beans in the microwave and the bread in the toaster, of course. Now the bastards were waking them at the unearthly hour of 6.00a.m. and before they could scoff their cornflakes and toast, they had to endure an hour in the frigging gym. This was not basic; every piece of punishing equipment, every torturous machine was there, as were their wardens, who liked to call themselves 'personal trainers'. Sadistic fucks were what they were.

Dave thought many times that he'd have loved to jack it all in and go back to sleeping half his life away but the truth was, in a masochistic way, he was quite enjoying the strict regime and the increase in muscle power. He did get a buzz from having 'personal trainers' get him to kick the shit out of himself. As Spalding had already made clear anyway – there was no turning back. Strangely enough, none of them thought about the reason for the trial anymore, it was just them against the world. None of them wanted to be the pussy that would crumble. They egged each other on, the banter both inspired and cruel, when the situation required it. Dave thought it was something akin to institutionalization. Inspirational phrases and big, fucking words, who's the daddy?

This went on for a month or so, but to be honest they lost all track of time. They were all getting pretty toned with the increasingly severe arse kicking routines they were enduring, and Dave couldn't remember ever feeling better. Man, he was a fucking coiled spring.

On a Friday, Dave thought it was Friday, before they tucked into their cornflakes in came the slimy, scrawny shite. As soon as they entered the gym every morning, all they could think about was the reward that was their meagre breakfast. Now here he was coming between them and those lovely, golden flakes. But then came the next stage of mind fuck.

FOUR

Spalding stood there and if they didn't physically curl their lips, they were all doing it mentally. There are some people that are hated but most don't deserve such intense emotion. Like the bloke in the post office who made a point of sighing when Dave took in bags of twenty pence pieces, waiting for him to replace them with crisp ten- or twenty-pound notes. His attitude pissed Dave off and he'd say, 'I hate that miserable bastard', but he didn't, not really. Like the phrase 'I'm going to kill him'. Just words and phrases, used but not meant in a literal sense. Dave had never been brilliant at expressing himself, but he could say, with all honesty, that he did hate, in fact despise, the streak of piss that was Christian. Just looking at the bastard, before he even opened his gob, the old nostrils flared and, yeah, the top lip curled. Real hatred is a powerful emotion and should not be belittled by feelings of the pissed off variety.

There he was in his hand stitched suit. Dave had never seen this man in casual clothes or witnessed a hair of his thinning thatch daring to be out of place. At times he entertained fanciful notions that he may be a synthetic version of human sadism, and this was even before he found out that he'd been issued with a pass for the time travel express. Dave had always been a great mental meanderer; it helped when one was unemployed with so many empty hours to fill. His thoughts sometimes bordered on the slightly poetic – or so he thought.

He was shit at English at school, never knew a pronoun from a proverb, not to mention adjectives and adjunctives and all that bollocks. He always wondered why you needed to know what a verb or a noun was or an adjective if you knew where to put the little bleeders. They didn't need to have titles, they're all just words that go where they go. To all the English teachers out there – stop making something so simple into such unnecessary, complicated bullshit.

Maybe he needed a soapbox or a mental restrictor. As stated earlier, he was a great mental meanderer and, on occasions, meandered, unchecked, for a considerable time. Time to continue, however, with this weird and, at times, wonderful tale.

"We are very pleased with your progress," said their gaoler. "The next phase will depend on your commitment, your strength and, more importantly, your trust. We have what you may call a mission, an adventure or, simply a test of your abilities. At this stage that is all I can say. I can, however, tell you that if you are successful in this challenge, you will all find your bank accounts no longer in the red but with a credit of one quarter of a million pounds sterling. Further intensive training will be required as the mission will involve combative elements. It will be a military style operation and will therefore be necessary for you to become a closer unit than you already are. All the other participants in this 'so called' trial have been paid and dismissed. Your group is the only one considered able to complete the mission in question. It will be six months to a year out of your lives and at the end you will be wealthy. I can't guarantee your safety; that will be down to you. We will allow you to finish your gym work earlier today to discuss and digest what I have just said amongst yourselves and tomorrow we will begin your training."

This was insane. Not being backward in coming forward as his old dad used to say, Dave opened his gob.

"Don't you think we need to know what this 'so called' mission is?"

Christian shook his head. "You will only find out the purpose of the mission when I'm ready to divulge it."

"Don't you think that's a little unfair?" Frank asked. It seemed a reasonable question.

"All I can tell you is that it will be dangerous, possibly life threatening, you will be in strange surroundings and your success and survival will depend on your strength as a close unit. You will be on your own; there will be no back-up. If I told you anymore and then you decided to try and make a break for freedom, we'd have to kill you." He let out a barking laugh, but his eyes told a different story. The bastard wasn't joking.

"Now go and talk to each other and tomorrow morning we'll hope you have come to terms with our way of doing things. I will say one thing. Before you answered that ad, you were all living sad, useless lives. You complete this mission, and your lives will be worth living. To herald the start of your combat training, you will be served a full English breakfast in the canteen. Don't say I never do anything for you. Enjoy the rest of today, get a good night's rest and we'll see you bright and early tomorrow. By the way, the money you have already earned will be added to your fee, as will the rest you earn during your training. You are all strong, resourceful individuals, which is why you were chosen. For that, you are being rewarded. I'll see you in the morning."

He left the room, and they were, finally, allowed to go and refuel their grumbling bellies. As they tucked into their Corn Flakes, they all imagined how it would be to tuck into a full English again. Dave was already started to mentally dribble. He could picture the bacon, sausage, black pudding, eggs, every fucking thing possibly associated with a cooked breakfast.

"What do you make of it all?" asked Harry, through a gob full of cereal.

"The way I see it is – we have very little choice in the matter," Dave said. "He must have about twenty meatheads guarding him, and they have fucking Uzis."

"You're very observant, young Potter," said Frank.

Pete shrugged. "He's right though – what choice have we got?"

"We could start a tunnel. " Jack said. "Anybody got a pneumatic drill about their person?"

"At least we get a decent breakfast." Harry gave all their thoughts a single voice.

They all gazed into space, mentally piling on the bacon, sausages, and eggs, leaving the beans, mushrooms, tomatoes, hash browns, and black pudding in a big dish to be dipped into when needed. It was better than a wet dream.

"Did you see that fucker's eyes? He's an evil bastard." Pete said.

"His bedside manner requires a little work," said Frank. "But I do agree – he is an evil bastard, Peter." Nicknames had not been sorted at this time. Although they were mates, they hadn't become the close unit that, as described by bollock head, they would become.

They finished their light breakfast and were carted off to the gym again. As Dave and Frank were running side by side on the rolling roads, Dave said, "What do you reckon this mission is?"

Frank shrugged. "Who knows? One thing you can guarantee though – it ain't going to be nice. I dare say the bastard will tell us when he's ready. Don't sweat it, mate. Like you said, we can't do much about it. At this precise time, resignation is the order of the day. Let's just focus on the good things like the breakfast."

"That's only one thing."

"Sorry man, I'm not a magician."

They ceased to speculate and immersed themselves in their grueling routines. As 4.00 p.m. arrived, Jerome entered the gym. He wrinkled his nose.

"You boys do sweat, don't you?"

"We don't normally see you 'round these parts, partner," said Frank in his best John Wayne voice, which wasn't particularly good. He glanced at the clock. "Wow, all of an hour off. Cheers Jerome, I'm overcome – not."

Jerome looked apologetic. "I'm here with a little good news, "he said eagerly. "Christian has decided you deserve an evening of alcoholic stimulation."

"A night on the piss?" Jack said.

"Erm, I believe that may be one of the more colourful descriptions – yes."

"Lead on McDuff," said Frank.

Jerome wafted a hand in front of his nose. "You have an hour to shower and change and then there will be food and drink in the canteen."

"So, what's this mission?" Dave asked him.

Jerome's expression changed immediately. "I'm sorry Dave, it's not my place to tell you."

"But you know, don't you?"

"Er...I'll see you later."

"Jeez, he left the room like I used to do when my old man let off a real ripsnorter, after an afternoon on the lash," said Pete.

"Mmm, the plot thickens," said Frank.

"A piss-up though," said Harry. "Maybe he's not such a bad bastard, after all."

"And maybe I'm Mary fucking Poppins," said Dave.

"Well, I guess it's better than what we normally do, after killing ourselves in here," Jack said.

They all nodded, Dave and Frank sticking out their bottom lips to accentuate the point.

"Let's hit the showers and get our glad rags on then," Frank said.

They filed out of the gym and gave the showers a good seeing to.

A weird sort of portable bar had been wheeled into the canteen complete with bitter, lager and cider on tap and a whole row of optics. There were crates of mixers, buckets full of ice and even bowls of nuts, crisps and pork scratchings. They were like kids in a sweet shop.

"He wants us to get pissed," Frank said.

"That makes six us," Dave said, nodding to the Strongbow pump and almost salivating as he watched the barman fill a glass with the liquid gold.

Frank shrugged, ordered a pint of Carlsberg. "Just remember Dutch courage has been responsible for some seriously bad shit over the years."

Dave clinked his glass with his own. "Just as well mine was brewed in Herefordshire then."

They all laughed and for a time they drank and talked shit – sport, music, wenches – normal, shallow, bloke crap. Pete kept them entertained with a seemingly endless supply of jokes, some of which were actually funny. They were like a bunch of mates on a night out. After they'd been there an hour or so, the chef came in with plates of pizza, meat pies and pasties and bowls of French fries.

"Jeez, there are no bloody vol-au-vents," Pete said. "They should be served with every meal. Having said that, I am quite partial to pizza as well."

"Vol-au-vents?" Dave said.

Pete nodded. "I fucking love vol-au-vents."

"We might as well enjoy it while we can," Frank said. "Let's face it, after breakfast tomorrow, we're back to basics and who knows what's going to happen when we get to the...." He made inverted comma signs either side of his head before saying, "Mission."

Dave was sucking in cold air as he tried to get to grips with a red-hot meat and potato pie. "I've just burnt the rood of my mouth," he said, after finally managing to get it down.

"Blow it," said Jack.

"I beg your pardon."

They all laughed as Jack face reddened. "I meant the pie," he said.

82

"Can I just ask a question?" Dave said.

"I think you just did, sunshine," said Frank.

"Were any of you happy with your lives before all this shit?" Dave asked.

"No, I was bored to death, penniless and beginning to succumb to the lure of depression," Harry replied.

"So, I know we have no choice here, but the upside is we could possibly be changing our lives forever. Surely that's better than going back to nothing. I mean, fucking hell, none of us has a pot to piss in and no prospect of changing that."

"That's if we come through it unscathed," said Pete. "Don't forget the 'life threatening' bit."

"There is no point going on about it," said Frank. "What will be, will fucking be. Whatever it is, we'll kick its fucking arse. Am I right?" He raised his right hand, palm out. Dave gave him five first and the rest followed. "Now let's forget it for the time being and enjoy ourselves, yeah?"

The decision made, they made the most of the booze and food, having a good old bonding session. There was much merriment and laughter. It was probably the best day they'd all had in a few years. Dave had heard loads of people, in the past, say that alcohol wasn't necessary for a good time and, although he knew this to be true, it can't be denied, booze lubricates the laughing muscles.

At 10.00 p.m. The bar was wheeled out and a communal groan went up.

"I guess that's the end of that," said Dave, gazing at the Strongbow pump as it left the room.

"It was good while it lasted," said Frank. "And we've still got a full English to look forward to."

The tannoy suddenly burst into life. Spalding's not so dulcet tones blasted out.

"Please finish your drinks, gentlemen and return to your quarters. You have ten minutes to comply. I'm sure you all know what will happen if you don't. Goodnight."

"He sure knows how to put the mockers on things," said Pete. He drained his beer and set his empty glass on the table. Dave was thinking of going over the ten-minute curfew just to see what would happen, but he was knackered and the prospect of getting his head down was greater than his desire to rebel. He swallowed the last drop of cider and smacked his lips.

They had five minutes to spare when they left the canteen and made their way back to the room that masqueraded as a bedroom. They all lay down on their thin mattresses, fully clothed, and within minutes the room was filled with the sound of sleep.

FIVE

The morning arrived like a thief, silent and unbidden.
Dave sat up and yawned, his head fuzzy, his mouth dry.
The need to piss forced him to his feet and into the latrine
area. He relieved himself, splashed cold water over his face
and stuck his mouth under the tap.
"I know how you feel mate," Frank said, unzipping his
jeans. "It's bad enough when you're used to it. After such
a layoff, it sort of – kicks your arse."
Dave grabbed his toothbrush. "Mmm," was all he could
manage.
One by one the others joined them, all looking like death.
"Mind, it was a good night," said Harry, massaging his
temples.
Pete went into one of the cubicles, dropped to his knees
and hoofed.
Dave grimaced. "Nice one, Pete. You could have, at least,
closed the door."
Pete came out, wiping his mouth with the back of his
hand. "I'm ready for that full English now," he said with a
grin.
They all freshened up and made their way back to the
canteen. Once the aroma of bacon, eggs and sausage
permeated the air, they all seemed to perk up.
"Maybe, I could eat a morsel or two," said Frank.
They all grabbed a plate each and started piling them up.
They were allowed to eat a leisurely breakfast, without
hassle but after all the crockery was cleared away and they
were on their second cup of coffee, Christian and Jerome
entered the room.
"We hope you had a good time last night and have
enjoyed your breakfast. I think it's time to get down to
business," said Christian.
"Whatever that may be," Dave said flatly.

"So, what's our mission?" Frank asked.

"You'll be going to Scotland."

"Home of the Jimmy hat," Jack said with a chuckle.

"I don't believe the Jimmy hat had been conceived in the twelfth century," said Christian with a wry grin.

They all looked at each other, similar thoughts filling their working-class brains (they were working class, even if they didn't work). He's flipped, he's lost the plot, he's away with the fairies, he's a sandwich short of a picnic and any other figure of speech to describe someone who's as mad a fucking hatter.

Dave looked at Jerome, expecting to see the same thoughts reflected in his expression but didn't. He looked as sheepish as ever, but the only other thing Dave detected was resignation.

"Okay," Dave said. "I like a joke as much as anybody, but I feel we're all missing the punch-line here. What, pray tell, does the twelfth century have to do with anything?"

Christian looked smugger than ever. "Your mission is to travel to twelfth century Scotland, 1148 to be precise."

"Right," said Frank. "H.G. Wells has been in touch, has he?"

"Nothing so primitive," said Christian with a sneer.

Dave was starting to feel a little uncomfortable. The look on Jerome's face worried him, for one thing. All this twelfth century shit was, obviously, bollocks but something was going down here that he knew they weren't going to be best pleased with."

"I think it's time for cards on the table," he said.

Christian shrugged. "I think I have four aces, what about you Mr. Potter?"

Dave sighed. "Look, stop playing games. What the fuck have we signed up for?"

"I should have thought that, by now, you know I don't play games. Your colleague mentioned H.G. Wells and, presumably, referred to his novel, "The Time Machine".

Maybe he has read the book and, if so, is probably the only one of you that has. I imagine that you've all seen that ridiculous trilogy of films entitled 'Back to the Future' though. There has been much scientific speculation, however, concerning the subject of time travel. Concepts that appear to be ludicrous to men and women of limited intellect and no imagination will intrigue those with more analytical and adventurous minds. Imagine trying to explain the airplane or the computer to a twelfth century farmer. You, at this moment, are farmers not willing to accept that something beyond your current understanding could possibly exist. Most people in this sad world walk around with mental blinkers restricting their progress. H.G. Wells, along with subsequent novelists asked the question – what if? Although, probably, believing it to be impossible they still asked the question. And would be susceptible to the possibility and embrace it with the hope of enlightenment. You five must lose your farmer mentality and fire your imaginations."

"You expect us to believe that you have a time machine?" asked Pete.

"I will show you and you will believe – all of you. You have your mission." He became less animated. "You have no choice. It is not a case of believing or not believing. Truth is undeniable and you are soon to see that truth and make history by visiting it."

"You're mad," Dave said. He looked at Jerome. "Why are you with this nutter, man? Has he got something on you? 'Cos if he has, it must be something big."

"He's not mad, I'm afraid," Jerome said. "Hard as it is to believe, we do possess a machine that allows travel through time, although it is restricted at the present time." Christian waved a hand in his colleague's direction in a motion that indicated he wished Jerome to shut his trap. "We will come to that later," he said impatiently. "Once we've explained the mission, all will become apparent."

"Well you can fucking count me out," Frank said. "I didn't sign up for any mental shit."

"You signed up for a mission. A mission conceived and introduced by this group. Unfortunately, Mr. McGee, you have no further choices. You will do as you are told."

"The fuck I will. I ain't going and that's that."

Christian took some remote-control thing from his jacket pocket and pushed a button. Within seconds six military types were amongst them, all built like brick shit houses. Christian pointed at Pete. "Grab him and bring him to me," he instructed his henchmen.

"What the f…" was all Pete had time to utter before he was picked up like a child and carried to the front of the room, a massive, gloved hand over his mouth.

"Now McGee, let's see if we can't change your mind." He pressed his remote thing again and another dude came in with a medical bone saw. Dave was not a doctor or anything, but he'd seen his fair share of 'Casualty' episodes to recognize a bone saw when he saw one.

"I think we'll start with the left foot," Christian said with relish. He nodded and suddenly Pete's leg was yanked out and being introduced to the geezer with the saw. Christian turned his attention back to Frank. "Now, do we proceed to remove various parts of Mr. Davies' body or do you fall in line."

"You're bluffing," said Frank but we could all hear the uncertainty that we all felt.

"Dixon, proceed."

Bone saw man was like a robot. There was no emotion as he grabbed Pete's foot and brought the saw to bear on his ankle. He was about to start the primitive amputation when Frank rushed forward.

"Okay, okay. I'll do it, just leave him alone."

Christian waved Dixon away, who let Pete's leg drop with a thud. He didn't notice as his foot made a rather heavy contact with the floor. It was obvious he was in shock.

The meatheads let him go and he just stood there shaking. Frank put his arm around him and led him back across the room. "I'm sorry man," he muttered.

"As you should now have realized, all of you are dispensable. You follow orders and, hopefully, survive – or you die. It's your choice. It would be unfortunate to have to start the process all over again but if that's the way it turns out, so be it."

"One day I'm going to kill you, you son of a bitch," Dave said through gritted teeth.

The son of a bitch laughed. "I doubt that very much Mr. Potter, but I like your spirit. Keep hold of that, you're going to need it."

Over the next six months nothing else was mentioned about their mission and they were back on army rations and barrack-style sleeping arrangements. Their training was intense and, in addition to their normal martial arts shit, they were taught to fight with swords (heavy fuckers, at that), bows and arrows and staffs. They were prisoners. It wasn't as if they could tell the bastard 'bollocks' and suffer the consequences. If any of them cut up rough, one of the other four was punished. Through their mutual hatred of Christian and his goons they became like brothers. That was a phrase Dave had heard banded about many times before but had thought, 'what a pile of shite'. But the way he felt about his partners in slime was bordering on love. He was an only child, but he couldn't imagine feeling anymore for a blood brother than he did for these pillocks. As the weeks passed, they all grew stronger and faster and became tasty with their primitive weaponry. Frank found he was a natural with a bow and was as accurate as Phil 'The Power' Taylor was with his own type of arrows. The swords they had originally struggled to wield were slung about like toothpicks. So confident were they of their finely tuned abilities they even considered taking on the goons and attempting a break-out. The only thing that stopped them were the Heckler and Koch MG4s hanging at their sides. A sword, no matter how sharp, is no match for a machine gun.

So, they did as they were told and got on with it. Dave was a great believer that opportunities presented themselves at the most unlikely of times and so he was just waiting for the opportunity to gut Christian with his extremely sharp blade. He'd never killed anyone before, never had the inclination or need. Getting into scraps and giving some bloke a few digs is something many do on occasions, but to want to take another being's life is different. Hatred, real, unadulterated hatred burns inside and each encounter with the object of that feeling fuels the fire even more. That was how they all felt about Christian Spalding.

They trained, ate, drank, slept. That was how their lives were now, every day. They didn't even get Sundays off, not that any of them knew one day from the next. They had forgotten about the 'mission' and the ludicrous notion of a time machine. They were almost robotic. Then, as they were finishing another sweat drenched day, the bastard appeared. If they'd been dogs, they would have snarled in unison, as it was, they glared and clenched their fists, again in unison.

"I believe you are ready to begin," Spalding said with a smile that would have cut concrete. "Tomorrow you will be allowed to sleep until nine then be served a slap-up breakfast. By noon you will have become time travelers. Sleep well."

They still slept in the barrack room, although little sleep was had by any of them, considering their future prospects (or should that be past prospects). The breakfast however was something else, even by chef's exacting standards. It was more a mixed grill than breakfast, the meat tender, and the vegetables fresh and perfectly cooked. Dave had no idea what was in the sausages, but they really were to die for. He would challenge any King to find fault with their last meal of the 21st century. They were given plenty of time to eat and digest this glorious food and were even left to relax for a time afterward. Just before noon, Christian, Jerome and the platoon of goons joined them.

"The time has come my friends. You will all be given a photograph and a basic sketch of the same subject. As the sketch is something that could have been produced in the twelfth century, concentrate on the photograph and memorise it thoroughly. Before you leave, this will be returned. If any of you were found in possession of such a thing, there is no telling what could happen. Being burnt alive for being a warlock springs to mind, something I'm sure none of you would want."

One of the goons passed out the aforementioned items, a photo and drawing of a man's face. Dave had no idea what sort of paper the sketch was on, but it wasn't a sheet of A4, that's for sure.

"The man's name is Martin Poulson, although that matters little, as in the past he will have adopted a more suitable one. You are tasked with tracking him down and retrieving a valuable item he stole from us. What happens to the man himself does not concern me. If you must kill him to get what was taken, do so."

"How are we supposed to find this feller?" Frank asked. "It seems like a bit of a needle in a haystack sort of arrangement, if you don't mind me saying."

"The total population of Britain in the twelfth century was around two million, Frank," explained Jerome. "In Scotland it would have been around the forty hundred thousand mark, so, although not an easy task by any means, nowhere near as difficult as if you were searching for him today." He glanced sheepishly at Christian, swallowed, and said. "If at all possible, please try not to harm Martin, he's a good man."

"A good man who stole from us, Jerome," snapped Christian. "A misguided fool with no vision." He suddenly stopped and grabbed Jerome by the shoulder. "You don't share his views, do you?"

"N…n…no, of course not. I just meant that…er."

Under Christian's gaze Jerome's words petered out and he looked down at his feet.

He's frightened for his fucking life, Dave thought, how does this bastard have so much power? "What is this item?" he asked. "Sounds like he's nicked the crown jewels."

"Put it this way Mr. Potter, if you fail in your mission you will live in the past until your dying days."

"You're not really selling this," Frank said.

Christian's vampiric smirk intensified. "I don't need to sell anything to you," he said flatly. "You are now under my control and will do as I tell you. You are aware of the consequences, should you decide to try my patience."

He nodded to one of his goons who moved like a cat and cracked Harry across the shoulder with the butt of his gun. Harry winced but stood his ground, glaring at Christian.

"For fuck's sake man," Dave said. "There was no need for that. You're just a…."

"Watch your tongue Potter, unless you want to lose all your friends."

"Everything that goes around, comes around," Dave said with a smile. "There will come a day when there are just you and me and I will dash you into little pieces," he said, quoting Pink Floyd.

This time Pete received a massive fist in his solar plexus. He groaned and then said through gritted teeth. "Good on yer Dave."

Christian took in a deep breath and let it out slowly. "This is becoming tedious. I think it's time we got down to business. Follow me."

The goons (they were beginning to remind Dave of some weird things he saw on an old Popeye cartoon) closed in and ushered them forward, machine gun barrels digging into their backs. Poor old Jerome was bringing up the rear. Every time Dave looked at him, he gave Dave, what can only be described as, a sad, apologetic smile. Although they hadn't talked much, Dave really liked him. He was a good guy, obviously trapped in a load of shit, like the rest of their merry band.

They were pushed along; the guns being jabbed into their backs every few paces. They all gritted their teeth, muttering a variety of expletives under their breath. Dave considered spinning round and attempting to relieve the goon nearest him of his weapon, shoving it down his throat and pulling the trigger. The only thing that stopped him was the knowledge that he was not Bruce Lee or bloody grasshopper from 'Kung Fu' and he would end up looking like a colander. A look he wasn't keen on trying. The corridor they were being shoved down suddenly came to an end, a heavy, metal door barring their way. Again, to the right was a keypad. Christian punched in some number and being the filling of a goon sandwich, none of them had a chance to see what it was. He yanked the door open and a steep staircase was quickly illuminated, going in the downward direction. He led the way, and they were encouraged to follow, a little less forcefully. Dave guessed they didn't want their charges to trip and use the bastard as a surfboard to the bottom of the stairs. The idea appealed to Dave a great deal, he had to admit. They reached the bottom without incident. Another heavy, metal door faced them, which, once opened, revealed some weird shit.

"H.G. Wells eat your heart out," said Christian, arms outstretched like an American evangelist.

SIX

It was all fucking lights and silver and things beeping all over the place. It was like Dave would have imagined a spaceship to be.

"This is the doorway to history, my friends."

They all looked at each other and shook their heads. As Dave seemed to have adopted the mantle of spokesman, he felt it necessary to voice their mutual opinion.

"Cut the matey-matey shit," he said. "It doesn't suit you. Shall we just get on with your mental, suicide mission."

Christian looked him up and down and then a manic grin increased the insanity he embodied. "If you roll up in the twelfth century in your current attire, I believe your description maybe correct Potter. A major part of any con is to look the part. Behind that glass panel is a door to a small changing room. Your clothes are in piles marked with your names, as are your weapons. Your bow, McGee, is not of the calibre you've been used to but something of that nature would attract a great deal of unwanted attention, don't you think? If you would be so kind as to assume your new, or should I say old, personas, we can get down to business."

More gun barrel prods followed until they were in a tiny dressing room. Dave found himself wondering if up and coming pop groups had to squeeze themselves into such a small space. This was the first introduction of the old nickname thing when Harry asked Frank. "Did the Beatles ever have to suffer this shit, Ringo."

Frank beamed. "This is luxury to what they had to put up with in Hamburg, Coach."

It appeared they were on a bit of a roll with the old nickname business. It's funny how something as simple as calling someone a different, maybe freaky sort of name, brings them closer. Dave felt sort of jealous that Harry and Frank had sorted themselves out and he was still plain, old Dave. Pete suddenly changed that, not to Dave's liking, he had to say. "I suppose you've got to be a pansy," he said with a grin.

"Oh no, come on, more imagination please."

"Nicknames aren't about imagination," said Frank. "Even the thickest bastards have got to get it, otherwise it's pointless. It's no good having a nickname that only Mensa members can work out." His smile was wider than it should have been when he said. "So, pansy it is, Potter. You'll get used to it, don't worry."

Dave was still a little peeved at Pete and was trying to get his own back. Imagination had never been one of his talents but ever since he'd met the bloke, he'd always thought his face was the shape, with some of the undulations, of a parsnip. So out it came. "Tell Pete the parsnip to shut the fuck up," he laughed.

Frank was the first to join in, followed swiftly by Harry and then Jack. Pete joined in, and soon they were all in fits. Before anyone could even think about Jack, the bastard was back.

"Come on guys, you have a place and time to be and a thief to apprehend,"

"You'd better tell us what he nicked, what it looks like," said Pete.

Christian nodded and produced a pile of photographs that he handed round.

"I'd like to know how we get back," Jack added. "I think something of this nature would stand out a little in the twelfth century."

"A good point well put, Hardy," Christian responded. "If you fail to acquire the item immortalized in that photograph, I'm afraid you don't." The evil grin was back. Dave shook his head, feeling sorry for any spider that may lose its way and find itself in his bath. There would be no glass and card, no transportation back to the wild, just obliteration with a copy of the financial times or some other fucking broadsheet. It certainly wouldn't be a copy of the Sun. It's weird the shit that just springs into a person's head for no reason at all.

"Stop staring into space and look at the photograph, Potter."

Dave gave him a look and was about to add the finger. Luckily for his mates he sucked back in time and just increased the severity of the look instead.

"You are a pathetic, little lay-about with an attitude problem, Potter. Your childish glares are obviously intended to intimidate me. They don't."

Dave shrugged. "One day I'll hold a razor-sharp blade against your jugular and then we'll see if you're intimidated."

Christian laughed out loud, and Dave nearly lost it. The nails on his fingers were not that sharp but tiny crescents of blood appeared in the palm of his hand and his knuckles turned white as his fists turned themselves into miniature anvils. He couldn't stop repeating to himself – I hate this fucker and one day I will stop any more oxygen being wasted on him. He wondered how that grin would fare if they were alone in a locked room together.

"Try to curb your silly fantasies and concentrate on the job in hand. The sooner you realize that there is always a pecking order and that you'll always be at the bottom, the sooner you'll be able to accept your inferior position and do as you're told. Can you get that through your incredibly thick skull, Potter?"

Dave gave him a surprised look. "Sorry, what were you saying? I was picturing the blood pouring from the gaping wound that used to be your throat. I nearly got a hard-on."

He held Spalding's gaze and before he looked away Dave was sure he saw a hint of doubt or fear, or maybe both, cloud those gimlety eyes. Or maybe it was just wishful thinking. He did swear to himself, at that precise moment, that before his life ended, he would do everything in his power to end Christian's. He just couldn't get the picture of blood soaking the bastard's bespoke clothing out of his mind. That image carried him through a lot of the shit that was to come.

He looked at the photo and was surprised to see something resembling a metallic, honeydew melon. It appeared very low-tech compared to the bells and whistles of the futuristic time chamber.

"This is a bit of overkill for a rugby ball, wouldn't you say?" asked Frank, giving voice to the thoughts that puzzled them all.

"Have you never heard the phrase 'never judge a book by its cover' Mr. McGee? This "rugby ball" contains technological wonders, created by the man you are to seek out. The word genius is banded about all too readily but, believe me, Martin Poulson deserves the accolade." His expression turned into a sneer as he continued. "I believe your fellow Liverpudlian, John Lennon has been classed as such by poor misguided fools, only because he was shot dead at the age of forty. Had he lived he would have become a poor old has been like the rest."

Frank's rage was practically tangible. "You're not fit to say his name, you piece of shit. He is the hero of, not only one generation but many."

Christian's grin widened. "He was just a pop star, like Cliff Richard."

Dave stepped in before Frank did something that would cause the rest of them severe pain. "Leave it Frank (he didn't think using his new nickname would help at this precise moment in time), don't let him wind you up. Let's face it, do you care what a pathetic, puny prick like him thinks."

Out of the corner of his eye Dave saw the bastard nod to one of the goons and then to him. He saw the arc of the gunstock before it made contact with his solar plexus, but he tensed the old six pack and absorbed the blow. It hurt like a bastard, but he wasn't going to give twat-head the satisfaction of knowing it. He just returned the fucker's grin and took pleasure observing the expression of disappointment he was trying so fucking hard to hide. Mentally he chalked one up for the team.

"See what I mean Frank."

Frank smiled. "Indeed, I do, Dave. Indeed, I do." He launched into a reasonable version of 'Working Class Hero' and Dave joined in when he got to the line which contained the words 'fucking peasants', Pete, Harry and Jack adding their dulcet tones, making it a choral barrage. Dave had never known much about Lennon but, at that moment, he was glad of Frank's constant wittering about 'the great man' and his regular renditions of his songs. Christian's annoyance was apparent; he looked as though he was going to burst.

Dave looked at the geezer who had just bruised his guts. "How much is he paying you to act like a shit-head pal?" The goon stepped forward and Dave altered his stance, ready to take the meathead on. If he could get the gun, maybe he could put a bullet through Christian's miserable heart before the other goons turned him into a pin cushion. He felt a hand on his arm and turned to see Jack shaking his head. "It's not worth it mate," he said with a shrug. "Let's just get this thing done, yeah?"

Dave realized he'd been holding his breath and let it out slowly. His eyes were still locked with the goon's. "I never forget a face," he said. "When this is done and I've dealt with him, I'll be coming after you, soldier." He turned back to the bastard. "Fire it up."

"You'll find 12th century Britain, obviously a tad more basic than you're used to," said Christian with relish. "You will probably have to rough it a little." He grinned – one of his most sadistic. "You will sleep beneath the stars, most of the time, which I must add, without the pollution we suffer today, will be as bright as buttons. You may manage the odd night in a drafty old barn with shit stained straw for beds, if you're lucky. It will be a life where you'll have no idea whether you will eat from one day to the next, having to crap in the woods and swill some of the accumulative grime from your aching bodies in an ice cold stream. It will, hopefully, be hell on earth. A hell that will be permanent unless you locate the item in the photograph."

"We'll be back," Dave said. "I promise you that."

"I hope you're right Potter, for both our sakes. If you return our property, you will be free to go and will be wealthy individuals. I give you my word on that. If, however, you have feelings of a vengeful nature and attempt any form of misguided retribution, you will be disposed of." He shrugged. "The choice is yours, a bright new future or death. You'll have plenty of time to come to a decision. As I see it, it's, what's that ridiculous expression used by most of the unwashed and unemployed these days? Ah yes…a no brainer."

"As I've already said – fire it up."

"Two more things before you leave. One – the town that Martin transported himself to in Scotland back in the day, so to speak, was Jedburgh. Two – make sure you pinpoint your exact entry location. If you do this the egg will do the rest, if you don't, well, put it this way, there will be no emotional reunion, Potter. It will be goodbye and not au revoir."

"Will we be arriving in this 'Jedburgh'? Pete asked.

"Unfortunately, not, the machine has reverted to its default setting, which is London. So, you'll have a little bit of a jaunt, I'm afraid."

This time Dave did give him the finger. Spalding laughed. "If you'd all enter the chamber, we'll get this show on the road. Be lucky."

"Can I just ask one question," asked Pete.

"If you're quick, Davies."

"Why did this bloke take something that probably took him years to create back to medieval Scotland. It doesn't make any sense."

"Suffice to say that he disagreed with our plans."

"Which were?"

"Enough questions. Into the chamber." He nodded to his gun-toting lackies, who urged them forward, barrel ends jabbing into their lower backs. It was becoming a trifle tedious.

As he was pushed into the Tardis, Dave glanced back at the evil shit and mouthed, 'you're dead'. He was rewarded with a gun stock rammed into his kidneys and went sprawling onto the floor of the machine that was going to make them all into better people but test them to their limits. From now on they would not only live, they would be alive.

A cloth bag of what turned out to be counterfeit 12th century coins was thrown in after them, presumably to get them on their feet. Dave doubted that the beer slingers of their destination would have the means to detect the difference.

They stood and looked at one another as the door slammed shut, Dave rubbing his bruised kidneys. For a few minutes nothing happened. Then it did. All the shit shown at the pictures regarding time travel is total bollocks. It doesn't happen instantaneously, one minute the 21st century, the next eight hundred years earlier.

That's a fucking long time to travel. Consequently, it wasn't a brief, ear popping trip.

Dave didn't' know how long it lasted but it was definitely the best part of a day. And there was definitely no first class, or if there was, they weren't in it. They all agreed that a thousand trips to the dentist would be preferable to their first experience of time travel. Never mind ears popping, everything was popping, being pulled out of shape, and pulverized. It was a day of total abuse.

SEVEN

And then they found themselves up a tree, according to Pete – a horse chestnut. Dave just thought – who gives a shit, a tree's a tree and we're stuck at the top of the bastard, battered to fuck.

"Well that was fun," said Ringo. "I've always wanted to be hurled through the centuries from a catapult and end up with a branch sticking up my arse."

"Think yourself lucky," the coach moaned, rubbing his testicular region.

"Come on you miserable bastards." Dave laughed. "At least we're shot of Dracula and his toadies. And we've got dollars to spend." He put a hand to his ear. "I think I hear the pub beckoning."

They climbed, fell, tumbled out of the 'horse chestnut' and surveyed their surroundings. If this was supposed to be London, it was trying to find itself. At the moment, they were trying to find *it*. They spotted some primitive sort of dwelling in the distance and decided to ask for directions.

"Quiet for a Saturday," Jack said.

They all looked at him and burst out laughing.

The sun was shining as they trekked across plush green fields, the air so sweet and fresh, it was unbelievable. Dave suddenly remembered a family holiday at some camp site in Dorset when he was about ten and looking up at the stars at night. How clear and bright they all were, like a different world. He was looking forward to viewing the night sky of the 12th century.

As they trudged across the countryside, the birds singing, the warmth of the sun on their faces, no bastard sticking a gun in their ribs, Dave felt at one with the world. He didn't have a clue what the future held but, at that moment, his pals by his side, all relaxed for the first time in ages, it was a time to savour. Unfortunately, although

103

that feeling didn't last as long as he'd have liked, life did become interesting.

As they wandered leisurely up an incline toward a ramshackle, looking construction, they were in reasonably good spirits, for five blokes who'd been chucked back to the 1100's against their will. Suddenly Ringo stopped and fingered his bow.

"Hey, wasn't Robin Hood supposed to be out and about around this time?"

Not being a real history buff, Dave shook his head, thought about it.

"Fucked if I know," he said.

"Was he real anyway?" asked Jack. "I thought he was like Arthur and Merlin, sort of mythical, you know what I mean?"

"I have a feeling I read somewhere that he could have been some Earl or other, although I think the jury's still out on that," said the coach.

"Huntingdon, if I'm not mistaken," said the parsnip. "The Earl of Huntingdon."

Dave had to admit that he was feeling very historically challenged at this point. He'd heard of Robin Hood and his band of merry men, he'd even slept through most of a film with…Kevin Costner, he thought. But he hadn't taken much notice of when he was supposed to be around, if, indeed, he ever was.

Their chat regarding the man (mythical or not) in Lincoln green, riding through the glen brought them to a sort of wall/fence surrounding the primitive building they had first espied on their leafy arrival. Even to Dave's untrained eye it was aesthetically deficient and if practical, only just. It was a mishmash of stones, sticks and what appeared to be horse shit. It was roughly four feet high and Dave found himself wondering what it was meant to keep in or out. He immediately saw a gap in the market for a good, reasonably priced fence erection company. As they were all surveying this medieval masterpiece, a figure emerged from said, primitive building, which, incidentally, appeared to have been built by the same company as the fence. This appeared to be the 12th century version of DIY.

"Welcome friends," boomed an extremely deep voice, from a very red, and terribly, jowly face. A few wisps of straw-like hair protruded from a head, the size of a football. A nose, both ruddy and bulbous hovered above a grinning mouth, its few teeth, yellowed tombstones in a fetid graveyard. The smell of this geezer's breath could have been developed into a chemical weapon.

Dave smiled and held up a hand in acknowledgement.

"Hello friend, nice place you've got here."

Football head looked at him as if he were a Martian, which to him, he was close to being. Dave widened his smile, trying for 'friendly stranger'. He realized, once it was out, how stupid his opening phrase had sounded.

Unfortunately, they hadn't been given a course in 12th century peasant-speak.

"Where might we find the nearest inn, friend?" asked Ringo.

Smart-arse, Dave thought.

Old methane mush stood to one side and waved a hand in a southerly direction.

"You won't have much bother yonder," he replied with a four toothed grin. Dave hoped the rest of the population wasn't as dentally challenged as this chap. If they were, their little group would stand out like a carrot in a bowl of jelly, rather – five carrots.

They looked in the direction of football head's outstretched mitt and, low and behold, there were the unmistakable waters of the Thames, meandering untroubled and uncluttered. It took Dave a few minutes to realize that the haphazard collection of buildings below them constituted 12th century London.

Although they hadn't expected to see the Shard or the Eye or the BT tower, it was still a bit of a shock.

"I don't think they've built the Ritz yet," said Ringo. "We might have to slum it a bit."

Football head's furrowed brow added a new dimension to his already questionable appearance, Dave thought he might have spotted their over-populated gobs.

"Private joke, friend," he said. "You have a nice day now; we're off to the Hilton."

They set off toward the smoke, leaving their new friend scratching his sparsely covered pate.

It took them around thirty minutes to cover the distance between Methane's abode and the not so big city.

Although the buildings weren't the modern day wonders they were used to, the architecture was quite beautiful. Put it this way, they all put Football head's to shame. The stonework was incredible, as was the decorative wrought iron work added to some of the structures. They entered the town at Bishopsgate and could see the Tower not too far away. Wandering through a city, recognizable, yet totally different to what it will become was surreal. Dirt roads with the odd horse and cart were a million miles away from the congestion and pollution of the 21st century. Going back in time, initially, is like a breath of fresh air. Maybe like camping, although Dave had never had the inclination to try the old back to nature business. The five of them were in awe. Without the possession of one's own personal time machine, one could never possibly understand the overwhelming emotional deluge that floods one's entire being at such a ludicrous and momentous time. 21 had reverted to 12. A two- or three-hour flight induces jet lag, what does a trip of nine hundred years or so do? Dave forgot about the banter and allowed his feelings free reign. He thought he spoke for all of them when he said that they were at one with 12th century Britain. As they made their way to a hostelry with the dubious name "The Headless Body" with artwork to match, they were enjoying the laid-back feel of their new/old life.

Unfortunately, that feeling was not destined to last.

A warped, worm eaten door was propped open by a wooden bucket. After the polished chrome and glass of its 21st century counterparts, their first visit to a medieval inn was a bit of a culture shock. Dave had heard the expression 'spit and sawdust', but it wasn't until now he understood it. The stone floor was covered in wood shavings, a freshly laid carpet covering spilt beer, vomit and, yes indeed, spit, most of it of the green variety. The odour of this wonderful cocktail of aromas, coupled with smoke and severe man-sweat made him wretch.

"Jesus Christ," said the coach.

"For fuck's sake," added the parsnip.

Ringo breathed deeply and let out a satisfied sigh. "All it needs is a stage in the corner."

"With ye olde Beatles stomping about, I suppose," suggested Jack.

"This is a proper pub," said Ringo, with a nod. "Come on, I'll get the first round."

As they made their way to what was, obviously the bar, sawdust clinging to their boots, the spit, ale and sick, natural adhesives, a strange looking little feller lurched in front of them and banged a stone tankard down and demanded in drunken old English 'anuvver scrummy'. He slung a silver coin on the bar and the pot-bellied pig behind the bar poured some cloudy, piss coloured liquid into his mug. "Best make that your last, 'enry. That woman o' yourn'll be arter my blood 'swell as yourn."

'Enry staggered back to a table in the corner, (where Ringo yearned for a 12th century version of the fab four to be on stage, singing 'She Loves Thee' or 'I Want To Hold Thy Hand') the hand holding the mug as steady as a rock.

He plonked himself down on a wonky stool and took a hefty swig. Dave thought the furniture appeared to have been made by Football head – or him. It didn't require close scrutiny to spot the heads of a myriad of rusty nails lurking at odd angles waiting to tear into cloth and skin with impunity. If this were a 'proper pub', he wondered what an improper one would look like. Old Beatle-chops was at the bar giving it large with 'friend this' and 'friend that' whilst the rest of them settled themselves around a larger but equally dangerous looking table near to the door.

"He's loving it," Dave said.

"In his element," said Jack.

They watched as Ringo threw a few of the coins that had been chucked at them on their departure from normal life, onto the counter. The barman took two and pushed the rest back. Ringo brought five jugs of dubious looking liquid over to their table and grinned like a Cheshire cat.

"It's cheaper than Wetherspoons."

Dave looked at the shit floating in his and wasn't surprised.

It turned out that the coins Gobshite had thrown at them were counterfeit pennies and it was amazing how pissed you could get on a few of the little buggers. In films Dave had seen barmen taking coins and biting them to ensure their authenticity. Having glimpsed the gnashers, or lack thereof, of a few of these geezers, it was clear why this practice would be detrimental to whatever remained in their gobs. Maybe too much penny biting was a contributory factor to the widespread, dental demise. The thought made him laugh anyway, or maybe that was the apple treacle he was consuming. What is called Scrumpy in the twenty first century is like kids' apple juice in comparison.

"Where we kipping tonight?" Dave asked anyone willing to listen.

"Sorted," belched Ringo. "Our friend has a room above with five pallets."

"Pallets?" The word was spat through a spray of ale by the parsnip. "Pallets are wooden things that heavy shit gets delivered on, not fucking conducive to piling up the Zs."

"I did ask if he could direct us to the nearest Premier Inn but apparently it's fucking *years* away," said Ringo. "When are you lot going to realize that we're, literally, living in the past and embrace it?" He took another swig of whatever the fuck it was, stroked his chin and sighed. "Personally, I find it quite relaxing, you know, the pace of life. Plus, you don't have a bastard like Christian breathing down your neck."

At that there was a lot of communal nodding and murmurs of 'you're right there' and 'too true'. The only one of them not contributing was Jack. He was looking a whiter shade of green and swallowing repeatedly.

"You okay Jack?" The coach asked him.

Jack started to shake his head, then turned, and spewed a torrent of 12th century real ale onto the sawdust. Dave observed that travelling back hundreds of years had no effect on the mystifying carrot question. Even though it was about a week ago since they had last partaken of that vegetable, it was there, like a paranormal piss-take. At Jack's outburst, so to speak, a cheer went up among the other half a dozen or so customers and, as if by magic, a young lad appeared with a bucket of fresh sawdust and covered the evidence. Jack murmured an apology and the surprise on the boy's face was evident. He waved a hand and returned to his post as puke coverer, hidden from the naked eye, presumably refilling his sawdust bucket. It was surprising how much a covering of wood shavings did to reduce the stench.

"The local brew not agree with you?" Dave asked him.

Jack was about to answer when he heaved again. Luckily, the previous gusher must have drained him as this was a sort of guttural, dry rasp.

"I don't have the strongest of stomachs," he said.

"Probably not enough chemicals for you," said the parsnip. "We're all full of the bastards, you know."

"Well now's the time to get back to natural goodness," Ringo said, with a grin.

Dave looked at what was left in his pot and wondered how much of it was bordering on the good.

"I don't know about you bastards, but our unusual journey, coupled with a few jugs of this rot gut has taken its toll. I'm shattered," he said, stifling a yawn. "Them there pallets are sounding more attractive by the minute." Jack was the first to agree, followed closely by Harry and Pete. Ringo shook his head in disgust. "You're definitely a pansy Potter and the rest of you are no better. You'd never have made it in the Kaiserkellar, playing all night."

"Your obsession with the bleeding fab four is becoming a little tedious, to say the least," said Jack. "If you want to stay here, drinking this piss, fill your boots."

"Indeed, I will," replied Ringo. "The night is still young. You lot go and get some beauty sleep. Let's face it, it's well overdue. Night, night boys, sleep tight now."

"And don't you come falling about the place, waking us up either," said the coach.

Ringo waved a hand. "Go, pathetic creatures. It's the room on the right at the top of the stairs, the one with the en suite."

"En suite?" The parsnip was genuinely puzzled. Aided by the rocket fuel he'd consumed, the old brain cells were on a go slow, not far from a complete stop.

"Well it's more of a bucket in the corner, really," explained Ringo, with a grin. "But watch out, I think there's a hole in said bucket, dear Liza. If you're going to take a leak, I'd use the window. Just watch out for the nuns."

"Nuns?" The parsnip was near to shut down.

"Some story about his hero, Lennon, pissing out of a window in Hamburg onto some nuns," Dave said. "I wish I could switch off like you do, Pete. I just seem to absorb this shit."

"That's because you realize its importance," Ringo said, with a nod. "You're a sixties child, at heart, young Potter."

"Give it a rest, Ringo. Come on you lot, let's hit the hay – literally."

They shuffled off to the staircase behind the bar. Maybe staircase was a little over the top, it was more like a ladder with aspirations. The room itself was probably worse than expected and their expectations were not high. The pallets were dilapidated wooden troughs with a minimal amount of straw spread conservatively over their bases. The room stank of every bodily fluid imaginable and it was obvious that the cleaners were either on the sick or just fucking useless. Dave had heard people describe places as tips before, but they had no idea. It wouldn't have been so bad if the straw were clean, but a quick glance was enough to see it wasn't. But, as the saying goes, 'needs must when the devil drives', they were all knackered and were going to have to get used to a complete lack of creature comforts. Pete was done in and flopped, like a rag doll, onto the nearest pallet and was snoring within seconds. The other three of them followed suit and soon joined the parsnip in the land of nod. That was the first time Dave had the dream.

EIGHT

It all started with Christian yanking an empty syringe from his arm, a spot of blood becoming a smiley face with sharp teeth. Spalding was grinning like a maniac and wearing a Batman costume, Dave was naked apart from a blue nappy, held in place by a huge safety pin. This wasn't completely alien to him, just another alcohol fueled dream. It continued with a complete change of scene, a cross between the bar downstairs and his local from his previous life, full of men showing off their limited dental capacity, all watching a female dentist pole dancing. There was nothing to indicate her profession but, in the dream, he just knew she was a dentist. She didn't have a necklace of false teeth or anything, he just knew. Up to now it was just a common or garden conglomeration of recent events, embellished by 12th century scrumpy and total exhaustion. Then something occurred that, even in his dream state, was disconcerting. Like most, he'd had his fair share of illusionistic trips through slumber-land with their random images and rapid scene changes, but this was different. Although it, obviously, wasn't real, it was different. Dreams, even though they meander here and there and shoot off at a tangent are always constant in their feel. How many times had he said – I had a weird dream last night? But there had never been any doubt that it was a dream. What happened in this 'dream' was disturbing. He'd had loads of nightmares when he'd woken sweating and terrified, the images in his head real enough to cause such emotion but, even though they scared him shitless, the feel had always been the same.

When this white-haired bloke in a long black coat appeared behind a mono toothed, pot-bellied, leering Neanderthal, it was all wrong. He didn't belong there; it was as simple as that. When he pointed at him, Dave

nearly shat himself and then he beckoned him, and he was
begging to wake. Dave started to move towards him, he
didn't want to, but he couldn't stop his legs from moving.
By now he was screaming but the toothless brigade
ignored him, as if he'd become invisible. He started to
repeat 'it's just a dream, it's just a dream' and he was
punching his dream self in the face trying to wake himself
up. Still he followed that summoning finger, step by
miserable step. The man in the black coat turned and
walked towards the back of the pub and he followed like a
dutiful sheep, unable to stop his feet from shuffling across
the sawdust strewn floor. Suddenly a door, that hadn't
been there before, appeared before the man. He turned
back to Dave and held out his left arm whilst grabbing the
door handle with his right hand. Dave was powerless and
felt the man's arm around his shoulders, so that they stood
side by side. The man in black turned the handle and
pulled the door open. A blast of fetid air assaulted Dave's
nostrils and as the door opened wider a landscape of decay
and devastation was revealed. Although the view was
horrific, it was the feeling it induced that destroyed him. It
was a feeling of loss and total emptiness. This was how
futility felt.
He awoke with tears in his eyes.

The sun was shining through the window and it was a
welcome sight. The dream, or whatever it was, still
lingered like a bad smell, the feeling it had evoked slow to
dissipate. Dave was glad the other four were still piling up
the Zs, giving him time to get his head back together. He
looked at his wrist wondering how long it was going to be
before he got used to not wearing a watch. He was
bursting for a piss so went over to the window. A quick
check revealed a lack of bodies, nuns included, so he let
rip, the dream gradually going with the flow. As he was
pulling up his medieval pants, he heard a belch and fart

from behind. He turned to see Ringo had surfaced and was scratching his arse.

"That was a good night," he said with a bleary smile. "Got in with a couple of rough sorts and started playing skittles. Obviously, they weren't aware of my ten-pin prowess and I couldn't tell 'em, could I?"

"Stuffed 'em, did you?"

He held up the bag that Christian had given them, and it looked considerably heftier. "A good night on the piss, a bit of entertainment and I still came away to the good. Stick with me Pansy and you'll never go hungry, or thirsty, come to that."

The mention of hunger eradicated all left-over threads of the dream and started Dave's stomach rumbling. "Man, I'm starving."

"Yeah I could eat a scabby polo-neck myself," Ringo agreed, rubbing his belly. "I think I need to give them nuns a bit of a shower first though."

While he was emptying his bladder, Dave woke the other three. Jack was still looking a bit green around the gills.

"You all right mate?" Dave asked him.

"Yeah, I will be. Just need some grub down me."

"You're a fucking lightweight Hardy, what are you?" said Ringo, rearranging his trouser area.

"I just haven't got a cast iron gut, like you, that's all. When we get back, we'll go out and I'll drink you under the table, you'll see."

"If we ever get back," said the coach.

The look on his face was pained to say the least.

"Are you suffering as well?"

"Nah, I'm right enough, just didn't sleep too good."

Dave was about to ask if he'd had a bad dream but thought better of it. If he had, he didn't want to know. His expression was how Dave imagined his to have been when he woke up. Some things are better not said.

"Who's up for a bit of breakfast then?" asked the parsnip.

They all piled down the rickety staircase and found the lad with the bucket of sawdust re-carpeting the place. The landlord was nowhere to be seen.

"Any breakfast going?" Dave asked him.

"I can bring you some bread and cheese," the boy replied. "There might be some ham."

"Fawlty Towers has got nothing on this place," said Ringo. "Go boy; bring us the feast you described so eloquently"

The poor lad stood there, a look of total bemusement on his face.

"Bring the bread and cheese," Dave translated. "And the ham, if there is any."

Their first breakfast in the past consisted of stale bread, even staler cheese and ham that had more than a slightly green tinge to it.

The landlord appeared, bleary eyed, as they were forcing down the last of his severely out of date provisions. Ringo was up and at him. "You call this food? I wouldn't feed it to my pigs."

'You don't have any pigs,' said the parsnip.

Ringo shot him a look and returned his attention to our host. "If you think we're paying for this shit, you're mentally unstable."

The landlord looked at him, brow creased, waved a hand, and rushed out the back. They all heard the eruption.

"I hope you've still got some sawdust in that bucket, feller," Dave said to the young lad who'd served them their bacterially challenged breakfast. "I think your boss needs your services."

"That's my Da," he said. There was no pride evident in his tone.

Jack stood up and put his arm around the kid. "You make your own way in this world, lad"

The bemusement that had graced his features at Ringo's request for the breakfast returned and intensified.

"D'you think he's going put his name down for this year's plumbing course at the local college?" said Ringo. "This is the fucking 12th century, not the 21st."

The lad was looking from Jack to Ringo, bemusement replaced with fear. From being a bunch of oddballs, they'd become deranged and a threat.

"M...my Dad's six brothers'll be here in a minute," he stammered.

Dave looked at the kid and felt as sorry for him as he did for himself and his mates. "When they arrive, tell 'em they got a great nephew." He rubbed the lad's head, and they were out of there, on the road to find out, as Cat Stevens had once put it.

When he looked back to those first days in the past, he remembered them, in the main, with great affection. They'd already been used to having no phones, no telly, no internet, no cars; Spalding had made sure of that. Friendships mean much more when one of the group isn't trying to impress the rest with the latest gadget, they've got their hands on (in Dave's case, mostly illegally). Getting back to basics is a leveller.

They left the pub on a bright summer's day, their spirits high, the rank cheese remaining in situ, even in Jack's sensitive tum. They put the Thames behind them and struck out north, singing a Beatles medley, launched, obviously, by Ringo. Dave had to admit – those songs were timeless. They were halfway through 'Ticket to Ride' when he got the first flashback. It nearly knocked him bandy. It was brief but powerful. He must have staggered because Jack grabbed him by the arm and asked him if he was okay. Dave told him he was fine, and he was, if he ignored the feeling of complete dread that was turning his insides out. As they went their merry way, that feeling was like the early stages of tooth ache – you think it's gone and there it is back again, the bastard.

For the time being he was back in the past and enjoying the warmth and simplicity of a 12th century summer. With the ozone layer well and truly intact, no filthy emissions or any other form of pollution to cause it any grief, the air quality was amazing. As they wandered along the country tracks breathing in the scents of hedgerow blossom combined with the occasional musk of sheep or cow shit, he felt relaxed. It's strange how quickly man can adapt to the weirdest of situations, especially in the company of a bunch of good mates. After being cooped up in that glorified prison, to be out, feeling the sun on one's chops, enjoying the banter was, literally, a breath of fresh air.

"This living in the past shit ain't all that bad," he said.

"It's early days yet, Pansy," said cautious Jack.

"Ah, it's just 'cos you can't take the local brew, lightweight," Ringo said.

Jack made a face. "It's nothing to do with that pig swill. I mean, has anyone thought of where the next meal's coming from. It's not as though there's going to be a KFC or Subway or even a fish'n'chip shop round the corner. The next inn might be two days away. Will you be so enamored with the past when your belly's growling like a rabid lion?"

"I don't think lions get rabies," said the parsnip. "It's only dogs isn't it?"

"Whatever, you know what I mean."

"He's right," the coach agreed. "It's all well and good now. Our bellies are full of stale bread and out of date cheese, the day's a corker and we're glad to be away from the bastard and his goons. We should have thought about supplies though."

Dave nodded. "I guess all this is alien. I have to admit I hadn't even thought about grub, after our 'wonderful' breakfast."

"Something'll turn up. You're just a load of pessimists. You make your own luck in this world," said Ringo.

117

"Well I hope we do a better job in this one than we did in the other," said Jack.

So, they continued in a more subdued manner. Dave didn't know about the rest, but he was waiting for the old stomach to start rumbling. The open countryside seemed to go on forever. It wasn't until late afternoon, when all their bellies were growling like lions, rabid or not, that the coach spotted a structure in the distance. As they drew nearer, it appeared to be like old Football head's abode but in better repair.

"There you go," said Ringo triumphantly. "I'm sure we can buy something to scoff from our local farmer. You never know, he might even have some scrumpy, eh Jack?" Jack gave him the finger. "If you want to rot your guts, carry on."

When they reached the farm, the sun was low, and the wooden farmhouse was transformed into burnished gold. An old man was about fifty yards away struggling with some hay, cursing like a squaddie.

"Hello there, friend," called Ringo. "You look like you could do with a hand. We were wondering if you had any bread, cheese or fruit to sell to some wayfaring strangers." The rest of them looked at each other and it was obvious that the same word had entered all their tired brains – knob.

The farmer looked up and regarded them suspiciously but sighed and let the hay slip. "If you can help me tie this shite up, the wife'll put some more spuds and rabbit in the pot."

Dave couldn't help noticing how claw-like and deformed his hands were. Arthritis, it seemed, had been around for a long, long time.

They all mucked in and within about fifteen minutes had a dozen beautifully tied up bales of hay.

"My name's Will," said the farmer. "And I thank you for your toil. Come and meet the wife and daughter and fill your bellies at my humble table. It's nothing fancy but it's good and wholesome."

As the sun laid its lazy old head down and that clear, ozone intact upper atmosphere became a beautiful, orange fire, they entered Will's home.

His wife had, apparently, been watching the proceedings outside as our appearance was no surprise.

"Sit yourselves down young sirs and I'll do my best to fill your bellies. I thank you for your aid. Will still thinks he's forty-five and I love him for it."

"I will always provide, woman," said Will. "I know the years are passing and I'm no longer as fit as I was and I'm grateful for the help." He held up his hands. "It's the devil in these that does for me."

"My Nan suffered with Arthritis," the parsnip said with a nod.

"Arthur who?" asked a puzzled Will.

"Pay him no heed," Dave said, with a shake of his head, rather pleased with his Olde English-type speak. "He wanders." he added, the old twirly finger upside the temple, hoping this gesture originated pre twelfth century. Will seemed to understand, as he nodded with that funny, screwed up mouth thing people do when they're sympathizing.

They all sat around a table that had been made for six, at a push, on benches held together with nails. If dove-tailed joints had been invented they hadn't yet been released into the wild.

Will's wife carried steaming bowls of rabbit stew and vegetables to the table to accompany the hunks of homemade bread already there. Dave put her at around mid-fifties, her auburn hair liberally flecked with grey. She was an attractive woman, her cheekbones high and eyes an incredible, intense green. Her body was still slender. He guessed that was what happened when cupboards full of

chocolate and crisps weren't to hand; there wasn't a
takeaway at the end of a phone and hundreds of channels
of shite on the telly. As his mother used to say, you made
your own entertainment in those days. And she was
talking about the sixties, not the eleven hundreds.

"You haven't told us your good lady's name, Will," Ringo
said.

"I'm Anna," she said, as she put down a bowl of
something resembling bread sauce. "If you wait for him to
tell you, you'll still be here a month from now."

"Is your daughter out?" asked the parsnip.

Dave thought; please don't ask if she's out clubbing. Pete
was one of those people that opened his mouth before he
engaged his brain. It's wasn't that he was thick, he just had
a bit of trouble with focus, at times.

"Mary, food's on the table and we have guests," Anna
called.

From the only other doorway, a young woman entered the
room. Dave's eyes nearly popped out of his head and the
sucking in of his breath must have been audible. She was
beautiful, she had her mother's beautiful eyes and bone
structure but had taken it to a new level. She smiled shyly
and sat at the table, next to her father. She glanced at
Dave and smiled and when their eyes met, he was in
another time and place and gazing into the eyes of a black
Labrador dog. It was fleeting but it shook him. Weird shit
was happening, weirder than the old-time travel job. This
shit was in his head. He looked around at his mates' faces
for any signs that they were experiencing similar shit, but
they were all stuffing their faces and grinning dutifully.
Dave looked back at Mary and she smiled and for a few
seconds they were alone in her Dad's shack. She nodded
and then everything returned to the normality they had
begun to become used to.

Eating a hearty meal with such a close family was comforting. As they savored every mouthful, Anna left the room. When she returned, she was carrying a large stone jug. "I'm sure Will won't mind you sharing his precious apple juice," she said, as she plonked it on the table. "I'll fetch some mugs."

By Will's expression, Dave wasn't convinced. This was the look of a man trying to put on a brave face but not quite managing it, like the countenance of someone who desperately wants to fart but knows if they do, they'll follow through.

Anna returned with an assortment of mug-shaped receptacles, gave Will a look and a nod. Will sighed and began to pour his precious cider, the act patently paining him. He passed the mugs around the table and all, except from Jack, accepted enthusiastically. Jack smiled his thanks, took the mug reluctantly and put it on the table in front of him. Ringo was straight in, downing half of it in one gulp. "By God, that's good," he gasped. "100 times better than that slop we had at the inn."

"Which inn?" asked Will.

"The Headless Body," Dave replied with a grimace.

"Good God, you drank old Tom's brew. It's only thieves and beggars drink his swill. Talk is he puts dead rats in it. Others say he drinks it himself but don't let none go to waste, if you know my meaning," he said, with a hand gesture toward his nether regions.

Now anyone who has ever been told that they've drunk several pints containing liquidized rat and human urine, will know how they were all feeling at that precise moment. Jack was visibly upset, which is strange when you think he was the only one of them to purge his body of the evil piss. The rest of them had kept it down and let it become one with them. Only Ringo seemed unperturbed. "Ah, what don't kill you makes you stronger," he said with a shrug.

Jack had picked his mug up and was sniffing the contents but unlike a wine buff, he wasn't analyzing the bouquet, just sniffing for foreign bodies or bodily fluid. He took a tentative sip and beamed. "This is very good," he admitted, after a liberal slug.

"It ought to be," said Will proudly. "Made from the best apples and fresh water from the well, out back. I add a couple of other things when it's brewing but they stay in there." He tapped the side of his head.

Their appreciation of Will's home brew, coupled with a couple of mugs of the excellent concoction, seemed to have changed his view. He asked Anna to bring another jug-full and they all chewed the fat. It may seem strange how a group of 21st century refugees can natter with a twelfth century family when said refugees aren't able to reveal their origins. Ringo managed to transport The Beatles back, re-configuring them as a group of travelling minstrels and Anna, who said she liked a nice singing voice, seemed quite interested – emphasis on 'seemed', Dave thought.

The sun sank slowly, coating the horizon with its fire. They were all mellow, some more than others. Jack's eyes were in desperate need of a couple of match sticks to keep the buggers open and Will had stopped trying to hide his yawns behind his hand. Ringo was still holding forth and Dave suddenly realized he liked the sound of his own voice more than other people did. He decided it was up to him to do the right thing and let their hosts get some kip. "I thank you for your hospitality Will and now I think it's time to let you good people get some sleep." It was at this point Dave became aware that they had nowhere to rest their own weary heads.

Appearing to read his mind, Anna went off and seconds later came back with an armful of course, brown blankets.

"The barn's not the largest in Christendom but there's plenty of hay and these'll keep the chill off, if needs be." They thanked their hosts again for the wonderful food and drink and for supplying a billet, bid them goodnight and covered the few yards to the barn. Will had lent them a candle to light the way and Dave would have liked to have said the shadow of the barn loomed large in its flickering flame, but he couldn't. It was slightly larger than a small garden shed, plenty of gapping between the strips of assorted wood of its construction and he was glad it was the height of summer and not a blizzard torn winter's night.

"Cozy," said the coach.

"Just as well we're good friends," said Jack. "Otherwise this could be a little awkward."

Ringo yanked open the door, nearly taking it off whatever fixings held it on. Dave was guessing it wasn't a nice couple of metal hinges like the sort you get in Homebase. "Home from home," he said with a grin. He blew out the candle, left it outside and they all piled in, falling over and on heaps and bales of hay until they all managed to make themselves comfortable. Dave was expecting something akin to kipping on a grass verge. Once he'd managed to smooth out all the bits that kept tickling his nose, however, he couldn't remember being more comfortable. It was like a memory foam mattress – well close. Any road up, they were in and, as Jack had suggested, it was very cozy. After the meal and cider and the day's ramble, it wasn't long before they were all yawning and drifting off to kip. One of the others woke Dave in the middle of the night from a dreamless sleep, going outside for a piss, but he smoothed out the hay and carried on piling up the Zs. They all slept well that night, that was until the shouting tore them, unceremoniously, from their slumber, the sun up and shining through the gaps of their bedroom.

123

NINE

"Come on shitheads, we're needed." It was Ringo's voice.
The rest of them tumbled from the barn, immediately in
battle stance. Christian was a bastard, but the training he
had arranged for them was second to none. Dave nearly
felt sorry for the fuckers, they didn't stand a chance.
There were six ugly looking bastards; one was holding
Anna and one had a grip of Mary. The head honcho was a
foot taller than Will and was using the extra height in what
can only be described as an intimidating manner. He
appeared to be demanding money with menace.
"Take your hands off the ladies, if you want to keep 'em,"
Dave said, his sword arm emphasizing the point.
"And you," Ringo addressed the geezer towering over
Will. "Keep your voice down, it's annoying."
Will looked over at them and shook his head, his
expression turning from anger to dismay. "It's okay lads,
this is nothing for you to worry yourselves about. We all
have to pay our debts."
The leader of the gang turned his attention to them.
"Unless you want this to be your last day on God's earth,
I'd heed Mr. Tapler here and mind your own business."
"I think you like the sound of your own voice," said the
coach. "Now, either leave this family in peace or die. The
choice is yours."
By this time Will was visibly trembling, Anna was shaking
her head vigorously, tears in her eyes and Mary was
smiling. Gary Glitter nodded to his men and they all drew
their swords, trying their best to appear threatening. The
main man nodded again, and they lurched forward, swords
swinging this way and that. It was, immediately, obvious
that they had received no training whatsoever and just
relied on their bulk and ugliness to intimidate. When an
old man, his wife and daughter were probably typical of

their victims that would be enough. Unfortunately for them, those three people had been truly kind to Dave and his mates, and, in turn, they were obligated to show their thanks. They took a meathead each, playing sword pat-a-cake for a minute or so before they flicked the imbecile's swords in the air and ended their debt collecting careers. At that moment they were like the Red Arrows of swordsmanship and Dave could see old Gary appreciating it as well, as he had it away on his toes.

"Obviously not one of your 'lead from the front' types," said Ringo, taking his bow and nocking an arrow.

"Just stop him," Dave said. "I think we may need a few more words with the piece of shit."

"Your wish is my command," replied Ringo. "They don't call me Robin Hood for nothing."

By this time old Gary was about two hundred yards away. Ringo let his arrow fly and a second later the leader of the gang stumbled to the ground with said arrow, slap bang through his calf. His scream of pain was loud and even more annoying than his whiny voice.

"I think he may need a hand to walk back," said the parsnip. "I'll go make sure he's all right. In fact, I think he might be a little disorientated, he's trying to crawl off the other way."

The parsnip returned slowly with his charge, limping (that's old Gary and not the parsnip), with a severely pained expression. Dave imagined having an arrow stuck through the leg is not the sort of thing to cause fits of laughter, not that he could speak from experience, of course. It was, apparently, fucking painful.

"Have you got something to bandage a wound, Will?" Ringo asked.

"How are you going to bandage that?" Will responded. "That arrow's sticking out front and back, if you know what I mean."

125

Ringo grabbed hold of our captive's shoulder. "Now if you want this to hurt as little as possible, you had better keep still."

Gary was trembling like a frightened child as Ringo bent down and surveyed his handiwork. Luckily, the arrow had passed through the bastard's leg almost to the feathers. Ringo gripped the shaft just behind the head with his right hand and closed his left over the flight. He looked up at Gary and grinned as he snapped off the head and yanked the rest of the arrow from the poor bugger's calf.

Dave had never heard a man scream like that before. Ringo let him drop to the ground where he chucked up his breakfast and, yes, there were carrots. Anna had brought some strips of old sheeting and Ringo wrapped the wound tightly making our new friend scream some more.

"You shouldn't have done all of this, Robin," said Will, shaking his head, "He'll just send more men and they'll take everything we've got." He looked at Anna and Mary and his expression of terror said it all.

They all ignored the Robin Hood reference, Will's fear their primary concern.

"Who, exactly, is *he*?" Dave enquired. "And where can we find him?"

"His name's Thomas Daunter and he lives in the big house over the hill." Will pointed north. "All of us land-owners have to pay him each month, otherwise our houses are burnt down – or worse." Again, he glanced at his wife and daughter.

"I think we need to meet Mr. Daunter and point out the error of his ways," Dave said. "Are we agreed? What do say Robin?"

Ringo smiled. "It's why we're here. To take from the rich and give to the poor."

"What's this specimen's name," asked Jack, kicking the gibbering wreck in his bad leg.

126

"He's Henry Charter and he used to be one of us until he decided to take Daunter's filthy money." Dave was disappointed to find his name wasn't Gary, he had to admit.

"Well I guess we're off to seek an audience with Thomas then and take Henry here back to his master," he said. "He may be a little disappointed in his man's lack of ability to perform the simple task of extortion."

"They'll kill you," cried Will. "Especially after all of this." He waved a hand over the dead bodies of his former buddies, gone bad.

Ringo wrenched the pouch, containing the previous collections from Henry's belt and gave it to Will. "You know where this belongs. You'll soon have all that is yours. There is an expression where we come from – fight fire with fire. Daunter may have fire but he's about to witness a conflagration."

They were about to depart with peg leg when Mary put her hand on Dave's arm.

"You must keep him safe."

There are times in life when total weirdness makes sense. As she squeezed Dave's arm, his vision became monochrome as if he were watching a forties film – with one figure in startling colour.

As they dragged Henry/Gary (Dave was still having trouble with the new name) towards his employer, very slowly, as it goes, Dave was becoming a little concerned about his sanity. He'd always been a straightforward sort, fairly shallow in the main but with, what he liked to think of, as a mildly humanitarian streak. Even before he was trained to be a badass, he hoped that, if he'd seen a poor unfortunate getting set upon by a couple of thugs, he wouldn't have turned a blind eye and walked on. He imagined most folk liked to believe that they were, fundamentally, good. Until it's put to the test though, no-one really knows, self-preservation is a powerful force and sacrifice, a rare commodity. He turned his mind back to his recent feelings of mental instability. With the disturbing dream and the two weird things with Mary, he was thinking that, either he was getting ready for the funny farm or he was suffering some sort of time travel brain rush. He, obviously, had a pained expression, something his mother had always told him occurred when he was worried about something. Like when his school trousers were two inches too short because she couldn't afford a new pair and he looked a tit. He remembered his, so called mates, calling them ankle fresheners but that's another story.

"You all right Pansy?" asked Jack. In that moment of annoyance at his transparency and his concern for such, a name sprang into Dave's mind.

"Yeah, I'm fine, Ollie."

Ringo was straight on it. "Class. Why the fuck didn't I think of that?"

"Because he wasn't Liverpudlian or a mate of John Lennon's," Dave said.

"Who's Ollie?" The parsnip's face was so puzzled, it looked like an algebraic equation.

"You must have heard of Laurel and Hardy," said the coach, with a sigh.

"'Course I have. Which one was Ollie?"

"What's Jack's surname?" Dave asked, thinking, old Pete's a decent geezer and a formidable force in a scrap but at times, his brain seems to be somewhere else. The old light bulb suddenly went on over Pete's head, he wasn't that stupid.

"Oh yeah," he mumbled, his ruddy complexion becoming – well, ruddier.

So, there they were, in the twelfth century and all nicknamed up, what could be better? Sat in a comfortable armchair with a nice glass of scotch, it needn't be a malt or matured in an oak cask for forty fucking years, would probably be much better, Dave thought. They were all still on the road to find out with old Cat. It made a refreshing change thinking about Cat Stevens and one of his many fine songs. When being bombarded with Lennon and The Beatles constantly, a bit of Yusuf Islam, as he is now, adds a little variety.

After sorting out Jack's nickname and Dave putting his mental concerns to the back of his mind, they reached the summit of the hill and gazed down into the lush valley that was Thomas Daunter's garden.

"Time to meet your master, Hop-along," Dave said to Henry. "Best foot forward."

Dave had never seen a terrified glare before but that's the only way to describe the look on their limping friend's face. "Caleb will crush you, like a nut." Henry was trying for a snarl but fell painfully short.

"I think you mean 'crack', my old beansprout," pointed out Ringo. "A nut is cracked, not crushed. Now Caleb, whoever he may be, may suffer both fates. Now move your miserable arse."

Henry shut his trap and hopped along like a good, little prisoner, now with, what can only be described as, a sly grin plastered over his mug.

Now, in all the books Dave had read, the type of architecture of old structures and what they were composed of is normally explained at considerable length, whether it be Georgian, Victorian, Tudor, Sandstone, Granite or whatever other bloody brick the bastards are made of. This house, although not a mansion, was sizeable and was definitely made of bricks of some kind. The style was typical of twelfth century, he thought. Not being remotely interested in such shit, that's all he could muster. It was a big house, as already mentioned by Will, with some decorative archway business going on around the front door. Not enough glass for Dave's liking but he didn't suppose people were bombarded with offers from double glazing companies in this day and age.

They stood about fifty yards away and Ringo gave Henry a shove. "Go and tell your boss we'd like a word with him, there's a good lad."

The poor bugger nearly fell flat on his face. Dave thought it was weird how a body can go from despising somebody to almost feeling sorry for them in such a short space of time. He stressed the 'almost'.

Someone must have been watching their arrival because, as Henry reached the door, it opened, and he was dragged in.

"We'll give them five minutes and then we go in," said Ringo. It appeared that Lennon's little helper was becoming their leader. This wasn't a problem to Dave and, looking around at the others, he was reasonably sure they felt the same way.

He was just starting to daydream about a big plate of steak and chips with mushrooms, tomatoes, onion rings and, maybe, a nice mustard sauce and a few pints of lager, when the door opened again. He counted twelve geezers with broadswords and shields before this huge fucker ducked his head through the door behind them. He must have been about eight feet tall and the same across. He had a face like a boxer who'd lost most of his fights but, even at this distance, his eyes reminded Dave of a shark's, black and lacking any emotion.

"The bigger they are, the harder they fall," said the parsnip.

They all looked at him, thinking the same thought – 'twat'. Ringo surveyed the scene. "No fucking about, watch each other's backs. Try and take out the monkeys first. The way they're handling those swords I think they may be a little more proficient than Will's debt collectors." He let out a heavy sigh. "As far as King Kong's concerned, I think we're going to need all hands to the pump."

They spread out into a loose line, swords at the ready and Dave, for one, was, for the first time since their extensive combat training, a little apprehensive at the outcome. The old sphincter was twitching a touch as he took his position. Their strategy was the tried and tested 'divide and conquer' routine and, as there were twelve of them, not counting old man mountain there, he estimated they had two and two fifths each to deal with. Ringo held up his hand and as they waited for it to drop and leap into action a huge mother of an axe and a shield the size of a kitchen table was passed to the big man. Ringo didn't falter, his hand sliced the air, and they were off. Their adversaries closed ranks and disappeared behind their shields, their blades like the spines of a porcupine. Ringo yelled "Drop" and they did, sliding like bowling balls into the group, their feet taking the feet from under several surprised swordsmen. Surprise should be added to the old divide and conquer rigmarole, it's a must. It should be – surprise, divide and conquer.

Within seconds they were all on their feet behind enemy lines, jabbing and parrying and all those other fencing terms. Dave thought he could speak for all of them when he said they kept one eye on the scrap and one on their mates and Mr. axe swinging Kong. Luckily for them, martial arts were not too rife in the twelfth century and, just before he broke his jaw, he saw even more surprise on the face of one of Thomas' bodyguards as his foot connected with the fucker's chops. Out of the corner of his eye Dave saw a broadsword starting to invade his personal space. He dodged just in time but still felt the sting as it nicked his shoulder. He did a fair impression of a pirouette, before kicking his attacker's shield away and plunging his own sword into his attacker's guts. As he dragged it out another of the fuckers was on him and he couldn't help wondering where the other three fifths had come from. He was nearly knocked off his feet as a hefty shield nearly shattered his ribs. He staggered, channeling the pain, as he had been taught, feinted left, spun, heard the satisfying groan that always accompanies a foot to the bollocks and performed his first decapitation. He nearly threw up.

"Man down." It was the coach's voice and as Dave turned, he saw the parsnip on the floor, blood pouring from his nose, two of the remaining bastards towering over him, swords ready to strike. He had to give it to old Pete, he was still growling, his blade before him. "C'mon then," he roared.

Before they could 'c'mon' though an arrowhead sprouted from one of their foreheads and Ollie hacked the other's left leg off, impairing the poor bugger's balance a tad. Dave helped the Parsnip to his feet, and they surveyed their victory. Then the coach posed the most important question. "Where's the big fucker?"

They all shook their heads in bewilderment. "He was there a minute ago," said Ollie. "I saw the ugly bastard swinging that overgrown machete."

None of them saw him appear again until Ringo was flat on his back with the sun's rays being reflected by the blade of the 'overgrown machete' as it was about to split his skull in two. Everything seemed to slow down. It was like watching a film frame by frame. It was clear to the rest of them that there was no way they could do anything to save Ringo before that massive blade completed its arc. Even so, they all leapt into that slow-mo. soup, their swords
drawn back, their faces contorted into a communal "Nnnoooo."

None of them saw where the black Labrador came from, as it leapt and sunk its teeth into King Kong's wrist. His scream of pain was music to their ears but as he dropped the axe it continued its original arc. They were suddenly released from their torpor and they fell in a heap on Ringo. King Kong, the dog and, most importantly the axe was gone, as if figments of their collective imagination. "What the fuck," Dave said, and he meant it.

At least they'd all seen this disappearing act, or – axe. Going

back in time had, apparently, more drawbacks than first thought. Ringo got to his feet, brushed the dust off his arse. "Where'd the fucker go?"

"I haven't a clue," Dave said. "But you'd better think yourself lucky he went, otherwise your nut would have been cracked like a Brazil at Christmas."

"I was just lulling him," Ringo said, regaining his composure. "I could have took him anytime."

"'Course you could," the rest of them said in unison.

"Whatever. I think we still have business to attend to in the house, here, have we not?"

"I think we've taken all of his soldiers out," said Jack.

"And we need to make sure he doesn't replace them." Ringo said.

They walked to the front door and knocked, like the gentlemen they were. Strangely, there was no answer, so Dave kicked it open. It took them a few minutes to find their host and Henry hiding in one of the bedrooms. Old Thomas was a funny looking geezer, he was about five-foot four with a belly that belonged to a man of greater stature.

"You're partial to a pie or two, Tom, I see," said Ringo. "I think it might be time for a bit of a diet."

"Show me the money," Dave said, unable to remember which Tom Cruise film the line came from.

Little Tom was like most who pay other men to do their dirty work, a weak and cowardly piece of shit. Jack kicked him in the ribs. "Money," he said. "All that you've stolen from the hard-working farmers around here."

"Yes, it's about to be returned to its rightful owners," Ringo said. "And as you no longer have bodyguards, it's a waste of good swords to leave them lying in the dirt, so we'll take them as well."

Tom just kept nodding his head, his badly fitting wig slipping nearer to his eyebrows with every nod.

"Go on then, little man," Dave said. "Put your wig straight and go fetch the cash." He pointed his blade at Tom's codpiece and added. "Unless you want to start losing body parts."

He was up like a cat being chased by a German Shepherd and seconds later reappeared with two large bags of coins. "I…it's all there," he stammered.

"Every p. p. penny. P… please don't hurt me."

Dave pointed to Ringo. "This here is Robin Hood and we're his band of merry, fucking men. We rob from the rich and give to the poor, understand?"

Tom nodded again.

"We only give one second chance and you've just had yours. Although I doubt anybody else would take you seriously enough to allow you to try and re-establish your extortion racket, remember – we have eyes everywhere." Dave gave him the old two fingers from his eyes gesture and finished off with a cheeky wink.

They took the money and old Tom even let them have a horse and cart to carry all his obsolete weaponry. He appeared to be a reformed character. They all piled into the cart, Ringo driving, so to speak. He told them he had a way with horses, unfortunately this beast didn't appear to realize that. Somehow his indicators weren't working too well. A lot of shouting ensued, speckled liberally with expletives, as the horse plodded off in the opposite direction to the 'driver's' instructions. Needless to say, it took them longer to get back to Will's place by horse and cart than it had to reach Daunter's house on foot. But the day was warm and sunny and, apart from some rather painful bruising, they were all in fine fettle. A job had been well done and another greedy arsehole had been put, well and truly, in his place.

"How long have you been a horse whisperer?" Dave asked Ringo.

"Fuck off Pansy." His reply was pretty much drowned out by the laughter from the rest of the group.

"It's probably something to do with the time difference, eh Ringo?" The coach suggested. This didn't even warrant a reply, just a Liverpudlian glare.

"Come on chaps, he's doing his best, the poor lad. This old feller probably doesn't understand Scouse. Ain't that right, Ringo?"

"Go on, have a fucking, good laugh. I'd like to see one of you tossers do a better job."

They were a hundred yards away from Will's when the parsnip eased the reins from Ringo's clenched fists. "The horse picks up on your frustration," he explained. "You have to relax, let him feel your control without yelling like some demented............."

The parsnip was, obviously, having trouble finding the appropriate word. They all came to his aid – "dick."

The horse responded to old parsnip face like he'd known him for years.

"Why didn't you take the reins, when we left Daunter's?" Dave asked him.

"I might not be as sharp as the rest of you, but I enjoy a laugh, just the same," he said with a wink. He turned to Ringo. "Did the other horses you've come across in the past have little runners attached to their feet and rock backwards and forwards."

"Nice one, Parsnip," said Ollie, chuckling.

Ringo resorted to his witty banter and told them all to fuck off, unable to stop a grin gracing his rugged features. "No-one can excel at everything," he said. "Nobody is perfect."

"Yeah, but some of us are more perfect than others," Dave said, punching him in the shoulder.

"Okay, I'm not Lester, fucking, Piggott. A joke's a joke but let's not turn it into a full-blown pantomime. You've had your laugh, now let's get back to the business at hand."

Will was outside with the widest grin Dave had ever seen. His relief was practically tangible.

TEN

The parsnip parked them up and they jumped, not too nimbly, off the cart, a lot of oohing and aahing going on.

"We come bearing gifts," said Ringo. "Do you or any of your fellow farmers know how to use a sword?"

Will shook his head. "Why would we? We're farmers, not soldiers."

"Do you know anyone that could give you a bit of tuition?" Dave asked him.

"Not real...well I suppose there's old Jacob."

"And who might Jacob be?" Ollie asked.

"He was a sergeant in the King's Guard."

"Was? Did he retire? I mean, get too old to carry on?" Ringo enquired.

"No, he was badly injured."

"What, in battle?" This was starting to feel like pulling teeth.

"A wild boar made a bit of a mess of his leg. He was out hunting with the King."

By the smiles on the others' faces, Dave knew he wasn't the only one picturing Elvis, on horseback, hunting big, hairy pigs."

"When you say, 'mess of his leg'," Dave said. "What do you mean exactly?"

Will shrugged. "Well, it gored him fairly badly and he walks with a pretty bad limp these days but, otherwise, he's fine. He gets paid a generous amount each week for his trouble by the crown, half of which he slings over the bar at the

"Dog and Trumpet". There's a lot that'd change places with him."

"I have to say, he doesn't sound ideal," Ringo said.

"As long as you get him in the afternoon, after he's slept off his hangover and not started out on a new one yet," explained Will. "And, of course, pay him for his time." Dave turned back to the cart and retrieved the bag of coins. "I don't think there'll be a problem there." He handed the cash to Will. "Mr. Daunter kindly offered you all a full refund. I don't think he'll ever trouble you again, but it wouldn't hurt to become a little more proficient in protecting your interests." He jerked a thumb to the cart. "There's a pile of weapons in there, again kindly donated by

your new best friend."

"Yeah, like Pansy…er…I mean Dave says – the money and the swords are there, so, do yourselves a favour – never let yourselves get pushed around again. Don't forget, who dares wins." The coach said.

"R…right," agreed Will, unable to hide the confusion he clearly felt. "I don't know how to thank you all. You've changed our lives."

"Just part of the service. Now, Robin Hood here and his little band of merry men must be on their way. People to meet, places to see, you know how it is. Stay safe, Will and look after those two lovely girls of yours."

"Wait," said Anna. "Let me get you some food to take with you. It's the least we can do." She turned and hurried into the cottage.

"Give them a jug of cider as well, " Will called to her. She returned seconds later with a muslin wrapped parcel and a stone jug with a lump of rag as a stopper. Dave took them from her. "Thank you, Anna, that's exceedingly kind. Now, look after yourselves. It was a pleasure meeting you."

As they rejoined the road to find out, Dave wondered if anyone else had seen the black Labrador that had leapt to their rescue back at Daunter's place. As nobody had mentioned it, it was doubtful. And, if that was the case, why had he seen her? The vision had been so clear he even knew the dog was a bitch. This was becoming more worrying by the hour.

As they walked on, the parsnip interrupted Dave's reverie. "You've got to stop all this Robin Hood rubbish. You never know, we might bump into him."

"He's a myth," said Ringo. "Like King Arthur and Merlin. You're a good bloke, Pete but you are a bit on the naive side."

"And you can be a pompous twat," Ollie told Ringo. "You think your opinion is the only one that counts."

"Pompous? Pompous?" I've been called a lot of things in the past but pompous ain't one of 'em. Facts are facts, that's all I'm saying."

"And what's your view on religion?" Dave asked him, hoping to lose himself in a bit of useless banter, to take his mind off the strange, appearing/disappearing, black Labrador.

"Imagine no religion," said Ringo simply.

"Yeah, and no possessions," added the coach. "Like your hero did. He lived in a tent in Central Park, living on baked beans, I suppose."

"If all the politicians and kings and queens had, he would too. He was advocating a way of life. Not just for him but for all of us."

Dave nodded. "Yeah, I can see that. But then, maybe he should have set an example, shown 'em he meant business. We can all talk a good game; the secret is playing it."

It was obvious that Ringo didn't take kindly to having his hero's actions brought into question.

"And was he giving peace a chance when he was getting wasted with Harry Nilsson and throwing his fists about?" the coach continued. He was on a roll.

"He was in a bad place then; it happens to all of us. It just doesn't get into the papers when you or I get totalled and lash out at some dickhead who's pissing us off. I never said he was a saint, did I?"

"To hear you talk, he was God," Dave said. He was enjoying this little game. It appeared that winding Ringo up was not difficult at all. "He was just a pop star who liked the sound of his own voice."

Poor old Ringo was getting redder and redder in the face. "Have you ever seen the news footage of millions of people all over the world, in tears, when they heard about his murder. They didn't think he was just a fucking pop star who liked the sound of his own voice, did they?"

"They're winding you up," said the parsnip, spoiling the game.

"Yeah, I never realized how easy it would be," the coach said, with a grin. "I thought you were going to blow a gasket."

"He really threw his toys out of the pram," Dave said.

"He meant a lot to me, that's all. I wish I'd been a teenager in the sixties and lived through the Beatles years. It must have been awesome."

"Well, you never know when we get this over and done with, maybe Christian will let us take a little holiday," Dave said. "I quite fancy going back to the days of making love not war. All them gorgeous girls with flowers in their hair and skirts like belts. Go on Ringo, start us off on one of your Beatles medleys."

He didn't need asking twice and as they all sang their way through 'Please, Please Me', Dave almost forgot about that damned dog.

If any normal twelfth century dweller had heard them, they would have, without doubt, considered them troubled in the grey cell department, unless, that is, there happened to be a medieval version of George Martin in the vicinity.

They dragged their tired and bruised bodies northward, the sun still high and resplendent in a clear blue sky. For the first time in his life Dave began to believe that pollution was a bitch. Everything was sharper in their present today, the colours, the smells, the lack of irritating dickheads in their obligatory four-by-fours ferrying their kids to and from school. There wasn't much about his previous life he missed. The last few months of their existence in the twenty first century had been less than pleasant, cooped up in a facility akin to a prison, only allowed out in the grounds in the pissing rain. To be out and about in the vibrant countryside with not even a rogue tractor to worry about was kind of liberating. Belting out timeless classics with his old buddies, strolling through the lush green-fields, cooling themselves beneath canopies of healthy, majestic oak trees and the like felt good. Maybe it was true – less is more.

"Does anyone have any idea where we are?" he asked no-one in particular, hence the word anyone. Even a sign from the heavens would have sufficed.

"Probably about fifteen miles north of London, at most," said Ringo. "I'm afraid without the London to Glasgow express, it's going to take us weeks to be in the vicinity of our objective."

"Ooh, 'our objective'. I love it when you talk dirty," the coach said with a wink.

"Old John was a bit of a dirty bastard, wasn't he, Ringo. Didn't he have his photo taken with that Japanese sort, all in the buff, for some shit record?"

"Leave it Coach," Dave said. "We've given him enough stick for one day." He winked at Ringo. "We'll start again tomorrow."

"Fucking morons," was Ringo's short but pointed response.

They did indeed let it be, so to speak, and lapsed into a contented silence. A slight breeze had surfaced but did little to combat the summer sun. Even though, due to their latest 'scrap', Dave was feeling about twenty years older than he actually was, he was the most relaxed he had been in years. He'd never been much of a thinker – well, deep stuff, anyway, but as they embarked on their lengthy journey, the birds singing, the sky as blue as fuck, he realized something – we make our own stress. The brain is like a computer and, unfortunately, most people have little in the way of programming skills. There was a job opportunity there for some clever bastard. Everyone else needs to learn to chill and not load the stress apps. Maybe easier said than done.

The day was completely uneventful. They stopped around what felt like, according to their bellies, lunchtime and ate some of the home baked bread, cheese and pickles supplied by Anna.

"I can't believe how such simple grub tastes so bloody marvelous," the parsnip said.

"'Coz it's not full of additives and shit," said Ollie, through a mouthful.

They all nodded in agreement, savoring every morsel. They washed it down with a drop of Will's wonderful cider. They all felt so mellow, they lay down in the grass and grabbed forty winks. Well, maybe eighty.

They stirred and were up and at 'em around, what Dave estimated to be, mid-afternoon. It's weird how, when a watch isn't available, even the thickest are able to estimate the time of day purely by the position of the sun. Dave thought it was about three in the afternoon when they resumed their northward journey. For the first time, since arriving in the past, a few clouds were blotting the clear, blue sky's copybook. They weren't serious enough to alter the temperature though. As they walked, sweat glued their shirts to their backs and the friendly banter seemed to subside. Dave, for one, after a good, honest meal and a couple of hour's kip, aided by Will's homebrew was at peace with himself. The sun was in the sky, even if it was having to dodge the recent clouds, the countryside lush and un-spoilt and, for two or three weeks at least, there was nothing to stress out the old noggin.

"This is the life," said the parsnip, breaking a beautiful silence. They all nodded. Old vegetable face had hit the proverbial nail right on its bonce. What does it matter if some misguided sorts have to be shown the error of their ways from time to time, when the simple life, with the current bun on one's mush can be enjoyed? Dave found himself wondering what it would be like on the coast. The sky was bluer than in the pollution ridden 21st century which meant that the sea would follow suit. When he was a kid, he used to think the sea was really blue and could never understand how it turned to normal looking water when you took it from its natural habitat. Luckily, he never voiced his worries in that direction to anyone other than his old man who, he was sorry to say, wasn't the sharpest tool in the box. When he asked him why, all his dad said was 'I dunno, son'. It wasn't until he was on a school trip to Weston-super-mare when he was about eight or nine that he learnt the truth. It was on a day when the sea actually graced them with its presence, and this other kid, Nigel something-or-other said 'Wow, ain't the sea blue' and their Geography teacher, 'Grumpy' Grant, as they called him, said, 'Well, without a cloud in the sky, it will be'. Then, just to make Dave feel like a real dumbo he said, 'Some people think the sea is really blue and not merely reflecting the sky above it'. Everybody had a real good laugh at that, even Dave. How can anybody be so stupid? Anyway, it got him thinking.

"Why don't we angle our course eastward a bit and take a look at the old seaside?" He was expecting Ringo to shoot him down and put forward about ten reasons why that would be a terrible idea. Instead, he surprised him. He shrugged, then nodded.

"I don't see any reason why we can't aim for Lincolnshire and follow the coast up through Yorkshire and Northumberland if they're called that in this day and age. Might as well make the journey as pleasant as we can." Dave punched old parsnip head on the arm. "We're off on our holidays."

The Parsnip shook his head, rubbed his arm and told Dave he was just a big kid. And that's the way he felt, like he did when Mum and Dad used to take him to Torquay. It's true – men never really grow up.

ELEVEN

The rest of that day was spent exchanging holiday tales, the best one being the day the Coach had a crab latch onto his 'taters as he was creeping gingerly into a freezing cold sea at Bournemouth. "If you've ever had a crab grab hold of your bollock, you'll know what I'm talking about," he said, wincing with the memory of it all. The rest of them were in stitches, none of them having experienced a similar fate.

"It wasn't pissing funny at the time," he said.

"It is now," Dave said, in between waves of uncontrollable laughter. "It gives a whole new meaning to 'having crabs'."

As the light started to fade, they were still chatting and laughing. It had been a grand day.

"We'd best find somewhere comfortable to bed down," said Ringo.

As everywhere was grass, with the occasional copse-like area and a few rocks here and there, it wasn't going to be difficult. It seemed Ringo liked playing party leader, it made him feel important. It didn't bother any of the others, they just looked at each other with that 'here he goes again' sort of expression.

"Where do you suggest, Ringo?" asked Ollie, with a wink to the parsnip.

"Yes," Dave added. "We are in desperate need of your guidance."

Ringo resorted, once more, to the old Liverpudlian witty repartee and told them both to 'fuck off'. He had a way with words.

As the sun left their world to provide others with its welcoming glow, they dropped their gear by a couple of sizeable boulders and 'made camp'. The parsnip cracked open the rest of the bread and cheese, which they split in two, half for their supper and the other half for breakfast. "We're going to have to start hunting for our food tomorrow unless we happen on more farmers in need of our services," Ringo said.

"Well we've seen lots of little bunny rabbits," Dave pointed out. "Do you think you could put an end to one of their little, hopping lives with one of your nasty arrows?" he asked Ringo.

Ringo shrugged. "Needs must." The look in his eyes, however, didn't support the statement. Tonight, he would be praying for some other means of sustenance to present itself, Dave could tell.

It didn't take them long to eat their meagre supper but at least they had something in their bellies. Dave estimated by nightfall the next day they would be starving unless something happened, or they started to kill to eat. None of them were vegetarians but eating meat from animals that someone else has slaughtered is different to having to kill them yourself. Dave was just thinking that if he had a surfeit of vegetables and fields full of cows, pigs, and sheep at his disposal, if he wished to kill and eat them, he would become a vegetarian. As he was wondering what sort of exotic vegetarian dishes he could rustle up, a sound like twenty claps of thunder blew his thoughts to Kingdom Come.

The usual shouts of 'what the ….' were drowned out. Dave's head felt like it was about to explode, his eardrums assaulted by the equivalent of a dozen Ginger Bakers battering their way through 'Toad'. As the roar began to subside, in came an orchestra of screeching violin players. This was the nearest his ears had ever come to bleeding. They were all on their knees, hands over their heads, when the 'nails on a blackboard' squeal became a banshee's wail.

The air was sucked out of their world and the twilight turned into a sickly green fog.

"There's that bloody dog again," yelled Ringo.

Dave followed his gaze and, sure enough, his old mate, the black Labrador was battling her way through the murk, a gale that they didn't feel, flattening her ears against her head.

"Who the fuck are they?" The coach shouted above the cacophony.

Following behind the dog were three blokes and a vision of loveliness, the muscles of her long and shapely legs straining against weather conditions they could only observe. It was like looking through a window, watching the autumn wind stripping the trees and blowing wheelie bins across the road, whilst in the stillness and safety of a warm home. The trio of strangers turned and looked at them, the confusion Dave's group felt, mirrored in their own expressions. What made it worse was that the geezer leading the group looked very much like the chap from the dream Dave had had at the pub and the feller next to the tasty piece looked familiar as well.

"I think his name's Danny," said the parsnip, seemingly reading Dave's mind, as the volume was turned down.

Dave was just beginning to realize, either he wasn't mad or, if he was, he wasn't the only one, when there was a sound similar to the opening of a vacuum sealed jar and their new friends, dog included, disappeared.

"This is getting weird," said Ollie.

"I thought I was going mental," Dave said.

"So, did I," added the parsnip.

It turned out they'd all seen the dog at Daunter's place, but all thought they were hallucinating. Which was rich as the strongest thing they'd had recently was old Will's cider. The parsnip, Ringo and Dave had also had rather vivid dreams about one or more of the folks they'd just seen through the 'window'. Ringo's was about the girl with the legs, the lucky bastard.

"What does it mean?" The coach asked.

They all shrugged and then Ringo said, "You don't think the slimy bastard sent another group through before us, do you?"

Dave nodded, considering the possibility. "And they got caught in some sort of time bubble?"

"It's a possibility, I suppose," Ringo said.

"I don't think so," said the parsnip. "Did you not see the clothes. They were all wearing 21st century clobber, apart from the old dude, who looked like Charles Dickens."

They all had to concur, most, if not all of them, thinking of the hot pants worn by one member of the band.

"Strange days indeed," said Ringo.

"You're not wrong there my old drumstick," Dave added. "As if being forced into a 'Time Machine' and slung back to the 1100's ain't strange enough."

"Mind you, that was a lovely dog," said Ollie, with that expression that people only have on their chops when talking about babies or animals. "I've always loved Labradors. My Dad used to have one, used to go everywhere with him. He called her Maggie, after Margaret Thatcher."

"Why would anyone name a dog after that heartless bitch?" Ringo said with a sneer.

"Whoa," the coach said. "Let's not get political, for God's sake. We've got enough problems, as it is."

"The man's not wrong," Dave agreed. "I, for one, am a little concerned about this recent development. I was, kind of, getting to like the past with its simplicity. This is an unwanted complication."

"I've got a really bad feeling about it," the parsnip said softly.

"Well, whatever. I suggest we get some shut-eye and see what tomorrow brings," said Ringo, all business-like.

The rest of them nodded, although Dave wasn't sure how much kip they would get after that unwanted interlude. He was with the parsnip on this one. Some deep shit was coming their way. Nevertheless, they all stretched out beneath the beautiful night sky and tried to find slumber-land. His mind was doing somersaults, creating weird and wonderful scenarios involving their new friends. That was one thing he was sure about. The three geezers, the girl and the dog were not their enemies. Mary's parting words kept coming back to him, as well. 'You must keep him safe' was what she'd said. The more he churned it all over in his confused brain, the more he was sure she was referring to one of the blokes in the 'bubble'. But, if so, what was he supposed to do?

After about an hour of lying there with his mind racing, trying to fit pieces of one jigsaw puzzle into another with completely different shaped bits, the old grey cells had had enough. They shut down and he fell into a fitful sleep. He dreamt in technicolour, a tsunami of images rolling over each other, crashing and disintegrating or being whipped into a cyclonic twister. It was like one of those old horror films, like 'Tales from the Crypt' with a variety of short stories, only these mingled and merged. He had never taken LSD, but he would have imagined a 'bad trip' to be similar to his dreams that night.

When the morning sun touched Dave's brow with its soothing fingers, he awoke with a start, breathing heavily, the sour smell of the night sweats on his skin, The coach, Ollie and the parsnip were still twitching like sleeping dogs but Ringo was sat with his back against a boulder.

"Bad night?" he asked softly.

Dave nodded. "You could say that."

"What do you make of this shit?" Ringo asked quietly.

Dave shrugged. "It's mental. Before I knew the rest of you were seeing what I was, I thought I was. Going mental, I mean."

"You'd think once you'd got your head around time travel, there'd be nothing that could phase you," Ringo said. "But this is........far out."

"Yeah man, totally cosmic," Dave said, getting into the sixty's vibe.

"No need to take the piss, Pansy. I'm trying to have a sensible conversation here."

"Sorry, I thought I'd try and lighten the mood a little. I always resort to being a twat when I'm worried."

"So, you are worried?" Ringo said, a look of concern gracing his Liverpudlian features.

"Well, yeah. Aren't you?"

He ran a hand through his hair. "I don't know what to think. I just have this feeling that, I don't know, this is just the start."

"Of what?"

"I'm fucked if I know. I get the impression that our trip to the seaside might be dead in the water though."

Dave nodded and told him what Mary had said to him and how he believed it to allude to the bloke the parsnip had called 'Danny'. "I don't know about you but I'm beginning to think that we're destined for stranger days and we ain't going to have any choice in the matter."

"Destiny's a funny fucker," said Ringo.

"He's not making me laugh."

"Who's not?" The parsnip sat up, stretched, and farted. "Oops," he said, grinning.

"Destiny," Dave said, watching the parsnip's face crease in confusion. "Don't worry about it, chap, we were just shooting the breeze."

"Who's shooting bees?" Ollie yawned, adding more methane to the mix. Having never lived with a woman,

Dave wondered if they took on surplus gas overnight, the same as blokes seemed to.

"You're some dirty bastards," spluttered the coach, the overpowering stench wrenching him from his slumber.

"The gang's all here," said Ringo, waving a hand in front of his face. "I guess we'd better get some breakfast and make tracks."

They broke out the last of the bread and cheese, a definite feeling of trepidation surrounding their merry band, and munched in silence. Little did Dave know that his next night would be spent in a shitty cell and the following afternoon would find his head on a block.

They made the most of the last of their food, packed up their stuff and moved off. Dave didn't know about the rest of them but the weird shit they'd witnessed recently overshadowed his concerns about where their next meal was coming from. He wondered how Ringo was feeling, as it would have to be his arrow that had to do the business in the hunting department. He didn't envy him that, he had to admit.

As it turned out, his archery skills were not needed, at least, not that day. They walked for the rest of the morning and as the sun crept overhead, indicating p.m. was upon them Ollie spotted couple of sheep in the distance.

"Sheep," he said enthusiastically. "Bloody sheep. That must mean a farm." He was practically jumping up and down. Anybody would have thought, by his excitement, that food or water hadn't passed their lips for weeks.

"Steady on feller," Dave said. "You'll bust a blood vessel." A rabbit appeared from nowhere and hopped across their path, as if he knew he was safe. Dave could have sworn the little bugger winked at him. It was obvious that Ringo was relieved as he let out one of the heaviest sighs Dave had ever heard.

"We must make sure we get as much food and water as we can carry," he said.

"Depends on what they can spare," said the coach.

"Plus, they probably won't have some rip-off merchant that needs sorting," added the parsnip.

"Let's not cross any bridges," Dave said. "What will be, will be. And let's face it, we ain't starving, are we?"

"I could murder a leg of lamb," said Ollie, eyeing the sheep.

As they got closer, the farmhouse came into view, along with more sheep and a plethora of chickens but, more importantly, not too far away, was a village. It was about half a mile, the other side of the farm, and a welcome sight.

"At least you won't have to mug the farmer," Dave said to Ollie. Ollie gave him a 'fuck off' look and added the V's, as if to drive home the point.

"Who fancies a pint?" Ringo asked.

"Now you're talking" Dave said, the thought of Will's homebrew still fresh in his mind. "I just hope it's better than the last drinking establishment we encountered."

"Booze is booze," Ringo said.

Dave nodded – he had a point. "Let's go get shit-faced." He could taste it already.

They walked past the farm, the sight of the farmer's wife's enormous arse presenting itself, as she bent over feeding the chickens.

"A fine figure of a woman," said the parsnip, and he wasn't joking.

Twenty minutes later they entered the village. More medieval buildings greeted them, and Dave wished he knew more about architectural nuances but, hey, no-one's perfect. It took them about five minutes to find the local, a reasonable hostelry with the attractive name of 'The Mare's Head'. Dave wondered what the deal was with bodiless heads in this century. Anyhow, they entered and, for a time, enjoyed themselves. That's until fancy-pants and his entourage came in.

The ale at this place was a definite improvement on the swill served at 'The Bodiless Head' and slipped down a treat. The floorboards were oak and well-polished. No spit and sawdust here. They were having a good time, laughing and joking, putting the weird shit to the back of their minds. Living in the moment might have been the fashionable phrase from their previous life but they were definitely employing it here. They were quaffing the amber and generally chilling when in he came. He was all ponced up, like somebody from a movie about........twelfth century shit, with half a dozen heavies. They all did a bit of nudging, nodding, and winking, in a discreet manor, of course. This dude was dressed in satin and lace with some ridiculous, powdered wig on his bonce. Everybody fawned around him, it was sickening to watch.
"What a knob," said the coach.
"He's obviously a big knob," said Ringo. "He's got more minders than Justin Bieber."
"How many's *he* got then?" asked Ollie.
"Probably not as many as six," Ringo replied.
"I put you down as a closet Timberlake fan," Dave said. "And now I find you're down with the kids."
Ringo shrugged, held out his hands. "Appearances can be deceptive."
That's when the poncey twat interrupted their humorous exchange by abusing their own waitress, a lovely girl named Kathleen. By this time, Dave had watched her glide around the pub quite a bit, her auburn hair whipping back and forth as she served. The locals loved her, that was obvious. She flirted with the younger chaps and made the old geezers feel – not so old. She had a future in the future, where most waitresses he'd met had faces like slapped arses. Kathleen was a natural, she was pretty, had

153

an infectious personality and a cracking body. He was watching her hips sway as she took mugs back for washing when old 'Satin and Lace' was suddenly in her face, leering and practically dribbling. Kathleen's body language told it all, he obviously made her skin crawl, but she was also afraid to upset him.

"If he lays a finger on her, he's a dead man," Dave said.

"She looks as though she can handle him," said Ringo.

"Keep out of it, he's clearly some bigwig, who could land us in a whole heap of trouble."

That's when he started pawing her and the old red mist came down. Dave felt the parsnip try to grab him as he leapt up, his hand brushing Dave's arm. Dave was shaking with rage as he reached the twat. The rest is history, as they say. He had the pleasure of landing a solid punch on that smarmy mush and taking a few of his heavies down before the pub was swarming with soldiers and he was carted off. One thing that made it all worthwhile was when Kathleen blew him a kiss as he was bundled roughly through the door. Small mercies and all that.

This brings things full circle, so to speak. They had it away on their toes, as previously stipulated, Dave's neck still supporting his head in a very efficient manner. Bauminster would soon become a distant memory and, unfortunately, so would Kathleen. Dave wondered why real life never mirrored TV shows like 'Kung Fu' where the evil fuckers get their arses kicked and the good people walk off into the sunset, happy as Larry. Because life is a bastard, full of people who want to screw the little man, the government being the worst culprit. Dave decided to put the soapbox away and get back to his jovial self. Even though he'd chastised Ringo on his tardiness in the arrow department, he still owed the bugger his life and would never forget. He felt he had to make his feelings clear.

154

"Thanks mate," he said sincerely. "You, literally, saved my neck."

"Yeah, I did." Ringo said flatly.

Dave was expecting something like – 'no sweat, man' or 'you'd have done the same for me' sort of shit and was a little miffed with Ringo's high and mighty attitude.

"I'd have done the same for you, you know – and probably a bit quicker." Dave was upset, feeling as though his gratitude wasn't enough. It felt as though Ringo was throwing it back in his face. In all honesty, he was pissed off. His expression did little to hide his emotions.

Ringo sniggered. "I have to admit, I didn't think you'd be that easy to wind up, Pansy. Parsnip, yeah, but not you. I thought you were made of sterner stuff."

There was only one response and Dave gave it, making Ringo's snigger escalate to a full-scale belly laugh and causing Dave to join in.

"You're a Beatle-headed bastard," Dave told him.

"And you're a pushover," Ringo said.

Dave had never been a tactile sort of bloke, but he couldn't help giving the twat a big hug. That's what having good mates does for you.

"Whoa, steady on," Ringo said. "I was only getting a bit of target practice in, it's no big deal."

"You need to get in touch with your feminine side," the parsnip told him.

"I ain't got one." He punched his chest. "This is solid man." He winked. "Ask the ladies of Liverpool."

Dave suddenly felt an overwhelming affection for the four of them, a feeling he'd never experienced before.

"Thanks to all of you," he said, brushing a tear from his cheek. He held up his hand. "One for all and all that shit." They all high fived him, Ringo putting a little more force than necessary behind his. "Let's hit the coast."

Back on track, after their little, unfortunate interlude, the sun on their backs, the deep, blue sea only days away, they were in high spirits. Dave started to sing 'Don't Look Back in Anger' by Oasis but within minutes they were back on the Beatles' back catalogue. Let's face it Noel Gallagher had admitted that he nicked most of his songs from the Fab Four or their contemporaries. Listening to the radio, you'd be hard pushed not to hear The Beatles, even now, that's 2021 and not 1148, of course. There they were, singing John and Paul's songs, looking forward to their holidays when all hell broke loose.

PART THREE – THE SPLIT

ONE

When Danny regained consciousness the first thought he had was - how could he think when there was a construction site in his head. With his time away from the demon drink his ability to cope with an excess of the stuff had disappeared. He, quite simply, had the mother of all hangovers. His mouth was dry and rancid and all he could think of was another shot, the old hair of the dog. He remembered little of what had led to his present state, just a vague recollection of drinking scotch in his flat. After that it was pretty much a blur, although there was a feeling that he'd done or said something that he should be ashamed of. Pretty much the stuff hangovers are made of. He looked over to the bedside clock and was surprised to find, not only was it no longer there but the table that had supported had done a runner as well. He sat up, wincing with the effort and, even with the road drills in his head and cognizant thought a struggle, it was obvious he wasn't at home. The room was small, the walls an unsettling white, the flimsy curtains allowing too much of the summer sun through. He was just about to brave it and swing his legs out of the bed and, maybe, find out where he was, when a piece of this whiteness swung inward.

"Ah, I see you're back in the land of the living Danny," said a man who was strangely familiar. Danny found himself wondering where the man's long, black coat was and, suddenly, a Bob Dylan song covered by Joan Osborne sprung to his ravaged mind. And then a name rose like a phoenix from the old fiery remnants.

"Seth."

"Very good. I'm glad to see that alcohol has not destroyed all of your brain cells."

A teapot, cup and saucer and a couple of slices of toast were on the tray Seth held.

158

"Ginger tea," he explained. "Very good for hangovers, I believe. Make sure you have a cup before you try and eat anything."

As he walked over to the bed, an extremely attractive, dark skinned girl followed him into the room. Again, she appeared familiar, but no name came into Danny's head this time.

"Why are you pussyfooting around this waste of space," she asked his host. "He's just a weak, suicidal drunk. I mean, look at the state of him."

Seth poured the tea and handed Danny the cup, "Drink it all, you'll feel better. Then eat the toast, there's no butter or any sort of spread, it needs to be dry. Trust me."

"Trust me," mimicked the girl.

Seth turned slowly and sighed. "The Machine has chosen him, just like it did with you. Let's face it Phil, you were hardly a model citizen when I first met you."

"I wasn't a waste of space drunk."

Another sigh. "No, you weren't."

Danny was drinking the tea and it seemed that the pneumatic drills were taking a tea-break as well. The only part of the exchange between Seth and Phil that had really penetrated his slowly recovering brain was the phrase about being chosen by The Machine.

"Which of you is Finch and which is Reese?" He asked, having watched a few episodes of 'Person of Interest'. "Has my number come up?"

Seth looked confused. Phil told him it was an American TV series.

"This is not fiction Danny. Am I correct in assuming that you no longer believe in God?"

Danny took another swig of the hangover cure and gave him the thumbs up.

"Good, because you're about to find out what makes the world go round. And it's not love."

"Was that a joke?" Phil asked with a bewildered expression.

"I think it possibly was," said Seth.

In most books or films when somebody wakes up in a strange place, they all ask, 'Where am I?'

As Danny really didn't want to be on this earth at all, he didn't give a fuck where he was. He was a little curious but even curiosity loses its appeal when you intend to depart this miserable life quietly and without the involvement of others. This was still a course of action that he intended to continue with when he could get rid of these two weirdos, or rather, extricate himself from the silly bastards.

He put down the cup but found it extremely difficult. His arms seemed to be losing all their strength and although the idea in his head was to get out of this bed and return to his flat and his plans, his legs wouldn't move.

"I'm sorry Danny," said Seth with what appeared to be genuine regret. "But we have to talk to you and need to ensure that you listen. There was a rather strong muscle relaxant in your ginger tea. You'll be fully engaged, mentally, but won't be able to move, at all. I apologise profusely but needs must when the devil drives, as they say."

Danny tried to yell but nothing came out. He wasn't even sure if his eyeballs were glaring as he intended them to do. He was a prisoner in his own body. All he could do was lie there and listen, while mentally cursing this twisted bastard at the end of the bed.

"Although the drug in your system is, initially strong, its effects wear off in a couple of hours. You will suffer no side or aftereffects. I hope, however, that your frame of mind will have altered considerably during that time."

Phil sighed and muttered, 'Get on with it."

Seth shot her a look and cleared his throat. Even in his present state, Danny could tell he was nervous. He reminded him of one of the pitchers from 'Dragons' Den' and even though he didn't want to be, he was intrigued. He'd been abducted, given a drug to render him immobile and now someone was about to try and convince him to join some merry little band. He wondered if Seth was a master criminal planning a heist and he needed Danny's fruit and veg skills to pull it off. If he'd had the use of his facial muscles, he would have laughed. Mentally he echoed Phil's last statement.

"Earlier," Seth continued. "I asked if you believed in God and you responded negatively. You may have, in your younger years, entertained the notion of a supreme being who, having created this earth that we desecrate daily, watches over us. However, when you lose everything you hold dear, that notion becomes impossible to even consider. Don't get me wrong, faith can be a great help to many but man's varied vision of the object of that faith corrupts and destroys. It isn't God in Himself that is the problem it's just that men create so many versions of Him, each believing their version to be superior to the rest and are willing to kill to try and prove it. The fact that there is no supreme being makes no difference. I know this for a fact but to convince all those Christians, Catholics, Muslims, Hindus and all the rest that their belief is misplaced would be futile."

Seth paused and took a sip from a glass of water passed to him by Phil. He handed it back and coughed again. "You see Danny, this world we inhabit exists and continues to exist because of The Machine. In this technological age is that not more believable than a white-haired old man, sitting on his throne in heaven?"

Danny had suspected that his captor was maybe a little deranged but now he was certain that Seth was as mad as a box of frogs. He was right, Danny had been brought up to believe in the existence of God and, although never a church goer, the idea of the man on high had always lurked in the back of his mind. Seth was wrong, however, when he assumed, after all that had happened, that that belief had simply dissipated. Danny needed someone to blame, some entity to hurl his feelings of anger, hurt and utter loss at. If anyone had asked whether he still believed in God, he would have said – there is no God, as if denying His existence would be the best way of getting back at Him for taking away everyone he had ever loved. Whether He existed or not was beside the point – he never really had any interest in the 'God versus The Big Bang Theory' scenario. It seemed that he had been right to ignore such a ludicrous debate now he knew the truth. It's a Machine, of course it is. Even though the drug prevented him from collapsing in fits of laughter, inside he was in pieces. If he weren't about to shuffle off this mortal coil (once he had control of his faculties again), he would, maybe, have been concerned for his safety. As it was, if this lunatic did the job for him, all well and good. He suddenly wondered where this Philomena fitted in. Apart from being a feisty sort with some sort of martial arts training she seemed relatively normal. Maybe Seth had brainwashed her. The bollocks about this wonderful Machine had not phased her in the slightest. If Danny didn't know it was impossible, he'd say she believed it. He watched, that's all he could do, as she handed Seth the glass again. He took a swig, let out another nervous cough and continued with his ridiculous monologue.

"You've obviously heard the term Artificial Intelligence, A.I. for short. It's something that scientists strive to achieve, not realizing that they are already fine examples of it themselves, as we all are. Mankind is a great creation, that is undeniable, but God, in whatever form is your preferred flavor, cannot claim credit. The earth has existed for millennia but was only populated just over two thousand years ago. There was never a B.C. or A.D. come to that, only vague theories filtered into the original

162

programming. It had to be a new beginning with only the chosen few still aware of the past. When I said that the world as you know it exists and is maintained by a Machine, it was a little too simplistic.

The Machine is as much organic as technological. Its creation was a necessity to alter this planet's atmosphere to accommodate the continuance of a species. Unfortunately sacrifices had to be made and adjustments endured. Before reaching, what is now known as, planet Earth, our ancestors' own planet was destroyed. Most perished as their home imploded. Only a few hundred were lucky enough to survive and all had to become part of The Machine as The Machine became part of them. Their previous lives were deleted and new, although primitive, paths were configured. The subject taught to you in school as history has some elements of truth, but the majority is pure fiction created for heritage purposes. Without history we don't exist."

Danny found it difficult, being a prisoner in his own body, without the ability to express any emotion at all. Not able to yell or just walk away from someone who was boring the shit out of him by spouting total bollocks was hard for him. But still it continued. Old Seth was obviously getting into his stride, Danny's inertia seemingly spurring him on. "I'm aware that when you've been brought up to believe in a God or, indeed, if you've decided to discard so called religious education altogether, opting for death as a total finality, the truth will be hard to swallow. I'm sure if you could speak and your face was able to show emotion, I would be subjected to a barrage of abuse whilst your expression would show your absolute belief in my insanity. Once I was in your position and although the guardian responsible for my induction didn't feel it necessary to chemically subdue me, he certainly received more than his fair share of vitriol, misguided though it was. You will be shown proof and you will have no choice other than to accept the true way this planet operates. It has been accepted over the generations, however, to prepare selected inductees before plunging them into an alien world. I will let Phil tell you about her own personal …er…how shall I say…troublesome will suffice…revelation. It was because of her reaction that I thought it prudent to try and prevent a similar situation." He stepped back and motioned Philomena forward. Had Danny not been in a state of drug induced impotence, he thought he would have experienced a little stirring in the nether regions as she took Seth's place. His feelings, had they been allowed full reign, were pure lust. For a person who had felt little over the past few months, this feeling was unusual to say the least. As was the unexpected interest that had formed since she took the floor.

"First," she started. "I don't know why a fucking alcoholic, suicidal waste of space like you has been selected." She shrugged and her breasts followed suit. Danny had the feeling that the drugs were beginning to lose their grip.

"Yeah I thought it was total bollocks when this one," she nodded at Seth. "Put the arm on me. I've never been good with authority. Let's face it most people that have power over us plebs are either sadists or fucking downright twisted. Anyway, he gave me the spiel and I felt the same as, I imagine, you do now. I told him to fuck right off and was about to leave. He tried to stop me and got a smack in the mush for his trouble. It was a beauty, wasn't it?" She looked at Seth for confirmation and received it with a nod. "He went down like a ton of bricks and I felt kind of sorry for him. I mean, look at him, he ain't no spring chicken. He begged me to let him show me and I thought, what the fuck. I wasn't in any hurry to be anywhere else and I wasn't afraid of him. Mind you I ain't afraid of anyone, I can look after myself." She looked at Seth and he nodded again and urged her to go on.

164

"So, he showed me and that did scare me, I don't mind saying. So, I guess all I have to say to you is keep an open mind and just hope it don't get blown away totally man. It took me a couple of days to get my head round it. It's a total mind fuck but the man don't speak with forked tongue."

"We're going to leave you to digest all that you've heard whilst the drug wears off. It should take about another thirty minutes or so before you regain the use of your limbs. I would beg, as I did with Phil, to allow us to prove everything we've said is true." He paused and his expression saddened. He let out a heavy sigh and continued. "If after that you wish to continue with your previous plan of ending your life, there's nothing we can do to stop you. No-one can make you fulfill your destiny. The choice must be yours. I will pass on a little more information that may or may not influence your decision. If you do decide to destroy yourself, you will not be absorbed. The organic force that has helped give your individuality will slip into a state, akin to that of drowning but without the finality. A constant struggle to regain life without the release of death. That will be your hell."
With that, he and Phil left Danny to use the only part of his body that he could, his brain. To be spun such a ludicrous tale was madness but to have two individuals convinced of its truth and trying to convince him to boot was even
madder. Danny had never really been into sci-fi or fantasy novels, although he'd seen a few films of that nature. He could imagine some sci-fi nut swallowing the whole thing, only because he wanted it to be true. Aliens bringing life to earth and keeping it real with a bloody Machine. But Seth had said he'd prove it. Suddenly a weird video that he'd seen on you tube came to mind, where this magician put a woman's torso on a bloke's legs and vice versa.

There is some strange shit about, and Danny began to wonder if this weirdo was some sort of illusionist and this was going to be some trick, and Phil was his extremely attractive assistant. The more he thought about it the more this scenario made sense. He was going to be the dumb bastard that everyone would piss themselves laughing at when the video went viral. He was the unbeliever, dragged unwillingly into their little scam, so Seth would look like a God of the magical world, creating and making him believe in a ridiculous fantasy. It would probably be on the scale of making airplanes disappear or swapping peoples' bodies. Danny was going to become the stupid arse running about on a pair of woman's legs. The situation was instantly more bearable. He had to admit that a certain part of him had begun to doubt his own sanity. He realized that over the last hour or so, his mind had been more active than it had in a long time. Whatever Seth's game might be, it had certainly dusted off the old grey matter and allowed it to pop its head above the surface of the sea of destruction it had been slowly drowning in. That would be hell, he reminded myself, with what was almost a chuckle. Whatever Seth had shot him full of was starting to lose its effect. He found that he could lift the index finger of his right hand and slowly, very slowly feeling reintroduced itself to the rest of his body. He came to a decision. He'd go along with their trick but at the appropriate time he would turn the tables. Strangely all thoughts of suicide had sunk to the bottom of his list of things to do and making sure these two jokers got what they deserved was straight in at number one.

TWO

Sure enough, after half an hour he was back to normal, apart from having a raging thirst. Seth had left a jug of water on a table by the window, which he drank in a couple of long, satisfying swigs, straight from the jug. He moved back to the bed and had to steady himself as a wave of nausea washed over him. Maybe he wasn't quite back to his old, miserable self just yet. Although he'd been drugged and put to bed, the only items of his attire to have been removed were his shoes. When he'd got his sea legs back, he slipped his feet back into his trainers. At that moment, the door opened, and his hosts re-entered the room.

"Good to see you back on your feet, Danny," Seth said with an apologetic smile.

Danny held his temper but glared at Seth and shook his head. "Sure, you are."

Seth sighed. "You're an intelligent young man, I'm sure you can understand why I had to ensure your cooperation."

"If I'm an intelligent young man, then why was it necessary to pump me full of drugs?"

"Well, in your current state of mind, without them we could have had a volatile situation on our hands. You were suicidal and quite drunk, not a combination conducive to calm conversation of a revelatory nature. I'm sure you can see that."

"Is that what you call this nonsense, 'conversation of a revelatory nature'?"

"You've just got to show him, man. You can talk till you're blue in the face, it ain't going cut any ice. You've known this weird shit for years and you've forgotten what it's like to have your world turned upside down, but for the likes of us, the more spieling, the more we're convinced you're a nut job. He needs to see for himself," Phil said. "There are times when I think you like the sound of your own voice, Show him the fucking badlands."

"I wish you wouldn't call it that."

"Well it's a better description than 'The Grid' and kind of sexier. When you're gone everyone that comes after is going to know it as the badlands, I'm going to make sure. Anyway, whatever it is, he needs to see it. He needs to see the shit he'll be dealing with if he decides not to be a pussy and top himself and to accept his 'destiny'," she said, indicating parenthesis with her fingers.

"I wish you wouldn't make fun of everything, Phil. To be chosen is an honour and should be taken seriously."

"Get over yourself. I'll do my bit, but I intend to have a laugh in the process. Mind you, looking at him, he's going to be more miserable than you. I hope this other bloke is an improvement. Now are you going to show him or try and talk him to death. None of us are getting any younger, especially you."

"Very well. Danny would you look out of the window for me and tell me what you see."

Danny thought, here we go, here comes the piss take.

"Why what am I going to see, the hanging gardens of Babylon or a herd of wildebeest, maybe?" He seemed to remember something like this being said by John Cleese in one of the Fawlty Towers episodes his dad loved so much. Seth looked puzzled, obviously not a Fawlty Towers fan.

"If you'd just humour me, Danny – please."

Danny shrugged and shuffled over to the bedroom window, his legs still a little wobbly from whatever shit Seth had pumped into him. There were no wildebeest or hanging gardens, just a small handkerchief of a lawn with an empty flower border and a paved path leading to a tiny shed. It was just another terraced house back garden, like millions of others. It was his turn to be puzzled.

"What am I supposed to be looking for?"

"Just what you'd expect to see from a bedroom window, a small, nicely kept garden."

This was becoming tedious and, from the way Phil was fidgeting and sighing, Danny was sure she shared his view.

"Very nice," he said. "Now if you'll excuse me, I've got things to do."

"Why do you have to milk it, Seth," said Phil. "Just show him. If you don't get a bloody wriggle on, he won't have to top himself, you'll bore him to death."

Seth cleared his throat and pointed to the door to the left of the window. "I'd appreciate it if you'd open that door for me."

It was just a normal wardrobe door. Not only was this tedious, but it was also pissing Danny off severely. "Why can't you open it?" His mind was returning to the magic trick scenario and wondering if this was climax. "In fact, if you want it open, open the fucking thing yourself."

"For Christ's sake," muttered Phil. "I've had enough of this crap. I don't mind a joke, Seth but bollocks to a pantomime." She marched over to the wardrobe and yanked open the door.

Despite himself, Danny let out a gasp. The hangers draped with various items of clothing, he had expected to see, weren't there. He still couldn't get rid of the idea of all this being some elaborate trick but, if that were the case, it was a bloody good one. Then he thought – it's a painting. It's a wardrobe that has been de-clothed and had a wardrobe sized painting fitted to the back. Thoughts were flying back and forth in his head but, somehow, whatever explanation the logical part of his brain came up with, the rest of his brain-cells shook their metaphorical heads to. They were telling him to believe his eyes. He must have been staring, open mouthed because Philomena laughed

169

and said. "Some fucking wardrobe, eh? It ain't no picture either. Danny meet the badlands, the badlands – Danny. Sorry Seth, Danny meet The Grid. Apparently, we're going to become incredibly good friends."

Danny stood and looked from the window to the door and back again. A herd of wildebeest would have been easier to stomach, metaphorically, that is.

It was a window to another world and not a better one. The scene Danny was confronted with was one of decay and fetor. The tidy, little garden he had seen through the bedroom window had turned into an abominable landscape of stinking detritus, where pools of what appeared to be slime reflected the sickening putrescence of a sky, the colour of decomposed waste. From inside the room he could feel the terrible stillness, unable to shake the feeling of oppression. He couldn't help thinking how Phil's description of this place had fallen short. The badlands suggested a place where danger lay in wait at every turn, it certainly didn't seem to apply to this ravaged, mephitic wasteland.

"Nice ain't it?" said Phil, with a sly grin.

"What is this?" Danny asked, his resolve leaking silently away. "This is some sort of trick, a bloody illusion of some...sort."

"Come on Danny boy, get real man. Stop trying to find logical explanations for something that don't have one. It's what it is. The badlands. Stink, don't they. He," she angled a thumb at Seth. "Assures me it gets better the closer to The Machine we get. More dangerous like, but kinder to the nose. I suppose you can't have everything."

Seth held up his hand to silence her. She made the motion of zipping her mouth shut with a mischievous wink.

"To begin with The Grid was akin to a printed circuit board working to keep the earth functioning, laying beneath the surface. It still is. But over the years things

170

have changed. The part of what we now call mankind, influenced by The Machine was the control over baser instincts unknown to our forefathers. Apparently, something undetectable in this planet's atmosphere cultivated feelings of a negative nature. For centuries all worked well or seemed to. But then, gradually, it became clear that these emotions were increasing in strength. Aggression, an emotion unknown to our race previously, became rife and flourished. What had begun as confrontations between individuals grew. Gangs formed and, eventually, factions evolved, and wars ensued. Jealousy and fear were added to the pot and there was little The Machine could do to counteract this mayhem. It became a support to the violence by continually breathing life into this planet. That will never change, unfortunately. Unlike the so-called technological products, you purchase in this world, The Machine will never break down, never freeze, never need repair. It is infinite. The people of this planet will do everything they can to destroy it, but they cannot. The Machine will not allow it. It was conceived to allow a peace-loving race to continue but, without the time to complete an extensive exploration of this planet, it merely aids all that it originally prevented."

Danny had never heard someone come out with such a ludicrous statement, that, literally, made him laugh out loud, and then proceed to prove to him that, not only was what they'd told him possible, but really quite probable. What he was seeing and what he was hearing was ridiculous, it was mad but, in his mind, disbelief had meandered into possibility and was now perched on the edge of probability.

He looked from Seth to Phil to the corruption displayed through the wardrobe door and back again.

"Catching them flies again Dan," said Phil, with a grin.

"Still, I guess I did a fair bit of it when he first showed me.

Takes a bit of getting used to. Wait till he tells you the rest of it."

Danny was speechless. He closed his mouth, opened it to speak but nothing came out.

"Close the door, Phil," Seth instructed. "We don't want to risk an unwanted entry, do we?"

"We certainly don't, boss," she replied, stepping over and shutting the wardrobe.

Danny felt like he was in emotion overload, there were so many vying for supremacy. Everything he had been thinking or feeling prior to this ridiculous revelation was gone. Something deep inside seemed to be stirring, something that had been locked away all his life. Until everything in his life went to hell in a handcart, he had felt destined, not for greatness but for something else, something different. As he lost the people he loved or they fucked him over, that feeling was drowned in an ocean of self-pity that he had floated in since. Whatever had created that feeling appeared to be awakening and with it a savage truth. He was destined. All those emotions crashed in a heap as realization hit him with its knockout punch.

"We are The Machine," he said.

"Ah, the penny has finally dropped." Phil said. "It didn't take that long with me, did it?" She looked to Seth for confirmation.

"It wasn't as quick as you think, young lady."

Danny was still puzzled. It was as if hundreds of memories were flooding his mind at once, a deluge of discovery. One thing was clear though.

"You're next," he said to Seth.

"Indeed," Seth replied. "But much has to be done first."

As the waves of knowledge passed Danny homed in on the more relevant pieces.

"There should be four of us."

"He's definitely picking up the pace now," said Phil.

"And you are becoming extremely irritating," Danny said. "You want get a chisel and knock that chip off your shoulder."

"I'll knock your head off yours, if you don't watch your mouth, sonny."

Danny was beginning to enjoy himself and was about to wind her up another notch when Seth put an end to it.

"We do not fight amongst ourselves," he said. "Save your aggression for when it's needed. Philomena, you are out of order. Apologise."

Danny gazed expectantly as she struggled with the concept, enjoying every second of her annoyance and discomfort.

"Soz, I took the piss," she said, through gritted teeth.

Danny was all set to make her squirm a little bit more when Seth shot him a look.

"Enough, we need to make contact with the last of our group."

THREE

From being a waste of space, having but one objective, to vacate and allow that space to be filled by a more deserving candidate, Danny had the beginnings of a fire in his belly. Although his present situation seemed to be the beginning of a novel by H.G.Wells or the more contemporary Stephen King, who both possessed the ability to make the unbelievable into matter of fact, it was not fiction. He'd always thought that sightings of UFOs were the product of over-zealous imagination coupled with intense desire to transform the ordinary into the extra-terrestrial. Over a short period of time his blinkered opinions would be blown apart, big time. He didn't know what would be coming next, but he knew it would stretch and change the way he looked at existence completely. He had never professed to be a saint, he had many bad points, as most do, but one thing he'd never been, was a liar. His dad used to say, 'tell the truth and shame the devil' and that's what he'd always done, apart from the occasional white lie to save someone's feelings. When his mum had asked him if her bum looked big in a particular dress, he didn't tell her it never looked small in any dress, he told a white lie, as anyone would unless they had cause to hate their mother, of course.

They were now three and needed to become four before their journey could begin.

"I think we need to build up our strength before we introduce ourselves to Sebastian. Are you recovered sufficiently to follow us down to the kitchen, Danny?" asked Seth.

All effects of the drug had faded, aided by his newly acquired motivation. Although, until now, the thought of food hadn't crossed his mind, filling his face suddenly seemed remarkably high on his list of priorities, he was starving.

"Lead the way," he replied, his stomach growling like a rabid dog.

They all trouped down to the small kitchen, where a large pot simmered on the cooker. The aroma was amazing. There were already three large bowls on the pine kitchen table. Seth took the pan off the hob and ladled generous helpings of steaming, vegetable stew into them. A plate with hunks of crusty bread lay in the centre of the table. For about five minutes they sat and ate in silence, the only sound that of metal against china, or maybe metal against cheap pottery.

Danny was just about to compliment Seth on his cookery skills when Seth sighed, rubbed his belly and said. "That was amazing, Phil. It's a pity we'll have no need of your talent in The Grid."

Danny's enjoyment of Phil's culinary prowess was such that he didn't even consider asking Seth for an explanation.

Once they were all suitably replenished, feeling at one with the world (it's weird the feeling of total well-being that fills the soul after a good and satisfying meal) it was time to progress.

"Where does this Sebastian hang out?" Danny asked.

"He has a small flat in Battersea," replied Seth.

Immediately the cover of Pink Floyd's album 'Animals' came to mind, with its view of Battersea Power Station, complete with flying pig. Once again, he was reminded of his dad and his excellent taste in music. This was quickly replaced by a picture of Paul O'Grady hugging an emaciated terrier at the Dogs' Home.

Phil was, obviously, on a similar wavelength and showed her softer side.

"Ah, is it near the doggy place?"

Danny had to admit, he was about to take the piss, but Seth shot him another look and jumped in before he could get a chance.

"No, it's not near the Dogs' Home, it's about a mile away. When our digestive systems have dealt with that wonderful meal, we'll make a move."

"What are we doing, catching a train?" Danny enquired, teasing a bit of onion from between a couple of molars with his tongue.

Phil raised her eyebrows and shook her head. It was her turn to receive one of Seth's glares. "You weren't aware of The Grid's facilities before I revealed them, Philomena," he said sharply. "If this attitude of yours continues, we will have a problem." He paused, then said. "Are we going to have a problem?"

Up until now Danny had found Seth intelligent, likeable but not really an authoritative figure. As Phil lowered her head and mumbled 'no', he altered his opinion. This was a man of substance. In time he would revere him and wonder if he would ever fully know and understand him. Seth's hidden depths were many and, in the main, surprising. After putting Phil well and truly in her place, he turned back to Danny.

"The Grid allows us instant access to all necessary locations, Danny. A train, although a very pleasant mode of transport, will not be needed. The door to your left will place us in close proximity to the final member of our team."

"That's the back door," Danny pointed out. "It'll put us in close proximity to the back garden."

"Open it," was all Seth said.

As Danny stood up and reached for the door handle, he knew that when he opened the door, he wouldn't be looking at that tiny lawn with its narrow path to that, equally, tiny shed. He didn't have a clue what he'd see, but he knew it wouldn't be that. His fingers closed around the

176

metal and he pushed the handle down tentatively. He was aware that he was holding his breath as he pulled.

It was like the opening credits of 'Only Fools and Horses', a grubby, dilapidated high rise, bordered by a tired, pot-holed car park, the odd, ravaged vehicle resting on bricks or worn, deflated tires.

"What a shit hole," said Phil. Danny found no reason to disagree and just nodded.

"Haven't you heard the phrase 'Never judge a book by its cover'?" Seth asked, his expression of distaste, insinuating that the pages of this one may not hold any surprises. "Come on, we have work to do."

They ambled across the car park, avoiding the numerous piles of dog shit, ranging from freshly produced to the ancient, bleached, crumbly stuff.

"Very quaint," Danny said.

"A salubrious neighborhood indeed," said Phil.

Despite himself, Seth couldn't help smirking as they approached the entrance. The double doors hung open, the screws holding the top hinges to the frame hanging by a thread. The black and white floor tiles were cracked and stained with what appeared to be more faeces, whether canine or human was impossible to discern. Phil's original description was becoming more relevant with each step.

"Sebastian's on the twelfth floor," Seth said.

Phil and Danny looked at each other and grinned. "Of course, he is," Danny said.

Seth pressed the call button at the side of the lift, and they waited. No illumination was visible, either behind the button or behind the floor display above the door. If it was working, it was both secretive and extremely quiet.

"It's probably been out of order that long, it would need a sign to say it was working rather than one to say it was out of order," said Phil, with a tired shrug.

"I think we are 'sur notre pieds'," Danny said, pointing to the staircase.

"Oooh, monsieur," said Phil with a wiggle of her hips. The pair of them burst out laughing and even Seth couldn't prevent a little chuckle escaping. "Very amusing. Onwards and upwards, I guess."

The staircase was no different to the hallway, apart from having more graffiti adorning the walls, an excess of poor illustrations of various sizes and styles of genitalia teamed with the usual expressions, mostly misspelt, Danny thought. Phil and he had both decided to call it a day with the disparaging remarks, more would be overkill and boring. The three of them climbed the stairs in silence. Danny was warming to Philomena, she was feisty, could be an irritating bitch but quite funny as well. Maybe they just got off on the wrong foot. Time would tell.

They arrived at the twelfth floor and the exertion didn't appear to have affected any of them. They were all breathing normally and, although Danny didn't know how old Seth was, he was, obviously, a lot older than they were, but just as fit, it seemed.

"Flat 1008," he said, striding down the corridor.

As Danny and Phil followed, Danny suddenly realized he only knew Seth and Phil's Christian names, well the same for this Sebastian. Before he could give voice to his thoughts, Seth stopped and rapped on the door in front of him. Within seconds it was yanked open and there stood someone who resembled a younger Stephen Hawking, the eyes behind the steel rimmed spectacles a sharp and intense blue.

"If my calculations are correct, you're late," Sebastian said, stepping to the side.

"Maybe you didn't include all of the variables," suggested Seth, indicating Phil and Danny with a thumb.

"Um, maybe," replied Sebastian, his steely eyes scrutinizing them as closely as a CAT machine. "Yes, indeed." He paused before waving a hand. "Enter."

The flat was in stark contrast to the communal areas of the block. Although there was little free space, there was a place for everything and everything was in its place, as Danny's mother used to say. The front door opened directly into the living room, well, the room that was, obviously, designed to be such. One wall was a huge bookcase, and a quick glance was all that was needed to see a lack of thrillers and what Danny had read somewhere described as 'Man fiction'. There seemed to be a wealth of hefty tomes on science, physics, mathematics and nature with several biographies, one of which was indeed Stephen Hawking. There was no sofa, no television, just one black leatherette chair with wooden armrests. Along the wall opposite the bookshelves was a long work bench with weird looking structures, like adult versions of Meccano and two laptops. As Danny was about to return his attention to the man himself, a black dog padded into the room, sat and stared at them with suspicion.

"Aahh, here boy," cooed Phil, bending and tapping her thighs.

"She's a bitch," said Sebastian, quite clearly irritated at Phil's poor observational skills.

Phil shrugged. "Sorry young lady, I think I've upset your dad."

Both Sebastian and the dog regarded Phil with a similar expression, one that questioned her sanity.

"She is a Labrador, four years old and canine. I find it quite aggravating when individuals debase these beautiful animals."

If looks could kill, Sebastian would have had about ten knives buried deep in his chest. "I don't debase animals," said Phil, through gritted teeth. "You're not fit to be a pet owner." She patted her thighs again and did some more cooing. The dog sat and retained her confused expression, Sebastian held out his hand, made eye contact with the dog and made a kissing noise. The dog trotted to his side, sat again and gazed up at her owner. Sebastian reached down, rubbed her ears and she let out a contented sigh.

"What do you call her," Danny asked him.

"I re-homed her when she was 11 months old. The rescue centre had named her 'Blue' and I saw no point in confusing the issue by changing it."

"Hey Blue," Danny whispered and made the same kissing sound, kneeling so they were on the same level. The dog eyed him with interest, her tail moving in a slow, singular arc. She looked up at her master, who nodded. She waddled over to Danny, her tail increasing its speed. As he stroked her and rubbed her ears, she licked his face. Although he'd never owned a dog, he'd always wanted one and felt a weird sort of affinity with canines in general. On several occasions, he'd heard the phrase – he/she doesn't normally like strangers. He glanced up at Phil and winked. "Dogs are very good judges of character."

Phil gave him a 'piss off, smartarse' sort of look and then addressed Sebastian.

"It's a shame you'll have to leave her," she said and then as an afterthought. "Both of you."

"Where I go, she goes," said Sebastian. "That, I'm sure, won't be a problem."

They all looked at Seth who looked a little uncomfortable. "Well, it wasn't something I had planned on but, on the other hand, I can find no salient reason to object."

They were now four at last – or five. Although a lot of stuff had fallen into place, the details of their new life were still a little sketchy to Danny. He knew they were bound for The Machine where Seth would remain and fulfil his destiny, as they all would in time. He was also aware that he would eventually take his place and become the 'recruitment officer' for the next set of 'guardians'. It was the bit between that needed a fair bit of fleshing out. As they were now a full complement and, presumably, set for the off, he thought it was time to get to the bones of the operation. Before he could say a word, Phil jumped in.

"Okay we're good to go," she said. "Am I the only one needing a little clarification here? I mean, I know the gist of it all but there's a lot of shit I need explaining. Am I right?"

Danny nodded enthusiastically and Sebastian followed suit, a little less fervently. Danny was beginning to get the impression that their latest member was used to being in control and was not happy when he wasn't.

"Well," said Seth. "You all know our destination and the reason why we are making the journey. I said before that The Machine will never fail, never break down – and that is true. As long as the guardians carry out their roles this world will continue. Whether that is a good thing or not, is a matter of opinion. We must believe it is and that the population will eventually cease trying to kill each other, using some God or other as an excuse for their bloodlust. Unfortunately, the original idea of a supreme being looking down and judging has evolved into so many different versions and as many horrific manifestos. People lose their lives every day under the guise of some religion or other."

"It shows no sign of improving," Danny said, "In fact it gets worse by the day. Why not let it all fade away if that's possible?"

"Firstly, you will find you have no choice in the matter. Now, you feel no pull from The Machine, and you may think you can walk away, leave it to die and this world with it. The idea of blasting all the terrorist factions into the ether is very alluring but along with the bad you destroy the good, the loving families, the peacemakers, the innocent. Maybe there is even an argument to support that. The fact is whatever you believe is immaterial. If you had chosen to take your own life, your replacement would have been brought forward. Mind you, when you witness the lost, what you would have become, I'm sure you'll be relieved that you didn't."

"What are the lost?"

"The poor unfortunates that found this life unbearable and accomplished the act you were on the verge of. This was supposed to be another deterrent. You commit suicide, you don't enter heaven. The fact is that if a life is ended prematurely it cannot be absorbed by The Machine and is left to the horrors that now inhabit The Grid. These are not the lost, they are the rejected, the murderers, terrorists, rapists etc. They are trapped in The Grid, in their millions and they will do everything in their power to corrupt the machine and prevent the guardians from renewing its energy. Suffice to say, our journey will not be without its problems."

FOUR

"So, when do we start?" Phil asked.

"I wouldn't be so eager, if I were you, young lady," said Sebastian. "You have no idea what you'll be dealing with."

"And I suppose you have."

"Actually, he does," said Seth. "You see his mother was a guardian and although she would have tried to protect him from her experiences, she would have been powerless to stop them from being absorbed genetically by her son. The connection between guardians' family members is intense and a kind of telepathy exists. The human part wants to hide the horrors from her or his offspring, but The Machine has a different view. So, you see, Philomena, Sebastian does have an incredible insight into everything we will face. In fact, it is testament to his courage, that he is still prepared to follow in his mother's footsteps."

"My mother meant everything to me," said Sebastian. "And soon we will be reunited within The Machine. That's all that matters to me."

"My mother was a drunk and would have sold me for a bottle of scotch," said Phil, glaring at the floor. "My father brought me up, until he drove his car into a wall when I was fifteen. From then on, I've had to fend for myself. I don't give a shit what's out there. Whatever it is, I'll kick its arse."

"Commendable, I'm sure," said Sebastian. "But I feel your confidence might be ill placed. What you are about to face is not a few Neanderthals in a pub, where a well-placed boot will suffice."

Phil looked him up and down. "Okay sunshine, you might be good with words and putting other people down but, by the look of you, you ain't going to be a lot of help on the other side."

"Battles are won, not by brawn, but by the brain power of superior tacticians. You may be 'handy' with your fists and your feet but faced with five men or women who are equally as 'handy' you will be beaten to a pulp. The way to win such a fight is to be tactical, know your opponents' weaknesses and play on them, know how to manipulate, how to divide, how to make the fight more equal. I can guarantee that if you came at me with a knife, I could kill you before you had any chance to do the same to me."

Phil laughed. "Bring it on, Yoda."

Sebastian picked up a letter opener from the surface and threw it to Phil. She caught it by the handle and flicked it round. "When you're ready," he said, not moving.

Phil looked away and then as she turned to launch her attack, Sebastian muttered what sounded like 'feet'. Phil started forward and promptly fell in a heap as Blue leapt forward and nipped her ankles. Sebastian was immediately over her with a rolled-up newspaper against the back of her head like the barrel of a gun. To emphasize the point, he shouted 'bang'.

"That's cheating," said Phil.

"It's called 'using your resources'. Something I happen to be exceptionally good at. We all have strengths and weaknesses; the trick is to know that and to be able to compensate for your own weaknesses whilst exploiting your rival's."

Danny looked at Sebastian in a new light.

Phil picked herself up, still glowering at Sebastian. She had been bettered and didn't like it one bit. She was, obviously, used to having the upper hand. I imagine, as Sebastian had pointed out, she was used to dealing with drunks and brainless thugs, the sorts that were predictable and, overall, a lot slower than she was.

Sebastian held out his hand. "You do the fighting and I'll do the thinking, that way we'll save each other's lives.

Come on, shake my hand Phil, we're on the same side, after all."

After a few seconds, she shrugged and grabbed his hand and held it. By the way Sebastian winced, it was clear she was squeezing for all she was worth. When she finally released him, Sebastian shook his hand and muttered, "Firm grip you have there."

Although this little display had been entertaining, Danny was keen on getting the show on the road. "When and where do we start?" He asked.

"I suggest we have a good meal and a good night's sleep before we begin our journey," said Seth.

Although it didn't seem that long ago since they'd eaten Phil's wonderful stew, Danny found his stomach grumbling again at the mention of food.

As if reading his mind Seth said, "I know it wasn't long ago that we ate but travelling through The Grid's portals depletes one's resources."

"A nice Chinese would go down a treat," said Phil. "I'm guessing they don't have takeaways where we're going."

"Indeed not," Seth said. "Not that you will be yearning for one. You see, once we enter The Grid, the need for food and drink will disappear. The power of The Machine sustains everyone and everything, no matter what their agenda. Supporters and antagonists are nourished equally. When it was conceived, there was no reason to believe there would ever be those wishing to obstruct or damage it."

Phil looked devastated. "So, no eating at all – I like eating, and drinking. In moderation, of course."

"You won't even think of it, Phil, I promise you. You only think of food when you're hungry and you will never be hungry. As far as drinking is concerned, it's good that you will never experience thirst as most of the water that has formed in The Grid is stagnant at best and toxic at worst. There are some oases, but they are few and far between. I won't try and dress up what we're about to do. It is a serious business with little to commend it. Once inside The Grid, we will all be focused on our goal and we will achieve it, no matter what. You will see things that will terrify you, face battles that will require every ounce of your strength and more. It's good that we won't have the distraction of hunger and thirst to impair that focus. Now, how about that meal?"

Sebastian went to the kitchen and returned with a hand full of menus. "Chinese, Thai, Indian, Italian and good old fish'n'chips. Take your pick."

They plumped for a good old Chinese Banquet Special, placed their takeaway order and settled down to wait with a nice glass of Chablis, supplied by Sebastian.

This was going to be their last supper and they were going to make the most of it.

The meal arrived and it was one of the best Danny had tasted. He didn't know if it were because he knew it would be his last but thought that would make a difference. By the time they'd finished, there were only a couple of prawn crackers left. Sebastian threw them to Blue who caught them in mid-air and disposed of them in a matter of time not classified yet. By the time they'd drunk a second bottle of Chablis, they were all nicely replenished and very relaxed. Sebastian offered Phil his bed, being the gentleman, he was, and she refused, being the furthest thing from a lady as was possible. Her words. Danny thought he was more in touch with his feminine side than she was. Sebastian and Blue retired to the bedroom, after Sebastian had accompanied the dog down to the car park to relieve herself. Danny wondered if he found this a bind every night but the look on his face as they returned told him – no. This was a match made in heaven and he realized that the phrase 'dog is a man's best friend' didn't even come close. Sebastian loved Blue and she loved him back. They were inseparable.

Sebastian brought them blankets and pillows and the three of them slept on the floor. Danny was away in minutes, maybe still suffering the aftereffects of the drug that Seth had pumped into him, along with the wine, taking their toll. He dreamt about Beth and how they used to be, then Joey appeared as a vampire but latched his fangs into Danny's leg and started to suck his life away. Then it switched and he was in the car with Dad and Sam and Tara and they were all screaming as this lorry was hurtling towards them. Danny looked over and saw his dad's dead eyes. They were all about to die when he was wrenched from the car and found himself in a wilderness, the reek of stagnation heavy in his nostrils. He was making his way up a crag, pulling his way around the boulders strewn there. His left arm hung at his side, practically useless, its shape not quite as it should be. He struggled on, a one-armed man in a ragged, inhospitable landscape. All he knew was that he was trying to avoid death, someone or something was stalking him. As he was about to reach the summit, he heaved himself around another rock and howled. The thing he'd been running from was ahead of him. He looked into those black, soulless eyes as the primitively fashioned spear was about to be pulled back and launched at his heart. He was about to close his eyes and embrace death when the point of a sword erupted from the monster's chest and it fell in a heap at his side. A man yanked his blade from the creature's back and wiped the blade on his ragged trousers. "I hate those fuckers," he said, grimacing. "You all right man?"

Danny woke up, the night sweats drying on his skin, the image of that shark-like face still vivid, his savior's face fading quickly. He tried to hold on to it, but it slipped away like sand through his fingers.

Seth was already awake and looking concerned, Phil was still fast asleep and snoring. Sebastian entered the room, rubbing the sleep from his eyes, Blue stretching behind him. When Sebastian saw the expression on Seth's face, the remnants of sleep disappeared in an instant. "There's a split coming, isn't there?"

Seth nodded and then shook his head. "I don't understand it, there's only ever been one split before."

Danny looked from one to the other. "Is one of you going to tell the uninitiated, what the hell a split is?"

"You're going to find out sooner than I could explain it," said Seth. "Any choices any of us had are gone. Wake Phil and get ready for the worst fairground ride you could ever imagine."

Danny shook Phil as a rumbling sound began to fill the room. "What the f...," was all she had time to say.

"Hold on to each other," yelled Seth, the rumble growing quickly into a roar. He threw his arm around Danny's waist. Danny, in turn, grabbed Phil, she held onto Sebastian, who was hugging Blue, his hand through her collar. The roar became a shriek and Danny thought his eardrums were going to rupture. The floor shook and then buckled and then disappeared. They were in the midst of a tornado, hurtling to God knows where, the stench of decay filling their nostrils and clawing at their throats. Danny tightened his grip on Phil and was vaguely aware of a werewolf like howl competing with the ear-splitting squeal. Within seconds, although it seemed longer, they hit the ground of their new world with some force. Various cries and moans ensued, the worst from Sebastian who had broken Blue's fall. He lay on his back with her on top of him, licking his face. Surprisingly, apart from a plethora of bruised body parts, none of them appeared to have broken any bones.

As they brushed themselves off and massaged the bits that hurt the most, Seth said, "That was a split."

"That was a bastard," said Phil, rubbing her thigh. "Normally, we have the choice of when and where, to some extent, we cross over. And the journey is not quite so bumpy, shall we say. In the case of a split, which I have to say I've never experienced before, The Grid rips through its creation, depositing its guardians unceremoniously where they belong."

"You said it had only happened once before," Danny said. "When?"

"The year, in your time, was 1492 when Leonardo Da Vinci came close to inventing a time machine."

"He was a painter, painted the Mona Lisa, everybody knows that. He wasn't an inventor," said Phil, with the authority of one who knows.

"He was many things, Phil. One of the greatest minds and talents of this earth's history. His invention was enough to cause the only other split and dump him and his fellow guardians here in a similar way, presumably, to us."

"He was a guardian?" Danny suddenly wanted to see a list of previous guardians.

"He is the only one known to subsequent guardians and only because of the split."

"So, what, do you think, caused this one?" asked Sebastian.

"To be honest, I have no idea. But whatever it is, it must be monumental."

"Will it have any effect on us?" Danny asked him.

He nodded his head. "As we didn't cause it, I can only assume it will. What that effect will be is anyone's guess. We must do what we have to, if who or what caused the split is going to aid or hinder, we must act accordingly."

They surveyed their surroundings. The Grid was nothing like a printed circuit, that's for sure. For as far as the eye could see, which wasn't that far, due to a strange green-tinged mist that hung like cobwebs over the desolate landscape, a dusty desert spread, patches of strange, ugly looking foliage adding to the general murk.

"Not what I would have chosen for a holiday destination," said Phil with a wry grin.

"No, I'm having trouble finding any redeeming features at the moment," Danny agreed. "How long before we reach The Machine?" He asked Seth.

"Impossible to say. Each time a group enters The Grid, the location is different, the trials to be faced unknown, plus, with the split, there will be massive changes to The Grid itself. Although I've been here three times before, I can tell you little of what is ahead, only that it will test us all to our limits."

Danny suddenly remembered his dream, the young bloke with the sword, who, he was sure, was like them – a stranger to The Grid. "Is it possible to have more guardians, that you don't… sort of… know about?"

Seth shrugged. "It's never happened before. But the last split was caused by one of the guardians, this wasn't. The simple answer Danny is, I don't know. We're all in unchartered waters, I'm afraid. Nothing, however, has changed for us. The Machine is our destination and, as all seems quiet at present, I suggest we make a start."

Phil held up her hands. "Which direction?"

"Now that I can help with," replied Seth. He took out something that resembled Dr. Who's sonic screwdriver and flicked a switch. He waved it in a slow arc until a blue light flashed on and off. "That way, I believe."

They trudged off into the unknown, a small band of misfits with a common goal. Danny was glad to have some direction back in his life. After the train wreck that his life had become and the emptiness that had followed, death had seemed the only viable option. Now he was looking forward to a journey that, according to Seth, was going to test the limits of both their mental and physical capacities. He should have been terrified but he wasn't.

There was a fire in his belly again, He had a purpose, a reason to be. To put all the shit behind him and, maybe help mankind. That's if mankind started to help itself. He was abruptly ripped from his reverie by a shout of 'Look out' by Sebastian.

FIVE

From nowhere a group of figures rushed at them, their intent obvious. They were immediately fighting for their lives. Something that resembled an orc from Tolkien's tales launched itself at Danny, its jaws trying to latch onto his throat, whilst he tried to parry a hand clutching a short, spear-like object. He punched and kicked, twisted and turned, avoiding the gnashing jaws and then the spear was being pulled back for a kill shot. Danny rammed his fist into the thing's throat and grabbed the wrist of the hand with the spear and twisted. There was a squeal of pain and the spear dropped. Danny grabbed it and rammed it into his opponent's neck. Some putrid liquid gushed from the wound, but it looked and smelled nothing like any blood he had come across. The 'orc' fell dead at his side. In a second, he was on his feet. He gaped at Seth, he was like the Keanu Reeves character from The Matrix, his long black coat swirling as his limbs dealt out death. Phil was just ramming another of those spear jobs up into the guts of another of the ugly bastards, while Sebastian appeared to be engrossed in some form of calculus, his feet shooting forward every few seconds, sending one of their attackers sprawling, Blue savaging the hands that held the weapons. As Danny rushed to aid Phil, he saw Sebastian stab two of the bastards in the back. Within minutes, between them they had dispatched eight of the creatures, were all breathing heavily and wiping what passed for blood with these horrors from their hands.

"What the fuck were they?" asked Phil with a look of total disgust.
Danny's earlier view, likening them to the orcs from Tolkien's fantastic stories, turned out to be a little

misguided. They were slim and rangy in stature, their skin a slimy, mottled brown hue. To say their faces were ape-like would be an insult to primates but their jaws jutted forward, more Neanderthal than ape. The eyes were large, sunken and black, above the nostrils of a long-time cocaine user. They made the skin crawl, even dead. When their putrid breath was suffocating you, Danny thought, and those large, misshapen teeth were trying to rip out your jugular, you were, literally, struggling with the jaws of hell.

"I'm afraid there will worse than that to come," said Seth. "And with the split, the sky is the limit."

Danny couldn't help seeing the look of admiration on Phil's face. "You bust some pretty good moves for an old timer, man"

Seth shrugged. "There's still life in the old dog yet."

"And the young one," Danny said, pointing to Blue.

"Like I said, we're a team," said Sebastian. "We look after each other, don't we girl." He rubbed the Labrador's ears. She leant into his leg and let out a satisfied whine. This really was man with his best friend and Danny was jealous. To see such love between two beings was overwhelming, especially when he'd lost everyone that had ever meant anything to him. Blue wasn't going to betray Sebastian by finding a new master. They were inseparable and they would stay that way until death claimed one or the other. Whichever that turned out to be, the one that was left would be devastated. Danny prayed that if the time came, they would go together, if this nightmare that was The Grid took Sebastian before his time, it would take her as well.

"So why are they so repulsive?" asked Phil.

"Everything from their lives before being returned to The Grid has been stripped away, so all that's left is the core. As I said before most beings within The Grid are evil, some more so than others. And that is what you will see, the degrees of evil and how they are without the trappings of human life."

"But surely evil is evil," Danny said. "Once the...er...façade has been removed, all that's left is evil, pure and simple."

Seth shook his head. "In both good and evil, there are various levels. Take the man who gives to charity every month, pays his taxes, is a model husband and father – he is a good man. But then compare him to another who dedicates his life to alleviate the suffering of others with no thought for himself. They are both to be applauded but if awards were to be given, who do you think would win. The same with evil, there are rapists who, although their crime is deplorable, they would never consider taking their victims' lives. The same applies to most paedophiles and thieves. These are all abusers who go about their sordid business under threat and retribution to their prey, but the idea of murder never enters their heads. Faced with discovery, they would, more than likely, take their own lives. Then there are those who take their loathsome pleasures and then enjoy even more gratification by watching the life drain from their poor victims. Who gets the award there?"

"What he's saying is, the more evil the being was on our earth, the greater that evil will be in The Grid, the more powerful." Sebastian put it in a nutshell.

"You said that if I'd topped myself, I'd be sent back here too. What happens to all the suicides, do they turn into these monstrosities as well?" Danny asked.

Seth shook his head. "No. Unfortunately they believe they're escaping a living hell on earth only to find themselves in a worse hell here in The Grid. On earth there are various forms of help available to them if they'd have chosen to go down those routes before ending their lives. When they return to The Grid, they are weak, pathetic beings, easy prey to the rest. Most are destroyed quite quickly but some find a new and remarkable strength. To decide to take your own life is one thing but to have others take that decision away is another. A small percentage find the ability to fight back and, as they are not driven by the urge to kill, they still have the capability for cognizant thought. There are small groups of these poor individuals throughout The Grid."

"Like resistance fighters?" Phil said.

"I suppose there are similarities," agreed Seth. "Mainly though, they are only trying to survive. Not attempting a military coup."

"What happens to them or any of these bastards, come to that, when they are destroyed here?" Danny asked.

"You've already said the reason they're here is that they can't be absorbed by The Machine." He waved a hand over their ex-attackers. "What happens to these bastards now?"

"Within a short time, they will become part of the putrid dust that covers The Grid."

"And that's it?"

"Yes, they cease to exist."

"So why do the suicides fight, why don't they just let these things rip out their throats and drift away."

Seth was about to reply when Sebastian jumped in.

"Because even though they wanted to end their lives on our earth, that option is no longer available to them. Once returned to The Grid the need to survive is paramount. Fight or flight is amplified and even the weakest will fight to the death when cornered. They were returned to The Grid because of their decision to end their earthly lives and, once here, any thoughts of that nature are deleted. Basically, you kill or are killed, there are no grey areas, no fifty-fifty, phone a friend or ask a psychiatrist. You are slung here amongst the murderers, sadists and rapists and you run or fight. As Seth said, some have the newfound ability to do both and to outwit the rest of the barbarous residents of this wonderful world."

Seth smiled and nodded. "I couldn't have put it better myself," he said.

"Probably waffled on a bit longer though, eh?" Phil said ruefully.

"If you mean, explained it in more depth. Quite possibly."

In this desolate, rancid landscape they all laughed, even Sebastian. Danny didn't think he looked totally comfortable, as though turning that frown upside down had never been high on his list of priorities. A first for him was to see a dog grinning. Many dog owners maybe familiar with this but it amazed him when Blue added her smile to her master's. Something like that creates a warm feeling inside and if Danny had known how rare that would be from now on, he would have embraced it more.

They set off in the direction indicated by Seth's gizmo, keeping their eyes peeled. It seemed that the inhabitants of The Grid could appear from the barren vista in the blink of an eye. In the distance the grubby wasteland rose into savage looking crags and Danny hoped there was a way around them. At the moment they seemed to stretch across the horizon like broken glass. Phil must have been pondering the same question, asking Seth, "Do we have to climb over that shit?"

"I have no idea Phil. As I said before, each time I return to The Grid, it's never in the same place and if it were, it wouldn't make any difference as it's constantly changing. If we must go over, then that's what we will do. Until we get closer, your guess is as good as mine."

"A lot of help you are," said Phil.

They walked on in silence, their mood in keeping with their surroundings. After a couple of hours Danny found himself yearning for another attack to relieve the utter boredom. It was soul destroying walking through a land of such desolation with no change, mile after mile of nothingness. They might as well have been blindfolded. As they moved closer to the mountains, the chance of finding a way around became slimmer. The peaks looked treacherous, to say the least, but Danny found himself looking forward to the challenge. Anything to get the blood pumping and the brain working.

"Anybody fancy a game of I spy?" asked Phil.

They all, immediately, burst out laughing and within seconds tears were streaming down Danny's face. When the shaft of sunlight appeared, he thought his watery eyes were responsible for this impossibility.

The laughter died out quickly as they gazed in disbelief.

"This split is something else," said Sebastian.

Seth was, clearly, concerned. "There has never been a rupture before. This could be catastrophic. The Grid has only ever been accessible by the guardians and only at designated points. If this is an isolated occurrence and The Grid can repair the rift, maybe no harm will be done. If not, if more ruptures appear and the world The Grid maintains merges with The Grid itself there could be an implosion. This makes our journey more urgent. The Grid, currently, is at its weakest. Until I can reach The Machine and renew its power, the earth you know is in a very precarious position. From now on we must pull out all the stops."

Suddenly the ground shook and, what sounded like a heavy sigh, rolled over the jagged teeth of the mountains. Slowly the sunlight faded as if some invisible fingers were stitching together a split seam. They watched in amazement as The Grid repaired its defenses. Seth let out a sigh of his own. "Let's hope that was it. The power required to mend such a rupture is substantial and now, will have left The Machine depleted."

They continued their journey with more urgency than before and within about an hour they were gazing up at the ominous peaks, their sickly hue bleeding into the rank atmosphere of The Grid. The ground was covered in rubble and the ascent, although not too steep to begin with, looked treacherous.

"Keep your wits about you," Seth said softly. "I wouldn't be surprised if we're being watched already. Concealment in such terrain is simple."

"We'll be too busy watching where we put our bloody feet to look out for them slimy bastards," Phil said gloomily.

"Well we'll just have to multi-task, won't we?"

"All right keep your hair on Keanu. I was just saying."

"Less talk and more thought wouldn't go amiss. Now, come on, let's get moving."

Phil pulled a face behind Seth's back and gave him the finger.

"And being childish doesn't help either," Seth called over his shoulder.

"Have you got eyes in the back of your bleeding head?"

"I don't need them when you're so predictable. Now, stop behaving like a spoilt child and follow me."

Danny couldn't help grinning, which earned him a punch in the arm. He mouthed 'spoilt child' and received another; this time much harder. Not hard enough to take the smile off his face though.

The going was difficult, the loose stones slipping beneath their feet and it wasn't long before Danny's calf muscles ached with the effort. So far, the slope was a wide-open area, with nowhere to lurk in wait, so he wasn't too worried about an attack. About three hundred yards away, however, the first of the craggy monoliths stood in a jagged line with only a narrow gap for them to continue their ascent. That, he thought, would be an ideal spot for an ambush. As they covered the remaining distance, he

198

forgot about his painful calf muscles and concentrated all his attention on that gap and the surrounding area.

They were about twenty yards away when Blue started to emit a low growl and stopped in her tracks. She looked up at Sebastian and then back at the gap.

"Good girl," was all Sebastian said to her.

"I guess she's our early warning system," Danny said.

"Yes," said Seth. "It's a shame she can't tell us how many of them there are."

"The more the merrier," Phil said. "Doesn't matter, we'll kick their arses. Doesn't matter how many there are."

Seth shook his head and sighed. "There could be fifty of them and that gap is only wide enough for two of us. Do you really think you could kill twenty-five of them before they did the same to you? Being a 'badass' is one thing, being a stupid 'badass' is another."

Phil was about to retaliate when Sebastian crept forward, his head down, as if he were looking for something he'd dropped. "I thought so," he said. "We can't go through, we go over." He stamped his right foot and the ground opened before him, the gap widening until it he slipped forward and down. Soon they were all sliding into an abyss and Danny couldn't help thinking about frying pans and fires. He seemed to remember a similar scene in an old film, the old Jules Verne classic, A Journey to the Centre of the Earth, with James Mason playing the professor. His dad used to love films like that, and Danny would be lying if he said he didn't enjoy watching them with him. He remembered being about six years old, sitting on the sofa, his dad's arm around him, a big bowl of popcorn on his lap, feeling safe, watching scary films. He missed those days, being a kid with loving parents. Mum hadn't started drinking then either. His dad's belly, however, had begun to outgrow his trousers. He remembered him blaming Mum, at first, for shrinking them in the wash, until it was obvious to all of them that he wasn't the lithe figure he used to be. The rest, as they say, is history.

These thoughts passed through his mind as they slid and bumped toward the centre of The Grid and he couldn't help wondering if someone was watching this with a bowl of popcorn in their lap. It seemed to go on for an age but was probably only a matter of minutes before they came to rest on the floor of a large cavern. A weird, green radiance allowed them a reasonable view of their surroundings, whilst an aroma like Sulphur assaulted their nostrils.

Phil was on her feet in an instant and in Sebastian's face. "What the fuck did you do?"

"As our path above ground was uncertain to say the least and, no doubt, life threatening, I discovered an alternative route. Although I wasn't expecting any thanks, I resent your aggression and having to wipe your spittle from my face."

"I didn't see it," was all Seth said.

"It was well hidden," explained Sebastian, rubbing his face with a white handkerchief.

"What was well hidden?" Danny asked. He had to admit that, as well as being as bruised as an apple that had fallen from the top of the tree, he was totally lost. He could understand Seth knowing a load of shit about The Grid, but he was confused as to how Sebastian was so knowledgeable.

"Throughout The Grid there are alternate pathways, only visible to the sharpest eyed of the guardians. Sebastian has proved himself to be such," Seth said.

"How do you know so much about The Grid, if, like Phil and I, this is your first time here?" Danny asked Sebastian.

"I told you that Sebastian's mother was a guardian," said Seth, before Sebastian could respond. "This is a rare situation but not unheard of. The information learnt by the parent is automatically downloaded to the son or daughter when the offspring enter The Grid."

"I suppose that bloody dog knows more than him and me," said Phil, indicating Danny with her thumb.

"Quite possibly," said Sebastian, his patience running out.

"Come on, we're supposed to be a team," Danny said. "All this bickering isn't helpful." He turned to Phil. "We should be grateful we're with two people who can steer us in the right direction."

Phil's eyes suddenly widened. "I don't think there's any question there," she said. "What the……?"

They all followed Phil's gaze. From a small gap in the cave wall to their right teemed a group of strange creatures. They appeared to have reptilian torsos which they dragged across the floor of the cave on six stumpy legs. Two huge nostrils twitched constantly whilst insectile antennae waved back and forth. As far as Danny could discern, they relied on both to find their way, as smooth skin covered the rest of the head with no eye sockets visible. There must have been about thirty of them and the group of guardians remained still and silent as they slithered across their path about ten metres away. The leader of the pack turned its head in their direction its nostrils flared, its antennae pointing towards Blue. The Labrador was also sniffing madly, a low growl beginning in the back of her throat. Sebastian stroked her head and whispered, 'easy girl'. For a few seconds no-one moved, the loathsome group clearly aware of the group's presence. Suddenly the leader opened its mouth and let out an ear-splitting screech, showing teeth that looked as though they'd have little trouble ripping through flesh. Although the repulsive creatures were no bigger than large mice, Danny had no desire to have half a dozen of the filthy, little beggars crawling all over him, their jaws snapping as they tried to rip him to shreds. At the sound of the screech, Blue snarled and dashed forward before Sebastian could stop her. With unbelievable dexterity she feinted left, the first of the creature's jaws following her motion. As its neck was stretched Blue, quick as lightning, clamped her jaws into the back of its head, swung it upwards and shook. They all heard the snap as its neck was broken. Blue slung it back amongst its clan, scattering them. Within seconds they reformed, a new leader taking the place of the one Blue had dispatched with such efficiency. They scurried off and disappeared into a tunnel to the left, leaving their dead compatriot on the cavern floor.

"Well, what the hell were they," asked Phil.

"You'll meet various weird and wonderful creatures here, Phil. Did I not mention that?" Seth replied, rubbing Blue's ears. "You, young girl, are proving to be invaluable," he said to the dog.

"No, I think I'd have remembered if you'd told me about ferrety, slug-like slime-balls. You're a devious fucker, Seth."

"To be perfectly honest, Phil, I've never seen anything like that before. I don't think they'd have attacked us anyway. Blue just aided their decision making."

"What, exactly, have you seen?"

"It doesn't matter, whatever I've encountered here before is immaterial. The corruption within The Grid nurtures itself and evolves in its own peculiar way. The best advice I can give you is – expect the unexpected. Now, shall we proceed."

He took out his sonic screwdriver lookalike waved it until the blue light flashed and they were off again, expecting the unexpected.

SIX

The cavern was a rough circle with a diameter of around fifty metres. The sickly, green hue revealed six tunnels leading off in various directions and Seth's magic wand had chosen the third on the right. They passed Blue's 'kill' and even she showed no interest. She had done her duty and was happy to move on. As The Grid took away their need to eat and consequently the desire as well, she didn't bother to give the thing a cursory sniff. Seth and Sebastian took the lead, chatting about everything Grid related, the dog, as ever, at Sebastian's side. Danny and Phil followed, a few feet behind. For the first time Danny realized he knew nothing about her, apart from how big a chip she carried on her shoulder. As the other two were deep in conversation and the scenery was limited, to say the least, he thought it might be a good idea for them to get to know each other a bit better.

"So, what's your story?" He asked her, thinking, immediately, how cheesy and patronizing he sounded.

"Who the fuck d'you think I am, Charles Dickens?" She replied sharply.

"Sorry, I didn't mean to sound like a dick," he said. "It's just that I get the impression Seth knows a bit about me, although I don't know how, and I guess he passed it on to you, from some of what you've said. I, on the other hand, know nothing at all about you."

"My 'story' is probably like a load of others," she said with a shrug. "It certainly wouldn't make the best seller list."

"I've always thought they were overrated – best sellers, that is. It seems like we're in this for the long haul, so we might as well get to know each other." Danny gave her his best puppy dog eyes.

"Were you really going to top yourself?" She asked him.

He thought about it for a few minutes to make sure he told her the truth. To be honest, it seemed an age ago and it seemed strange to think that something so monumental could be so easily forgotten.

"Yes."

"I thought about it a few times," she said. "But then I always thought – no, fuck it, I'll show the bastards."

"Which bastards?"

She glared at me. "You know fuck all."

"Well, educate me then. I'm not one of the bastards, at least, I don't think I am."

This brought a short laugh followed by a long sigh. "No, you ain't a bastard." She paused. "My old man wasn't a bastard either, he was just married to one."

Danny fell silent, as Phil stared at the tunnel wall, the years falling away.

"I loved him, my dad. And he loved me," she said softly. "Trouble was, he loved her as well and she killed him."

Danny got the impression that the torrent of emotion that followed had been restrained behind a mental dam for a few years. The expression – there's always someone worse off than you – is clearly true, but most of the time, one of those unfortunates is not walking beside you.

"She was a whore, she treated him like shit. And he sucked it up day after day." She let out a short laugh. "The stupid bastard even worked two jobs just so he could keep her in fags, booze and make-up. I mean, what silly fucker does that?"

"They say love is blind," Danny said.

She shook her head. "Nah, she paraded her conquests in front of him and laughed in his face. I'll never forget the hurt in his eyes, those sad, pathetic, eyes."

She wiped tears from her cheeks and sniffed. Danny went to put his arm around her, to comfort her. "What the fuck are you doing?" she snapped. "I'm not some silly little tart, and you're not my dad. The last bastard that tried that ended up with a broken arm."

Danny held up both arms. "I'm sorry Phil. About everything."

"She destroyed him. He tried to hide it from me, but I saw the life drain away until he couldn't take it anymore." She paused, wiped away more tears with the heel of her hand. "He drove his car into the wall of a disused warehouse. By the impact, the coppers reckoned he must have been going about seventy. The engine cut him in half."

"I'm so sorry."

"I was thirteen years old and I still remember the bitch moaning that she wouldn't get any insurance money because he took his own life. She was calling him all the names under the sun. That was the first time my temper really surfaced, I flung myself at her, wanting to claw her eyes out." She shook her head and sighed. "Trouble was, I was about six stone, ringing wet and just a silly, little girl. That's what she called me when she slapped me – a silly, little girl."

This time Danny kept quiet. He was under the impression that this was, probably, the first time she'd verbalised her feelings.

"From then on, I was treated like a skivvy, cooking, cleaning, doing the washing, which included some of her latest fling's shitty underpants at times. I hated her but I was trapped. Then, this piece of shit called Ronnie, arrives on the scene. He wasn't content with the whore; he wanted her daughter as well. He got her comatose on vodka and then came after me. I was in my room, reading some boring book from my English Lit. course, I think it was something by Hardy or Trollope, I can't remember. Anyway, there he is in the doorway with this drunken leer plastered across his face, fiddling with himself. I was terrified. 'Should Uncle Ronnie help you with your homework, pretty girl?' he slurred and then started to unzip his jeans. I threw the book at him, literally, and as he tried to dodge it, I was up and off. I was just sneaking past him when he grabbed my hair. I curled my fingers into a fist and punched him in the bollocks. He let go and doubled up and I was out of that house in seconds, running like the devil, himself was after me. That's when I smashed into Patrick.

"Who was Patrick?" Danny asked.

"Patrick was, and is, a wonderful man. He taught me to be strong, to not take shit from anyone." Her voice wavered. "Patrick was my saviour, without him, I would, probably, have gone the same way as my dad." Phil gazed, seeing nothing of our claustrophobic conditions, her mind in the past. "I was delirious when I ended up in his arms, a stupid, little girl. He calmed me down and asked me why I was running like a bat out of hell. Through the tears, I just managed to tell him what had just happened. I'll never forget the way his face changed. His eyes were soft and gentle, his smile reminded me of my old man's. After I'd told him about Mum's latest boyfriend, all the softness left his face and all I can say is, prior to that moment, I had never seen that expression in real life – in movies, sure. But never in real life. He said, "Where is he?"

I pointed back to our house and he was off. He shouted over his shoulder, telling me to wait." She paused again but this time I think she was relishing the memory.

"He stormed up to the house and seconds later Mum's boyfriend was rolling down the path like a bowling ball. Blood was pouring from his nose and he was hugging his left leg like it was about to fall off. Patrick followed, grabbed him by the throat, yanked him to his feet as if he weighed no more than a bag of sugar. Before he hurled him onto the lawn, he whispered something in his ear, which I didn't catch. All he would say to me, afterwards, was that he had a quiet word with him. Whatever it was, the shit-heap was up on his feet and limping down the road as fast as he could, glancing back every few seconds to make sure Patrick wasn't coming after him."

"I'm guessing you didn't see him again."

"Nah, he was history. Others came and went but none of them tried it on, although one or two looked at me as if they wanted to. In the meantime, Patrick taught me how to look after myself. He was a black belt in Judo and Tai Kwon Do, had been an amateur boxer and had devised his own martial art, incorporating all three. No-one could replace my old man, but he became the next best thing."

"He sounds like Billy," Danny said, looking back to the good, old days, before everything went to hell in a handcart.

"Who's Billy?" Phil asked.

"He taught me to box and, like Patrick, not take any shit. But never mind that. This is your story; I'll tell you mine later. Go on."

She smiled. "Maybe we ain't so different, after all then, Danny boy." She cleared her throat and continued.

"Patrick had a garage that he'd converted into a kind of gym. Before he would show me any of his moves, he had me weight training, doing sit-ups, road running, all the boring crap that goes with becoming fitter and stronger."

Danny laughed. "Yeah, I remember those days, wondering how much sweat there could be left in a human body."

"Too true." They looked at each other and grinned and then tears welled up in her eyes. Danny wanted to hug her, but he knew better.

Phil's affection for Patrick was clear as she continued with her story. She'd had a shitty life after her dad died and, Danny was sure, without Patrick's mentoring her life would have been totally different. The more she told him, the more he was sure that Patrick and Billy would get on like a house on fire. At times it was like looking into a mirror of his own past. They had both been subjected to bullying, albeit in different situations, before being shown, by someone special, that they were in charge of their own lives. Taught that no cowardly piece of scum had the right to impose their will on their own and, yes, shown how to knock seven bells out of whoever tried it. As she talked, she couldn't hide the hurt she had felt and, probably, always would. Her dad had loved her, that much was clear, but he wasn't strong. All he had wanted was a normal life with his wife and daughter. When that dream had been so thoroughly shattered, he had carried on with the pretence until he could stand it no more. If he had taken Phil and left the woman that was making both of their lives a misery, she would never have become the 'take no shit, badass' she now was. By what she had said about her dad, she would have enjoyed more affection than a lot of kids do with both parents in situ. Danny was listening, comparing their situations and contemplating on what could have been when her tone changed.

"Then she hooked up with this psycho called Brett, I mean, what sort of name is Brett?"

"I take it you weren't a fan."

The hatred in her eyes answered his rather flippant question.

"He was there when I came back from a session with Patrick," she continued. "I was drenched in sweat and just wanting a shower before I grabbed myself a microwave meal, watched some mindless crap on TV before crashing out. She was pissed, as usual. Didn't even acknowledge me. He did though. I could see the fucking lust in his eyes. He was a big bloke, not much fat on him, to be fair, better looking than most of the no hopers she managed to pull." She shook her head and gritted her teeth. "Hello little girl, he says to me, you're a pretty one. Fuck off, I said to him, just fuck right off. Your manners need some improvement, he says, you've obviously been missing a father's hand. That's when his eyes turned evil, that's the only way I can describe it. I don't mind admitting, I was

208

shit scared. I mean, sparring with Patrick and being faced with a real-life weirdo are two different kettles of fish." Phil licked her lips, this memory clearly painful. Danny waited for her to carry on, which after about thirty seconds, she did.

"Since my time with Patrick, it was the first and last time, I was taken by surprise. He grabbed my arms, and I could see the veins throbbing in his temples as he stuck his face an inch away from mine, those eyes burning into me. I'd better teach you a few lessons, he hissed and I'm thinking, he's going to rape me, and I'm petrified. Then I'm hearing Patrick saying – always use the other person's weight and balance to your advantage, an attacker is confident in his ability to inflict his own particular violence, especially if it is a he is dealing with a she. An attacker is intent on his own actions and is sure that his victim is just that – his victim. Whichever way he leans, normally into his victim, increasing the intimidation, go with him. Most people struggle and try and pit their own inadequate strength against the superior power of their assailant. So, I pushed backwards, pulling him with me, seeing surprise replace the malevolence in those baby blues. He let go of my arms to break his fall and I was out from under him before he hit the floor. From then I didn't look back. Brett's good looks took a severe battering that day and I like to think it taught him a valuable lesson. That was the last time I was afraid."

They walked in silence for a time, their footsteps in the dusty surface and Blue's panting the only sounds to break the ominous stillness. He felt that he and Phil were becoming closer, their sad lives similar on so many levels. He was more than curious, however, to know what had happened after she had beaten the shit out of this Brett creep.

"Am I right in assuming you left the happy home after your altercation with your mum's latest flame?" He asked her.

"Damned right," she snorted. "That woman was poison, and she didn't give two fucks about me. It took all of my self-control not to give her the same as I gave her boyfriend." She shook her head and when she continued, I could hear the disgust in her voice. "I can still remember the drunken cow looking at that bastard lying on the floor, slurring 'what have you done to….'. I mean, she couldn't even remember his bloody name. That's if she knew it in the first place, the whore."

"My mother's best friend was a bottle of gin," Danny said sadly. "The term 'mothers' ruin' is a good one. It certainly ruined her. Come to think of it, it didn't do me any favours either."

She looked at him in the gloom and let out a bark of a laugh. "Ain't we a couple of sad bastards. Come on then Danny boy, I've shown you mine, now let's see yours. Spill."

Danny intended to give her a brief synopsis of his life from his first encounter with Lawrence Carter to present but ended up giving her chapter and verse. Once he started, he couldn't stop and, he had to admit, with tears rolling down his cheeks, being able to offload was therapeutic. Feelings he'd kept inside were released and as he spilled his guts, he felt Phil's arm around him.

"What don't kill us, makes us stronger. Right?"

He nodded. "So, they say."

"Who the fuck *are* they?" She asked with another snort of laughter. "*They* don't do fuck all, but *they* say a fucking lot."

"That sort of language is not very ladylike, Philomena," said Seth, over his shoulder. "The English language has a plethora of words and yet you manage to utilise the same expletive three times in two sentences."

Phil rolled her eyes and was about to give his back the V's, thought better of it and, instead, asked Seth if this particular expletive was in the dictionary.

"Don't be ridiculous," he said shortly.

Sebastian shrugged his shoulders. "I'm afraid, through constant use, that ugly word has found its way into the O.E.D. following fuchsia.

"See," said Phil, gloating. "It's fucking official."

Seth and Sebastian both winced. Danny laughed. Is fuck a worse word than genocide, He thought not.

"That's better Danny boy," said Phil, punching his arm. "I don't normally do hugs, so I won't be making a habit of it. It's time to man up, sunshine."

"Yeah, sorry. I don't normally do blubbing either," he said apologetically. "I guess that's the first time I've let it all out."

"Well, let it be the last. The last geezer who let it all out in front of me wished he hadn't, I can tell you."

"I'm sure," he said with a chuckle.

SEVEN

"So, what's your story, Seb?" Phil asked Sebastian.
"Firstly," he pointed out. "My name is Sebastian. I have
never understood the overwhelming urge most people
have to shorten or bastardize the names they are
christened with. I do comprehend, however, that certain
individuals are not happy with the title their parents
bestowed on them and wish to customize it. I am not a
member of that clan, so I would appreciate it if you would
refrain from treating me as such. Secondly, I am not a
novelist, and so, have no 'story'".
"Pardon me for taking an interest in your sad life," said
Phil.
"Why do assume that my life has been sad, when you
know nothing about me?" Sebastian said. "To form an
opinion, one must be in possession of the facts.
Assumption can be an extremely dangerous thing."
"I bet I wouldn't be wrong in assuming you have no
friends," Phil said sharply.
"That assumption would be correct," Sebastian agreed,
"And if I were to hazard a guess, it would be that you're in
a similar situation. Would that be correct?"
"It might be," Phil said quietly.
"Come on, Sebastian. You've heard the 'train-wrecks' that
are our lives and, as I suspect we are to be spending an
awful lot of time together, it would be nice if we knew
something about you," Danny said, trying to calm a
prickly situation.
Sebastian appeared to be considering the situation. Seth
maintained his aloof, professor-like manner, as if watching
a debate between three of his students.
Phil shuffled along, with her head down and Danny
waited for Sebastian to make up his mind. In complete
silence, the gloom of the dusty cavern became more

oppressive. For the first time since entering The Grid, Danny realized that he had no desire to eat or drink and, when he pictured a large plate of steak and chips with a pint of ice cold lager by its side, it did nothing for him. He might as well have thought of Lawrence Carter's ugly mug, grinning its dentally challenged grin. Sebastian finally decided.

"It's true that, through your emotional outpourings, I know a great deal more about the two of you than I did when we first met. I will tell you the relevant parts of my past, without any emotion, I stress. Over the years, I have learned to control my feelings and channel my thoughts, to optimize my potential. I have been through my share of 'bad' times and yes, I believe the adage – what doesn't kill you makes you stronger. Here is my 'story'." Sebastian rolled his eyes before continuing.

"I was an only child. My father decided to shirk his parental and marital responsibilities when I was two and a half years old and left us both to shack up with a local prostitute, whose services he was, apparently, more than familiar with.

I have no memories of him at all and have no desire to seek him out and instigate a father and son reunion. I bear him no malice for abandoning us. We all have choices to make, throughout life, and he made his.

My mother, apart from being a guardian, was a lawyer, and an incredibly good one. Consequently, most of my early years, until boarding school, were spent in the company of Florence, my Nanny/Tutor. She possessed amazing general knowledge and a love for the poetry of Byron, Shelley, Keats and the rest of the so-called romantic poets. By the time I was shipped off to boarding school, a Victorian institution in Aylesbury named 'Waterbridge', a name that always puzzled me as there was no river or canal in the vicinity and, hence, no bridge, I was already on the way to being well educated. Unfortunately, in the main, most boys of six years old, are not appreciative of such and tend to treat those more intelligent and knowledgeable than themselves as something they stepped in. In the main, I was ignored, with the occasional derogatory remark. I found this quite satisfactory as there wasn't one of them, I could envisage having a remotely intelligent conversation with."

"There must have been other 'swots' there, surely," Phil said.

Sebastian sighed. "I was not a 'swot'. I didn't need to be. I have an I.Q. of 150 and an, almost, photographic memory. Combine that with a thirst for knowledge and the result is a magnet for unrelenting abuse from those less – committed, shall we say."

"I take it you were bullied," Danny said.

"Indeed, I was Danny. Unlike you, however, I possessed neither the inclination nor the ability to show my tormentors the error of their ways with the use of fisticuffs."

"Fisti…what?" Phil said, looking puzzled.

"Scrapping, to me or you," Danny translated.

Sebastian looked at her, shook his head and continued. "For months it was only verbal, expletives yelled by inconsequential morons. As the saying goes, 'sticks and stones etc'. I actually felt sorry for them, to have no direction in their lives, to channel all their energy trying to make another human being's life a misery; it was sad."

Phil was shaking her head, her expression displaying her feelings of disgust.

"Sad, fucking sad? They treated you like shit and you felt 'sad'?"

"As I said, this was only a verbal assault. Things changed when Dave Wynn homed in on me. I'd seen him swaggering about the campus with his entourage. It was just unfortunate that I ran into him, literally, when I was late for Physics, one day, I'd been engrossed in a biography of Disraeli and lost all sense of time"

Phil was looking at him with a bemused expression. "There's only one language bastards like them understand," she said, curling her top lip.

"Unfortunately, I have to agree with you," said Sebastian with a sigh. "If it had been an isolated incident, I would have grinned and bore it, but it wasn't."

Danny shook his head. "Once you allow yourself to become a victim, you are an easy target. Bullies get their kicks by showing their followers how hard they are by making the life of some poor unfortunate kid's life a misery. There's only one way to stop it, I'm afraid."

"Indeed," agreed Sebastian. "But as the saying goes 'there's more than one way to skin a cat'. There was no way that I could show this thug the error of his ways by, what would be classed as, conventional means."

"I'm intrigued," Danny said, with a grin.

Phil nodded. "Me too. Spill Einstein."

"For as far back as I can remember," he continued. "I have had a thirst for knowledge. I embrace technology. I spent most of my free time, either working on my laptop or with my nose in a book. I wrote my own programmes, I even constructed my own robot, maybe not as sophisticated as those used in the motor industry but capable of performing basic tasks. I'm digressing. My considerable ability with all things technological enabled me, with a little imagination to put a stop, once and for all, to Wynn's abuse and prevent any repetition by any prospective candidate with a similar nature."

By this time, they were all eager to hear the rest of his story, even Seth.

"There was a student in the same year as Wynn and me named Steve Goodwin. He was hard working, things didn't come easily to him academically, but he was a natural athlete, captain of both the rugby and the cricket teams. Although I never knew him to start a fight, he certainly finished a few. He was mild mannered and a nice guy. It was the idiots who mistook his demeanour for weakness that soon wished they hadn't. I chose him to be my champion, so to speak." Sebastian paused, a decidedly sly smile raising the corners of his mouth. "It was quite easy really. Like I said, Steve worked hard to improve his grades but struggled with a couple of subjects, especially Physics. It was no secret that I excelled in the subject as I did in a number of others."

"Nobody likes a smart arse," said Phil.

"That's where you're wrong, young lady," Sebastian told her. "This particular smart arse will prove that."

Phil let out a derisory snort. "I can't stand devious bastards."

"Well, maybe my 'deviousness' might save your skin, in the not too distant future."

"We have to use the skills we have," Danny said. "Go on Sebastian. I, for one, am dying to hear how Mr. Wynn got his just deserts."

Sebastian took a deep breath and continued. "Primarily, I offered to give Steve an hour or two of my time each week, to help with some of the finer points of the subject and ensure a pass in the end of the year exams. Although I found the time as his out of school tutor tedious, as I've already said, he was a nice guy. As expected, he was extremely grateful and a friendship was forged, as I intended." He looked at Phil and shrugged. "I did what I had to do and, in the end, the only person to get hurt was the one who deserved to. Anyway, Steve had been going out with a rather pretty girl, called Patty, from St. Martin's, a catholic school about a mile away, for about twelve months and, from all accounts, it was serious. Facebook was becoming more and more popular amongst my contemporaries, although it didn't interest me."

"Probably 'coz you didn't have any friends," said Phil. Danny glared at her and shook his head.

"Don't worry Danny," said Sebastian, with a resigned smile. "She's quite right. I've never really met anyone on my wavelength and I've always found the thought of making small talk with someone who is not my intellectual equal abhorrent. Plus, I really like my own company, but that's by the by. As I was saying, Steve was in a relationship with this girl and all in the garden was rosy. Steve and Dave Wynn weren't friends, in fact I got the impression that Steve disliked Wynn and his bully-boy antics - but it didn't affect him, so why should he worry. I needed to find some way where Wynn did affect Steve, and not in a good way."

By this time Phil had, apparently, shelved her 'holier than thou' stance and was as fascinated as Danny and Seth were with Sebastian's oratory.

"So, I hacked into Wynn's Facebook account and posted a defamatory statement about Steve and Patty."

"You're a hacker?" Phil was, evidently, impressed with certain aspects of Sebastian's 'deviousness'.

"It's not something I'm proud of, but I can normally find a way around most firewalls and codes, yes. This piece of hacking, however, didn't require a great deal of skill. At this time most of us were using Hotmail for our email accounts and most people just put an underscore between their Christian and Surnames followed by @hotmail.com. This was the case with Wynn, and, as he was a great fan of Liam Gallagher, always wearing T shirts depicting him or Oasis, it didn't take much imagination to crack his password – gallagher01."

"What was the post," Danny asked, feeling justice was about to be done and this Wynn character was about to get his.

Sebastian cringed. "I wrote, 'That Goodwin's a total wanker but his missus is a babe. She's about to feel a real man inside her. Know what I mean guys!!!!'"

"That's shit," Phil said. "Not even a Neanderthal would put something as lame as that."

Sebastian held up his hands. "Well it worked, what can I say? I showed it to Steve, telling him that one of Wynn's gang, who, for some reason, had been ex-communicated and thought Steve ought to know about it, passed it to me but didn't want to be involved. Steve was livid. Needless to say, Dave Wynn's days of bullying came to an end. In fact, if 'Horse-face' Williams, our P.E. Teacher hadn't pulled him off, I think Steve would have killed him. There was a lot of blood and, after that, Wynn's nose was not as straight as it had been."

"He was taught a lesson that all bullies should learn," Danny said.

He'd never advocated violence but, unfortunately, there are occasions when nothing else will do. No amount of reasoning or pleading would have altered Wynn's limited thought process. No amount of discussion would have convinced him that he was carrying out acts of intimidation, using his cowardly nature to persecute the timid and the weak. Danny said, "Maybe receiving a taste of his own medicine, made him into a better person."

"Shit will never smell like anything else but shit," Phil said with a sneer.

"I don't know," Danny mused. "Lawrence Carter ceased his bullying activities after I knocked his front teeth out. I think that once they realize that worms do turn and they can never be sure which will and which won't, common sense kicks in. As Sebastian says, they are all cowards who prey on those weaker than themselves. They are not fans of pain unless they're inflicting it. I have to say, I admire your resourcefulness."

"Yeah, I suppose," said Phil reluctantly. "If you're too much of a wimp to do it yourself, I guess by proxy works as well."

Sebastian looked at her and smiled. "An excellent description Philomena."

"Thank you, Sebastian," she drew out his name in a mocking tone. "But call me Philomena again and you'll need another champion." She held her fist in front of his face. Blue was immediately between them, her hackles up, her ears back and a low growl warning Phil that if she wanted to mess with her master, she'd have her to deal with as well.

"I believe I already have one," Sebastian said with a grin. "Nevertheless, from now on, I will address you as Phil although I think Philomena to be a beautiful name and to shorten it to a name associated with a number of dubious males is misguided and foolish."

Phil sighed and shook her head. "Whatever."

They all fell silent again, trudging through the seemingly endless tunnel, its oppression building by the minute. None of them knew how long it would be before they saw anything resembling light again. When the stillness was disturbed by a gentle breeze, they all thought that their time underground was close to an end. The breeze increased in intensity, slowly building until they were leaning into it as it howled around them like a swarm of keening banshees. Sebastian yelled above the screaming gale, 'What's happening?' Danny saw Seth shake his head. His expression was as confused as the rest of them. Danny turned his head away from the blast and saw a group of men staring at them, their clothing medieval. It was as if they were the other side of a window in desperate need of cleaning. "Look," he shouted. The other three turned their heads just before the figures disappeared.

The strange thing was that he knew one of them. He had made a guest appearance in his last dream before they entered The Grid. "What just happened?" He asked Seth. "I have no idea," Seth said slowly. "Whatever it was, it's never happened before."

He licked his lips and shook his head. "Sebastian?"

Sebastian shrugged. "I think we're in the realm of the unknown. What happens next is anybody's guess."

EIGHT

"Who the hell were they?" Danny asked.

Seth looked at him. "I don't know Danny," he said. "But I have a feeling we're going to find out."

Uncertainty was, suddenly, their new friend and their small group became split in two. Seth and Sebastian were ahead of Danny and Phil and deep in conversation.

"D'you get the impression, we're the thickos?" Phil asked.

"I guess, when it comes to all this." Danny waved his hand in a wide arc. "We are."

She nodded and sighed. "This shit is getting weirder by the fucking second, that's for sure."

Danny winced. The word 'fuck' had never really bothered him, but he was beginning to agree with Seth about Phil's over-use of the word. If he said anything to her, however, it would only increase its usage and have him become the target for most of it. He supposed he had been brought up not to swear, whereas, with her, it had probably been a daily occurrence, her mother and men friends using it constantly. She'd not had the best of lives, but she'd turned it around and become, what should be, a role model to many. What were a few swear words amongst friends.

"So, what do you make of all this?" He asked her.

"There's some other world these smart-arses don't know about, you'll see." She replied, with a wink.

"But you do."

"Fuck, no. I'm just playing Devil's advo.... whatever."

"Advocate," he said.

"Yeah, that'll do," she said.

Danny found himself following her meandering train of thought. Something was happening that neither Seth nor Sebastian had any idea about, that was obvious. The possibility of a dimension otherwise undetected was not unfeasible. As if he'd been a party to his thoughts, Danny heard Seth say to Sebastian. "There could be some corridor, some transitional waiting area."

"If so, why do we know nothing of it?" Inquired a skeptical Sebastian.

Seth shrugged and said nothing.

"Maybe, you don't know everything." Danny said, starting to feel a trifle pissed off with their attitude.

Sebastian looked at him and smiled. "Of course, you're absolutely right Danny, we don't. I'm sorry for being pompous and appearing superior, as I'm sure Seth is." He glanced at Seth, who nodded and muttered, 'Absolutely'. "It's just that, before recent events, we believed ourselves to be in a position to keep the group safe and on course. Now, everyone's input is welcome. We are sailing uncharted waters."

"So, we're not such dumbos, after all," said Phil, with a satisfied smile.

"No-one inferred you were," Sebastian stated. "It was a question of knowledge. That, now, does not apply. I believe that what lies ahead is beyond anything any of us can conceive. We go together into the unknown. Give me five." He held up his hand in a totally non-Sebastian stance and Danny and Phil slapped him 'five'. Seth decided to refrain.

"Could this 'split' have caused some...I don't know – door to open?" Danny asked.

Both Seth and Sebastian shrugged. "I really don't know, Danny," answered Seth. "I thought I knew everything about the way The Grid operated. This has just shown me, I don't. Anything I say will only be conjecture. I'm afraid, it's a waiting game."

"Waiting for what?" Phil asked.

"I can't answer that either, Phil. I just have a strong feeling that what we have witnessed so far is the start of something that can't be stopped. I believe we'll become better acquainted with the group of men we saw earlier. I may be wrong, of course. As I said, it's just conjecture."

"I hope you're right," said Phil, with a grin. "One of them was quite fit."

"I'm sure he felt the same about you," Danny said, unable to stifle a pang of jealousy.

"Thank you, Danny, you're a mate."

There it was – mates. If he was honest, that was how he was starting to see their relationship. He was just a bit pissed off that she didn't think he was 'quite fit'. Just an ego thing.

"What do we do now?" He asked Seth.

Seth shrugged again. "Just stay on track and take it as it comes, there's nothing else we can do. Our objective remains the same, although I think we may find it more difficult to achieve. But, having said that, it may be easier. Your guess is as good as mine."

They all nodded and fell into a thoughtful silence. Not long-ago Danny had been on the verge of suicide and now he was in the weirdest situation imaginable. Putting aside his ridiculous feeling of jealousy, he found the idea of doubling their number quite appealing. He had nothing in common with Seth or Sebastian (except for the bullying they'd both suffered) and, although, he and Phil were becoming mates, it would be nice to have a bit of male banter with some other blokes on his wavelength. He felt a strange sort of bond with the chap he'd already met in his dream, the one he was sure Phil was referring to. He didn't know how but he was convinced they were destined to become good friends. He hoped something monumental was going to happen because, the way things were shaping up, he was becoming bored out of his skull. Even an attack from the Grid-creatures would be welcome relief to the ennui. As it was, shuffling through this half-light, not even feeling hunger or thirst was making him think that death would have been preferable. To be absorbed by The Machine and find out what that entailed. Even Seth couldn't answer that question, so he guessed the old 'what happens after death' question remained even when God and heaven are not in the picture.

"I wish something would fucking happen," said Phil. "I can't stand much more of this shit."

Danny nodded. "Weird should be exciting, not bore you to death."

As if The Machine was pissed at their lack of appreciation, the banshees were back and wailing like there was no tomorrow. The cacophony grew louder, the wailing becoming a terrible screech, like a room full of novice violin players. Danny's eardrums felt as if they were about to burst. Like before, a gentle breeze quickly became a howling gale and they were all leaning into it, their hands over their ears, eyes shut. Blue added her voice to the mix and Danny thought he was about to pass out. They began to stagger, the assault to their hearing affecting their balance. Just as everything became echoey and distant and his knees started to buckle there was an almighty popping sound and he was thrown to the ground. The sudden silence, although a blessed relief, made him nauseous and he almost vomited. He opened his eyes and gasped. The cavern had gone. He looked around to see Phil's expression mirroring his own confusion. Seth and Sebastian were surveying their new surroundings with a great deal of animation, Blue was sniffing the lush grass, her tail wagging.

"What the.......?" Phil said again.

They could have been in the heart of the English countryside, surrounded by green fields. To their left a lake reflected the blue sky above, to their right, a quilt of greenery interspersed with patches of woodland stretched as far as the eye could see. Up ahead the ground rose steeply, and he could see the ruins of what appeared to be a church high on the hill. Blue had spotted the lake and was down at the water's edge lapping away. Danny's stomach growled and he was delighted to feel pangs of hunger but a stronger desire to slake his renewed thirst. "Do you think that water's all right to drink?" He asked. "If it's good enough for Blue, it's good enough for me," said Sebastian, walking down to the lake. Danny shrugged and followed, Seth and Phil falling in behind them. Minutes later, their thirst quenched, they sat on the grass and attempted to make some sense of what had just happened.

"Come on guys, what is this?" Danny gestured to their new environment.

Seth shook his head and looked at Sebastian. "Any ideas?" Sebastian stuck out his bottom lip, looked around and scratched his head. "None whatsoever," he admitted. "It looks as though we're back in, what we know as our world, but I don't see how that can be."

"No, I think appearances might be deceptive," said Seth.

"You're a lot of bloody good," said Phil, shaking her head.

"But we're feeling hunger and thirst again," Danny said.

"Yes, I know," said Seth. "That is puzzling in itself."

"Christ, this is like the blind leading the blind," said Phil.

"If you can do better – please, be my guest" snapped Seth.

"What about your sonic screwdriver/compass thing?" Danny asked. "Does that still work here, wherever here is?"

Seth's face lit up. "Good point, Danny. If we are indeed back where we started it will be useless. If not, at least we'll know there is still a way through this."

He took out his gizmo, flicked the switch and waved it in an arc. The blue light flashed, indicating the ruined church.

"At least we have direction," he said with a smile. "That is something, at least."

225

They sat for a few minutes more, enjoying a feeling of
normality. Well normal for Sebastian, Phil and Danny, that
was. Danny could smell the grass, feel the breeze and just
enjoy everything associated with a summer's day. He knew
they hadn't suffered the desolation of The Grid for long,
but it didn't seem that way. Tedium stretches time to its
limits.

Seth took a deep breath and let it out slowly. "I hate to
ruin the moment, but we still have a job to do. Shall we?"
He waved a hand toward the ruin above us.

Reluctantly, they all stood and let out a communal sigh.

"You're a bastard," said Phil.

"I think my parents would dispute that statement,
Philomena," Seth replied curtly.

"Only think?" she said.

"Come on Phil, give it a rest," Danny said, suddenly glad
he had no feelings of a romantic nature for her. The
words 'high maintenance' and 'nightmare' came to mind.

"I thought you were my mate," she said sharply.

"I am, believe me," he said. "But you can be a pain in the
arse at times. We are, after all, in this together."

She laughed. "You know, you're the first person to tell me
that and not get their teeth knocked out."

"That's because we're mates, right?"

She punched him in the shoulder. "Sure," she said with a
grin. "Let's do this."

Seth led the way and Danny, for one, was glad to get the
heart pumping and the muscles stretched. Shuffling
through dimly lit tunnels does little physically or mentally,
come to that, for anyone. It was nice to be in the fresh air
of whatever dimension or plain they were in. Although it
was a sharp incline, the distance from the bottom to the
top of the hill was relatively short and, after about ten
minutes, they were amongst the ruins of an unusual
building. From down below it had resembled a church
and, although not conventional, it was obviously a place of

worship. As they were searching the fallen stone and dilapidated archways for any clues as to where they had ended up, Danny heard a strange, whining. They all spun in the direction of the sound and were confronted by an odd figure, playing air guitar. The noise they'd heard was his vocal interpretation of his lead break. He shook his head to the imaginary music, a sparse thatch of white hair, hanging in thin tendrils about his age-ravaged face. He wore a tatty T shirt and dirty jeans, his grubby feet, bruised and cut, but shoeless. He looked at them, chuckled, said, "Yo," and carried on playing, his fingers picking out the notes like a pro. Danny recognized several bar chords between the lead runs and realized the man could really play. He bent over, an expression of deep concentration adding more lines to the road map that was his face, and hit the top of the fretboard, bending the notes, hammering on and off.

"Yo, yo, yo," he wailed. His fingers slid down the frets and he hit a massive, Pete Townsend-like barred F minor. He looked up, stopped playing, his eyes suddenly a startling blue. "You need to find the others," he said. "Follow the path of the spider and beware. Seeing is not always believing but belief will give you vision."

He turned away from them and disappeared behind the remains of a pillar, a distant 'Yo' resonating quietly through the crumbling stone.

"Well," said Seth.

"Well, indeed," added Sebastian.

"Who was *that?*" Phil asked.

"I'll bet he was a good guitar player in his day," Danny said.

Phil held out her hands. "What was all that path of the spider shit?"

"I have no idea," Seth replied. "But I have a feeling we're going to find out."

"We really are venturing into the unknown," said Sebastian, a concerned but excited expression gracing his features.

"Old Jimi Hendrix there obviously knows something; shouldn't we go after him?" Phil started to pick her way through the ruins towards the pillar where they'd last seen their air guitar playing friend. Danny shrugged and followed. It made sense to get hold of the old chap and pump him a bit. As Sebastian had pointed out, they were totally in the dark here and needed all the help they could get. He heard Seth say to Sebastian. "I think he's played his part."

They reached the edge of the ruin and looked down the hill. Open ground stretched out for a good mile or more before giving way to woodland. There was no sign of guitar-man.

"He can't just have disappeared into thin air," Phil said.

"Well unless he can run a two-minute mile, that's just what he has done," Danny said with a sigh. "I guess, we're on our own."

"That's unless we find the others," said Sebastian.

"Or they find us," Danny said. "I wonder if 'Slowhand' has paid them a visit too."

"Whatever," said Phil impatiently. "Are we going to make a move, or what. This place gives me the creeps."

"Phil's right," said Seth. "For the time being we'll follow our original course. Standing around here, deliberating is getting us nowhere. We need to move and just take everything as it comes."

Phil didn't need telling twice; she was out of the ruin and headed down the hill in seconds. Seth was a close second with Sebastian, Blue and Danny not far behind.

"What do you make of it all, really?" Danny asked Sebastian.

He let out a heavy sigh. "Honestly? I'm as much in the dark as you. My opinion, however, is that we're now in a plain or dimension that exists between The Grid and our world. Why, is another question; one I have no answer for, I'm afraid. It seems apparent that we are meant to be here as, indeed, the young men with the swords are. What our purpose is, if it differs from our primary course, is a total mystery to me. Speculation, at this time, would be fruitless and, frankly, create more confusion. I think Seth is right – we take it as it comes and, hopefully, as time passes, things will become clearer." He leant down and rubbed Blue's ears and Danny couldn't help thinking how much simpler life is for our four-legged friends. They have no problem taking it as it comes.

They strolled down the hill and, for the first time, since they embarked on this crazy journey, Danny felt light-hearted. They fell silent and he started to hum 'You've Got To Hide Your Love Away', one of his favourite Beatles songs, and one that Joey and he used to do a pretty good version of, if he did say so himself.
Sebastian sighed. "That brings back memories," he said, his expression wistful.
"Good, I hope,"
"My mother loved the Beatles, especially Lennon," he continued. "She was obsessed." He shook his head. "She even had a twelve inch, talking model of him; it used to say, 'Give Peace a Chance' and 'Power to the People'. To be honest, it used to freak me out a bit."
"Am I right in assuming that she played their albums regularly?"
"All the time. I was weaned on the Beatles."
"Me too," Danny said. "There are worse things to be brought up on, I guess."
Sebastian frowned. "I was never really into pop music, but I did like the 'Fab Four'."
"Who didn't?"

"One of my favourites is 'In My Life'. I don't remember which album it's on."

"Rubber Soul; a classic album," Danny said, enthusiastically. "It was my dad's favourite, with 'Revolver' a close second.

"I loved the cover of that," Sebastian said. "It was a drawing by ...er..."

"Klaus Voorman," Danny said.

Sebastian nodded. "That's him, yes."

Danny hadn't thought about his guitar for a long time but, suddenly, he missed it, the feel and ring of the strings, the diversion it created. He needed that sort of diversion now. But what you need is not always what you get. Guitars were the least of his concerns when Blue shot forward, snarling, her hackles up.

"What is it girl?" Sebastian shouted after her.

PART FOUR – THE RIFT

ONE

Within seconds the sky turned from a shimmering blue to black. The stillness of summer disappeared beneath gale force winds and torrents of rain. They were buffeted and drenched, the gale growing to titanic proportions. They lost balance and were drawn into the cyclone, spinning in its twisting swirl, the rain a savage wave. Dave thought he was a goner, he was spluttering, trying to spit out water as more replaced it. He thought he was about to experience drowning in a wind tunnel, it was akin to being thrown into a washing machine, he imagined. For what seemed like an age they were on a spin cycle, only as the water was sucked out, more poured in. At one point, Dave prayed for it to end, for death to take him. Then, as swiftly as it had started, there was a loud pop and they fell to the ground, breathless and soaked.

"Jesus Christ," Ringo managed to say, between sucking in air. "What the fuck was that?"

Dave pushed his sodden hair from his forehead, pulled his pants away from his testicles and grimaced. "That was probably like a mini tsunami. I really thought I was going to drown."

"I'm sure I saw my life flash before my eyes," said the parsnip.

"That must have taken all of five seconds," Ollie said, with a wink.

"Surely, not that long," added the coach.

"Piss off, all of you," the parsnip said.

"Ignore 'em, Pete," Dave said. "They probably ain't had a life to warrant a second glance."

"Cheers Dave."

"Hey up, what's happened to the old nickname shit?" Ringo asked.

"Well, it does get to be a little tedious, don't it," said Harry. "It's like being back at school."

There it was, after all the deliberation about Jack's nickname, they were back to being grown-ups. That was, apart from Ringo; he liked his and wanted to keep it. When Ringo is compared to Frank, it's understandable, no disrespect to all the Franks in the world, of course.

"Anyway, what just happened?" Dave asked.

Everybody shrugged and then Ringo shook his head. "It's all different, that wasn't there before." He pointed behind them. There was a hill with ruins at its peak. To their left was a lake. The landscape had changed completely.

"This time travel shite gets weirder," said Jack.

As if to confirm his statement, the ground rumbled, and shallow cracks appeared in the grassy earth. They were all poised, expecting a massive earthquake. The tremors subsided and they relaxed.

"Look, it's a spider," said Pete.

It was true, the cracks that had appeared, radiated from a small clump of grass, in eight directions, like the legs of a spider. One of the cracks was much longer than the other seven. They looked at each other, shrugged and followed the spider's leg. What else was there to do?

"Come on then, who's going to offer an explanation for what just happened?" Dave started the ball rolling. "And, more importantly, where we are now. Are we still in the past? Come on, somebody help me out here."

Ringo shook his head, again, Jack and Harry shrugged, again and poor, old Pete was like the Sex Pistols – 'Pretty Vacant'.

"Well, as I mentioned previously," Ringo began. "The landscape has changed, which means we're in a different place. At present, there is no way to determine which time period we're in and I have not got a scooby as to what just happened. Is that helpful?"

"Oh yeah, that does it for me." Dave grinned at the others. "What about you lot?"

"Ace," said Harry.

"Spot on," added Jack.

Pete was still with the Sex Pistols.

"And why are we following this spider leg thing? Can anyone tell me that?"

"You got any better ideas?" Jack asked.

Dave had to admit defeat in that quarter and said so.

"I think this is where that dog, the three blokes and the good-looking girl are," said Pete with a nod. He'd obviously left Johnny and Sid to their own devices.

"And what makes you think that my old parsnip?" Ringo asked him.

"I thought we'd dispensed with the nicknames," Pete replied.

"You may have, I couldn't possibly comment," said Ringo.

"What's that supposed to mean?"

"Didn't you watch 'House of Cards'?" Ringo's expression was one of disgust. "You're just a pleb; I'll bet you watch EastEnders and Emmerdale and all that shit."

"What's wrong with EastEnders?" Harry asked indignantly.

Ringo shook his head yet again. "Plebs," he repeated.

"This ain't getting the baby a new bonnet," Dave protested.

"What?" A 'what' by four people in unison, with a hint of harmony can be a bit intimidating.

"Just something my old man used to say," Dave said apologetically.

"Well I vote we carry on following the spider's leg," said Ringo.

"I agree," agreed Jack.

"Why not," said Harry.

"Absolutely," insisted Pete. "We can't do anything else."

"Do you know something you're not telling us, Pete?" Dave asked him.

It was Pete's turn to shake his head. "No. It's just a feeling, that's all."

"Do you have many of these feelings?" Ringo enquired.

"I've had a few," he admitted.

"Have they always been right?" Jack asked.

"Not always, no."

'Great,' Dave thought.

They followed the spider's leg, each dealing with his own confusion. The time travel shit was bad enough but now they were in an even stranger land, following a crack in the ground. Dave was wondering if it could become any weirder, when the air before them turned into an inverted mushroom.

"Aw, come on, this is taking the piss," he said.

"I think we're past that, mate," said Ringo.

"What do we do now?" Harry asked.

Pete stepped forward and held his sword out in front of him. He jabbed the mushroom and the blade disappeared. He pulled it back, inspected it, leant forward and put his hand where his sword had been.

"What are you doing, man?" Ringo asked him.

"I think it's just some sort of doorway," Pete said. "It's harmless, I'm pretty sure of that."

"Pretty sure?" said Jack.

Without another word, Pete walked forward and was gone. Seconds later he returned unscathed. "It's nicer on the other side," he said. "Even greener, you know?"

They indulged in a communal shrug and passed through the mushroom. Pete was right, the landscape had improved, there were a few trees dotted about and swathes of grass carpeted open countryside.

From nowhere, literally nowhere, this attractive but small, exceedingly small, young woman appeared. If blue was a shade of sunburn, she was slightly tanned.

"Alesh let in them," she warbled in a sing-song voice, "Help you have to."

Dave felt like they were in 'Star Wars' and listening to a pleading, female, azure Yoda.

They stood and stared at this strange, yet beautiful creature. She was about three feet tall but well proportioned. She wore a loose-fitting shirt-like garment, leaving little to the imagination, the nipples of her pert breasts obvious beneath the silken cloth, her legs the shapeliest Dave had ever seen.

Ringo ignored the perverted lust Dave felt. She was a full-grown woman – just a bit smaller than usual – and blue.

"Who has Alesh let in?" He asked. "And where?"

"Mothraqui," she said, pointing in the direction they were travelling,

They looked, they squinted, but saw nothing other than open land.

She saw their confusion, sighed and muttered something that sounded like a spell from Harry Potter. A village of rather strange looking constructions replaced the greenery.

"Jesus Christ," Dave managed to mutter, before this fifteen-foot-tall monstrosity hurtled in their direction, its intentions clear.

"What the fuck is that?" Jack yelled.

It had the face of the devil. Dave had no idea what the Devil looked like, if he even existed at all, but this thing was evil looking, really evil looking. It was a huge fucker, like something out of a horror movie. Not only was he an ugly bastard but he was swinging a luminous sword, its pitted surface appearing and disappearing.

"Go low," shouted Ringo. "Bring the freak down."

Like a well-oiled machine, they dropped and slid under the arc of the elusive blade, as it flashed in and out of focus. Dave had to admit, as he rolled beneath old Goliath's sword, he was praying for their old friend, the black Labrador, to make another appearance and help them out a tad, as it had at Daunter's place. As this giant raised and planted his steel-clad size twenties in the grass, his calves and thighs protected by similar armour, Dave was at a loss as to how they were going to 'bring the freak down'. They hacked away, doing no damage but, obviously, annoying the fuck out of the man mountain. The sword came closer and then a huge right foot hurled Jack into the air. The poor bastard landed in an ungainly heap and the sword rose. There was nothing any of them could do; Dave closed his eyes and prayed, something he never dreamed of ever doing. In a situation like this, he thought, when all other choices are fruitless and you are about to witness the slaughter of one of your best pals, what's left? This grotesque, gigantic fucker with a sword the size of Birmingham was about to end his buddy's life and he was powerless, so, yeah, he prayed.

TWO

"Oh, you beauty," Ringo yelled. Dave opened his eyes as something black flashed past. Goliath screamed and almost dropped his weapon as the hand holding it was savaged.

"Come on," Dave screamed.

The Labrador launched herself into the air, her ears flat against her head, her muzzle drawn back, showing her teeth. The dog's jaws clamped on the monster's wrist and it let out a guttural scream. Then this older geezer was leaping forward, yelling for a sword. Ringo obliged, chucking his seldom used blade. That wasn't meant in a derogatory way; it's just he was always more use with the old Oliver McQueen shit (for the uninitiated that's the DC comics 'Green Arrow'). The way the stranger moved put Bruce Lee to shame; he was awesome. Talk about using an opponent's body against him. He leapt onto the big man's knee, sprung up and brought Ringo's sword down into the fucker's eye. That did it for Dave; he was a fan.

The geezer pulled the blade from the giant's eye, wiped it on the grass and handed it back. "Thanks," was all he said.

When it had all calmed down and they were all looking down at this cross between Mighty Joe Young and a character from 'Zombie Apocalypse', an ugly bastard, to be sure, Dave felt it was time for a few introductions (between the normal coloured people that is, not their new, little, blue friends).

"Nice one, man," he said. "You put the rest of us young 'uns to shame." Why is it the realization of putting one's hoof in one's mush always comes too late. "When I say young," he back peddled. "I mean...er...less experienced?"

The giant slayer hit him with a steely stare and then burst out laughing.

"There's no shame in being old," he chuckled, a glint in his eye. "The shame is in covering yourself in it as if it's a comfort blanket."

"That's what I meant," Dave said, with a grin. "Anyway, my name's Dave and I'm glad to make the acquaintance of a real life 'Matrix' character, at last."

When a touch of confusion touched those grey eyes, the dark-skinned babe stepped forward. "Seth's not much into films, he's more hands on," she said with a smile that melted snow; well, would have done, had it been there. Dave's focus had altered, he didn't mind admitting. Seth was a legend, no mistake, but he didn't possess long, beautifully shaped legs, a face and eyes to bathe in and a perfume that could knock out the British army; she did. He grabbed her hand and gave it an untidy kiss. She looked at him as if he was alien."

"There are certain protocols that must be adhered to," she said.

"They don't call me 'Super Glue' for nothing," Dave said, grinning like an idiot. "I'm Dave, by the way"

"Of course, you are." She sighed. "Now stop being a twat. I thought you were alright – it seems I was wrong."

"I've been called worse," Dave told her. "But never by such a vision," he added a wink and dropped to one knee. "Will you marry me fair wench?"

"I'll kick you in the bollocks if you don't get up," she said, obviously loving the attention.

Danny stepped forward. "I'm Danny," he said. "The Matrix character is Seth, one man and his dog are Sebastian and Blue, and the girl you're trying to impress is Phil, short for Philomena, but call her that at your peril."

Seth nodded, Sebastian gave a wave, blue wagged her tail and Phil gave Dave the finger.

Dave laughed and blew her a kiss. "Well, I'm Dave, I may have already mentioned that, The Liverpudlian looking one there with the bow is Ringo aka Frank, next to him is Harry, then Jack and last, but not least, the parsnip that goes by the moniker Pete.

"Parsnip?" said Phil.

Pete shook his head, "Don't ask."

"We're pleased to meet you," Seth said, going along the line, shaking hands. "Have you any idea why we're all here?"

"Not the slightest," replied Ringo. "I was hoping you might be able to shed some light on that one. We're just your run of the mill time travellers who, for some reason, have slipped into some weird 'Lord of the Rings' thing with miniature blue people. No disrespect," he added, gazing around the group of blue faces that were gazing at them in wonder.

"Time travellers?" Seth asked, his excitement evident.

"Yeah, it's a long story," Ringo said. "The short version is that we were sent back from 2022 by a mad bastard to find some geezer up in Scotland and retrieve what he'd nicked from said mad bastard. We were about to take a bit of a detour and head for the coast when the mother of all storms hit and we ended up, staring at a fifteen foot gorilla that seemed intent on ridding wherever we are of little blue people. Again, no disrespect." He smiled at the band of upturned faces and they smiled back.

"That explains a lot," said Seth.

"Indeed, it does," Sebastian agreed. "Da Vinci caused a split by coming close to inventing a time machine. Now that one has been constructed and used, we have a considerably larger problem, in so much as, we have no knowledge of what is to come and, just as importantly, where we are."

Phil and Dave were indulging in a little more banter, ignoring their present predicament.

"We need to ask these good people some questions," said Seth.

For some reason, a song title from one of his old man's albums came to Dave's mind - 'Can Blue Men Sing the Whites' by the Bonzo Dog Doo Dah Band. They were surrounded by a sea of azure, adoring faces. Dave grinned and gave them a silly wave.

"You are a tit," said Phil.

"I know," he agreed, the grin making his facial muscles ache. "I'm just not sure how to deal with hero worship from blue Lilliputians."

"It's not you, it's him," she said, pointing to Seth. "He's the man of the moment. You just scuffled about pissing the big bastard off."

He was hurt. "That's a little harsh," he said. "We were doing our best."

Seth glared at them and they both zipped it. Dave mouthed a 'sorry'. Seth bent down so that his face was level with theirs. "Do you have a leader?" He asked softly. A crowd of little blue heads nodded in affirmation and then the pocket delight who had decried Alesh and spoke like a female Yoda stepped forward. Her eyes were wide and flashed gold and bright blue, the colour changing as she spoke. Dave was mesmerised.

"Geeshta is our queen," she said, totally un-Yoda like but in the same sing-song warble. " Already she knows of the great warrior who defeated the Mothraqui and saved her children. Come."

She turned and the group of misfits followed, the blue sea parting before them. Seth led the way and Dave could see a slight resemblance to Charlton Heston, who played Moses in the epic, The Ten Commandments. For a moment, he came over all biblical.

Phil and he were side by side. "Did you ever have a normal life?" He asked her. "Or is this normal to you?"

"Christ, no," she replied. "Until a few days ago, I was a badass in 2022, minding my own beeswax and encouraging others to do the same. What about you? How long have you been a time traveller?"

"Same – not long. It just worries me how easily I'm starting to accept weird shit."

"Tell me about it," she said. "I mean, if you'd seen these," she gestured to our miniature, blue friends. "A few days ago, you'd have freaked, right? Not to mention that fucker," she pointed to the thing that Seth had dispatched. Dave nodded. "Yeah, too true."

Ringo and Danny fell in behind Phil and Dave, who, appeared to be getting on like a house on fire.

"Love is in the air," Danny whispered.

Ringo smiled. "I think you may be right Danny boy."

Danny winced. "Just Danny, if you don't mind," he said. "Someone who I thought a lot of used to call me 'Danny boy'."

"I'm guessing it didn't end well," Ringo said.

Danny nodded. "You could say that."

"Sorry man, I didn't mean to – you know?"

"No problem, but if you'd could just keep it to Danny, I'd appreciate it. What about you? Is it Frank or Ringo?"

He grinned. "It used to be Frank, but I've sort of got used to Ringo."

"He was a good drummer," Danny said.

"Yeah, he was," Ringo agreed. "And he played on some of the best songs that will ever be written."

"You'll get no argument here, my dad had all of their albums, I loved The Beatles, still do."

Ringo held out his hand. "Put it there Danny. You and I are going to get on simply fine."

Phil and Dave stopped suddenly, and Danny grabbed Ringo's arm to stop himself barging into Phil. He looked around and saw nothing but open country. He couldn't see their little, blue girl-guide with Seth, Phil and Dave in the way.

He peered around Dave's shoulder. Their little friend dropped to her knees, held out her arms and muttered something in the same strange language she'd used earlier. The picture of the English countryside crumbled before their eyes, revealing a shimmering building.

It was not palatial, instead resembling a Tudor cottage. A short path crept up to a beautiful oak door. Weirder and weirder, Danny thought.

One second, he was looking out across the fields, the next, a house had taken their place. The roof looked as if it had been recently re-thatched, the walls between the oak beams, a brilliant white. This building was at odds, severely, with the rest of the tiny dwellings in the village.

Danny looked at Ringo, who shrugged. "Don't ask me," he said. "I just take everything as it comes now. Nothing makes any kind of sense. You've just got to accept it man; if you don't, you'll go mad."

Sebastian drew level with them, Blue by his side. "Wise words," he said. "Although, in the not too distant future, I think we may have our powers of perception tested."

"What's that supposed to mean?" Ringo asked him, visibly confused.

"I don't know yet," replied Sebastian. "But I will."

THREE

Their guide reached forward and pushed the oak door and
it swung inward. She nodded to Seth and left them to their
own devices. The inside of the cottage appeared dark and
gloomy through the partially opened portal.

Seth pushed it open wide and, the light it let in, showed a
hallway with four doors, two on either side and the
bottom of a staircase at the end of the passage. Seth
knocked on the first door on the right, waited about thirty
seconds and opened it. The curtains covering the window
opposite were worn and thin and allowed in a little light.
The room reminded Dave of his Nan's sitting room.

"This is just an old woman's home," said Ringo. "It's just
like my Nan's."

'Copycat,' Dave thought.

The other three doors continued the theme, a small dining
room, a spacious kitchen and a tiny toilet. Going from
defending a tribe of diminutive, blue people from
something from 'Clash of the Titans' to this throwback to
fifties Britain was peculiar, to say the least. They followed
Seth to the staircase and Dave, seriously, thought they
might find an old woman lying in bed, in the dark,
suffering from a migraine.

"Maybe she's got a migraine," he said. Seth gave him one
of his 'why don't you shut the fuck up' looks. Dave didn't
think he liked him very much.

"Or a hangover," said Phil with a grin, receiving a similar
glare from the big man. That made Dave feel better; it
wasn't just him; it was all flippant, young punks. He could
live with that.

"You need to chill a bit," Dave said to Seth, giving him a
wink. He always liked to push his luck; it had been a thing
of his for as long as he could remember. It had earned him

a few good hidings from the old man, in his younger days. Some people never learn.

"And you need to take life a little more seriously, young man," Seth said sharply. "Not everything is a laughing matter. Have you any idea how vital our mission is?"

Dave shook his head. "As you haven't told me – no I don't. And, one other thing, I hate patronizing bastards." Seth was starting to get on his tits with his high and mighty attitude. The way he had dealt with that big, ugly fucker impressed the shit out of Dave, but that didn't give him the right to talk to him like a was a snotty nosed, little kid.

Seth looked him up and down as if he were a pair of jeans, he was thinking of shelling out for. "I wasn't being patronizing."

The geezer with the dog, Sebastian, Dave thought Danny said he was called, opened his mouth, and Dave thought, here we go. He surprised him.

"You may not have intended it, Seth, but I'm afraid it sounded pretty patronizing to me."

Seth was taken aback. "Well, if that was indeed the case, I apologise."

"Dave," Dave said. "The name's Dave."

Seth sighed. "Okay, I apologise Dave. Now can we get on, please."

Dave gestured forward. "Go for it."

Danny and Ringo listened to the exchange between Seth and Dave. Ringo frowned. "Man, he's so uptight," he whispered. "I mean, what is his problem?"

"I think Dave might be a little too jocular for him," Danny replied. "He's not one for youthful humour."

"That's obvious."

"He's a good bloke though," Danny said. "Bloody useful in a scrap, as well. As you've already seen. He saved your arse."

Ringo held up his hands. "Okay, okay, I agree. He's a legend, a fucking hero and I wouldn't fancy going up against him. All I'm saying is – it wouldn't hurt him to lighten up a bit, that's all."

"He has his moments," Danny said. "Few and far between, I admit."

"This could get ugly," Sebastian said suddenly. "I think a little mediation wouldn't go amiss." He stepped forward. After he'd poured oil on troubled waters, Sebastian rejoined them, and they followed Seth, Dave and Phil into the house, Harry, Jack, and Pete bringing up the rear.

"This is just totally out of character," Pete said. "Does anyone else feel uneasy about this whole situation?"

They all shrugged. "You should be used to it, by now mate," said Harry. "Nothing is logical anymore. Just when you think you might be getting a bit of a handle on things; you get another curveball lobbed at you. Like Ringo says, you've just got to accept it."

Pete shook his head. "No, I know all that. I've just got a feeling, that's all"

"Oh no, not another of your famous feelings," Jack said with a sigh.

Ringo wasn't quite so dismissive. "What d'you mean Pete? What sort of feeling – good, bad, indifferent?"

"It's not a good feeling, put it that way."

Seth, Phil and Dave didn't hear this exchange, Seth already making his way to the staircase. The little group at the rear shared a look, Jack rolling his eyes, Ringo's brow furrowed, Pete concerned, Danny and Harry non-committal.

Danny nudged Ringo. "You don't think he has a sixth sense, do you?"

He shrugged. "I don't know." He paused. "All I do know is that I'm starting to get a similar feeling."

"What happened to taking everything as it comes?" Danny asked him.

He shrugged again. "What can I tell you? Despite the lunacy that now passes for our lives, I'm getting this feeling of.......foreboding, I suppose is the best word to describe it."

"You're both mental," Jack said, and, as they neared the bottom of the staircase, he moved forward to join Seth's group.

"Hey, Jack." Ringo reached out to him, but Pete grabbed the Liverpudlian's arm.

"Let him go," he said softly, nodding; his smile, one of resignation.

Ringo looked at him. "Why?" His expression became one of concern. "I think you're starting to freak me out a bit, Pete. You're not starting to see.... like.... visions, are you?"

Pete shook his head. "No. Like I said, it's just a feeling. I can't really explain it."

Watching the exchange between these two, and the way Jack had rushed to be with Seth & co. had got Danny thinking, so he waded in. "The dynamics are switching, aren't they? We came together as two separate units. Those are splitting and new ones forming. That's why you want Jack to go with Seth. Is that it?"

Pete shrugged. "I don't know. Honestly, I don't. I just get the feeling he needs to be away from Ringo and me. I don't know anything about new groups."

Danny thought Ringo would take the opportunity to start on again about how any of the new bands paled into insignificance compared to his beloved Beatles, but he didn't. He was looking from Danny to Pete, confusion dragging down the corners of his mouth and furrowing his brow.

"This whole, fucking thing is spooky enough without this shit," he said.

"I think," said Sebastian. "That you might be right, Danny. We have already split into two different parties;

only separated by a foot or so, granted. But, nevertheless, we have, inadvertently, formed new alliances. Over a longer period, that would not be unusual, but within the space of an hour or so, it becomes yet another extraordinary development."

"Does he always talk like that?" Ringo asked Danny.

"If you mean, properly," Sebastian answered. "Yes, I do. If, in future, you have a question relating to me, I would appreciate it if you would refrain from directing it elsewhere."

Ringo nodded. "Um....yeah......sorry. I guess."

"Apology accepted," said Sebastian.

As they climbed the stairs, Jack had pushed himself up to the front.

"Hello mate," Dave said. "Getting fed up with Beatle-head?"

"Nah, it's Pete and his psychic shit. Mind you Ringo ain't helping."

"What? Is the old parsnip getting his funny feelings again?"

Jack sniggered. "You got it. He's starting to do my head in."

"Ah, come on, he's harmless," Dave said. "And to be fair, he was right about us meeting these nice people." He smiled at Phil; she grinned and gave him the finger again.

"Let's forget about it," Jack said and shivered.

"Man, you're severely uptight about it," Dave said, shocked. "I didn't realize it was creeping you out so much."

He shook his head. "I had an Auntie, who was a medium. She used to scare me to death. She used to wear this bright, red lipstick and thick, black eye liner and call me 'little Jacky'. She'd stick her face right in mine, her breath stunk of rotten onions." He shivered again. "It makes my skin crawl, just thinking about it."

Dave laughed. "Poor little Jacky."

"Don't," he pleaded. "It's not funny. One afternoon, I crept into the room just before she did this séance thing. Halfway through, she threw her head back and this......stuff, came out of her mouth. It was fucking horrible, man."

"Ectoplasm," Phil said.

"Whatever," said Jack. "It's not the sort of thing a nine-year-old should see, believe me."

Dave nodded. "I'm sure. I don't think Pete's going to go down that route though, mate. Do you?"

He shrugged. "You never know, Dave. You just never know. Especially now. Let's face it, anything's possible."

Dave had to agree. Recently, everything they had taken for granted had been blown to fuck. Up was down, left was right, fantasy was reality – or was it? At that precise moment in time, he could, quite honestly, say, he had no idea what was real and what wasn't. For all he knew, it could all be a weird dream, but he didn't think so. He looked at Phil's posterior in those tight pants and hoped it wasn't. Once a shallow bastard, always a shallow bastard but then, nobody's perfect.

By this time Seth had reached the top of the stairs. Maybe the blue queen could shed some light on their current situation."

Danny tried to peer around Seth and the others as he pushed open the door on the left and then quickly reached for the handle of the door directly in front of him. From their position he couldn't really see what was going on. He did, however, hear him say, 'follow the path of the spider' and turn to his right.

"What's he doing?" Ringo whispered.

Danny shrugged. "I don't know. I think he was going to open the door at the top of the stairs, but something, someone said to us earlier, changed his mind, for some reason."

Dave must have heard him. "A bloody big spider came out of the bathroom and scuttled under that door," he said, pointing to the right.

"And he's following it?" Ringo asked.

"I think he's got a bee in his bonnet about following them," Dave said. "That's spiders not bees."

Seth reached forward, grabbed the door handle, took a deep breath, and twisted the knob. The door swung inward silently. The room beyond was black and Dave couldn't see a bloody thing. It was like a solid wall of thick, impenetrable darkness. He felt like they were in one of those horror films where some young tart's about to enter a room where everyone knows she's going to meet her end. The music's building and then it suddenly stops and the only thing that can be heard is her breathing. Most people are on the edge of their seats, mentally screaming – *Don't go in there, you silly bitch.*

Like the silly bitch, Seth entered and, ridiculously, they followed. It was the blind leading the blind. Dave had his hands out in front of him, unable to see his shuffling feet. As soon as he entered the room, it was as if the dark closed in around, mummifying him.

"This is taking the piss," whispered Phil, unable to hide the fear in her voice.

"I don't like this, one bit," added Jack, reaching out and grabbing Dave's arm. His grip was like iron.

"Steady on, feller," Dave said. "You're strangling my arm."

Just as he started to ease off on the pressure the door slammed shut behind them and it re-intensified.

"Shit," a number of voices blurted in unison.

"Try and keep calm," Seth said softly. "Are we all here?" After a verbal roll call, it appeared their group of ten had been reduced to four, Seth, Dave, Phil and Jack.

"Try the door," Dave urged anyone.

"It's fucking locked," yelled Jack, rattling the handle. "It's fucking, bastard locked. Oh God, what's happening?" The poor sod was practically in tears. Dave wasn't best pleased himself, He had to say. "Calm down, mate. We'll be fine. Seth?" He was after a bit of assurance from the big man. Jack was on route to becoming a gibbering wreck.

Normally when in a darkened room, a person's eyes become accustomed to the gloom. They begin to make out shapes and stuff; this just wasn't happening. They were in a big bottle of black ink. "Seth?" He tried again. "I'm as much in the dark as you," he said.

"Did you just make a joke?" Dave asked him, then to Phil. "Did he just make a joke?"

Phil was about to answer, Jack was back, wringing the life out of his bicep when a deep, ethereal gasp washed through the room like surround-sound.

"Oh m...m...y G...God," stammered Jack.

'You are the four rangers. The spider will guide you. Never stray from his path." The words seemed to be in Dave's head, formless but intense.

"Where are our friends?" Seth asked the darkness.

'The spider will guide you'. The communication faded to a breathless notion.

To their left a crack of light appeared as a, previously, unseen door swung outwards a tad. Their old friend, the spider disappeared through the chink. Jack was after him, in a shot, pushing the door wide and falling through. The room, this block of black ended at the new doorway but the light from beyond didn't penetrate it. Seth, Phil and Dave followed Jack into the light.

Danny and Ringo were standing on the top couple of stairs when Seth opened the bedroom door. Over Jack's shoulder, Danny saw only darkness, no glimmer of light. He began to share Ringo's feeling of foreboding.

251

"It's pitch black in there," he shared. Blue began to whine. "Sshh, girl," whispered Sebastian, rubbing her ears. She leant into his leg.

Danny looked back and watched Seth enter the room, Dave, Phil and Jack on his heels.

"This is turning into a horror film," Ringo said.

"I think we're about to start a new chapter," said Sebastian.

"And, what the fuck's that supposed to mean, Einstein?" Ringo hissed.

"Do you have a problem with me?" Sebastian asked him.

"As it happens, yeah. You, either talk in riddles or you act like a fucking teacher, and it's getting on my tits. Any more questions?"

Their new 'group' seemed to be having some teething problems. "Come on, Ringo. We're all getting stressed, and we're all dealing with it differently," Danny said quietly. Blue's hackles were up and, if a dog can glare, that's what she was doing – Ringo, the focus of her attention. To add a little menace, she emitted a low growl and twitched her muzzle, flashing her teeth.

"Easy girl," Sebastian said softly.

"Stop being a twat," Pete said. "There are some people who know more than you, and don't need to eff and blind all the time. Try acting more like John Lennon and less like John Dillinger."

Ringo looked as though he was about to launch into another verbal assault, then reason kicked in. He let out a heavy sigh and held up his hands.

"Sorry man," he said to Sebastian. "I thought I was dealing with this shit pretty well. Obviously, I was wrong." Sebastian held out his hand. "I have met many 'twats' in the past." It was clear that he was uncomfortable using vulgar slang. "Plus, I pride myself in being a good judge of character. I've forgotten it already." As if to reinforce his words, Blue became quiet and started to wag her tail, slowly. Apparently, she wasn't totally convinced.

Ringo shook his hand and muttered another apology. This exchange had taken their attention and, by the time harmony was restored, Jack was crossing the threshold of the bedroom. The gloom swallowed him. Danny went to follow him when the door was slammed in his face.

"Christ, Jack," he said, grabbing the doorknob. The door was locked or jammed. Either way, it wouldn't budge.

"Open the door, Danny," yelled Ringo.

He rattled the knob and it rattled back but the door stayed firmly shut.

"You try," he suggested, stepping away from the door.

Ringo rushed forward, grabbed, pushed and grunted but to no avail. The door remained shut. "What the fuck," was all he could manage.

"Wait," said Pete. "It'll open in a minute."

Ringo shook his head. "Oh Pete, man. You're starting to......"

There was a sharp click and a gap appeared between the door and the frame.

"I think," said Sebastian. "It's our turn."

While the rest of them stared tentatively at the door, Pete stepped forward, pushed it open and entered the bedroom. He disappeared beyond what appeared to be a dense, black curtain.

"Well, here goes," said Sebastian. "Come on girl."

He followed Pete, Blue by his side.

"There could be anything in there," said Harry.

"We haven't heard any screams," Ringo said. "I guess that's a good thing, yeah?"

"We can't stay here," Danny said.

"We could go back," Harry said.

"Nah, you should never go back," Ringo said, wiping his palms on his trousers. "Who dares wins." He vanished into the blackness.

"Come on Harry, best foot forward." Danny grabbed his arm and they almost stumbled through the door.

To be continued